Patricia le Roy was born in Liverpool, and educated at the University of Sussex. After working as a teacher, translator, secretary and journalist, she spent several years as a research editor at Radio Free Europe/Radio Liberty. Patricia now lives in Paris with her French husband and two daughters. *Music at the Garden House* is her third novel published by Piatkus.

Also by Patricia le Roy

The Angels of Russia
The Glass Palace Chronicle

Music at the Garden House

Patricia le Roy

First published in Great Britain in 2000 by
Online Originals, London

This edition published 2001 by
Judy Piatkus (Publishers) Ltd of
5 Windmill Street, London W1T 2JA
email: info@piatkus.co.uk

*A catalogue record for this book is available
from the British Library*

ISBN 0 7499 3261 9

Typeset by Palimpsest Book Production Limited,
Polmont, Stirlingshire

Printed and bound in Great Britain by
Mackays of Chatham plc, Chatham, Kent

In memory of
Virginia Gusovius
1942–1991

and Mary Lipton
1909–2001

Prologue

Axel

November 1999

My father had expressed the wish not to set foot in the new millennium, and the cancer that had been eating away at his intestines granted his request. He said he had seen enough already.

He had been born in a peasant's hut in Tambov oblast, and he died in the Moscow apartment they had given him when he became a general in the Soviet Army in 1976. My father had come a long way. He had seen patriotic war, cold war, fraternal war, the end of history, and the bombing of Chechnya. By the end, he was sick of it all. For much of his life, he had believed in Progress, the advent of Socialism, and the creation of a New Soviet Man. He had been disappointed on all counts. At the end of the twentieth century, Russia was plundered and destitute. Whatever was in store for the twenty-first century, he didn't want to see it. 'It's going too fast, I can't keep up,' he whispered to me the day I arrived from Germany. It was the week before he died. He had difficulty speaking by then, and he slept for most of the day. I was shocked by his appearance. In the six weeks since I had seen him, he had wasted away. His face had fallen in, his legs were like sticks, he was unable to move. He had to be turned over every two hours. I was amazed to see someone who had been energetic and decisive suddenly so helpless. He was beyond dignity and beyond hope. It seemed like a terrible way to end your existence.

My mother, my sister and I took turns sitting by his bedside. He had insisted some months earlier on moving his bed into his study, ostensibly to allow my mother to sleep, in reality to feel his life tangibly around him. The room was lined with books, photos and military memorabilia. During my spells by the bedside, I spent a lot of time looking at the photos and dipping into the books. It was like entering a foreign country. I had no idea why he had underlined certain passages in the books. I could not put names to the faces in the photos, with the exception of Yuri Andropov, glass in hand, with my father at some Kremlin reception. Why my father had been photographed with Andropov, I had no idea, and I realized that now I would never know. There were photos of some of the houses we had lived in, which I remembered more or less distinctly, as well as the rather palatial villa where my mother had been brought up in pre-war Koenigsberg, and the much more modest hut where my father had been born. I spent a lot of time staring at the latter, trying to discern how it had made my father what he was, searching too for some sense of my own links to that log-built cabin with the plank floor and the tiled stove. I could find nothing. My father's past was closed to me, and it was only now that I understood how much. I could not imagine how it must have felt to get up in that hut every morning and feed the animals and till the fields.

Without communism, my father was fond of saying, he

would not have got an education, never left Tambov oblast, not become what he did. Until the age of sixty, he had believed implicitly in the Party. Like so many military men, it was the war in Afghanistan that had made him see things differently. When the sealed coffins began returning from the battlefield, his faith in the Party was shattered. The young men in those coffins were my age. Though he never admitted it, he began to be thankful I had not followed him into the army as he had always wanted.

The three of us kept vigil alone. Irina's husband was in St. Petersburg, my wife was in Germany, the grandchildren were away at school or university. I don't think any of us missed them. This was the last time we would be together as a family, just the four of us, as we were in the beginning, when my father's postings took us across the length and breadth of the Soviet Union. Once or twice a day, we congregated in the study, all three of us together, and reminisced in low voices. The picnic in Rostov where Irina lost her doll, the courtyard in Kaliningrad where Axel used to hide behind the dustbins, Mama's friend Yulia in Vladivostok. Once, in a low voice, barely above a whisper, my mother told the familiar tale of how she had first met my father, in 1945, in what was still Koenigsberg. The war had been over for three months, and Germany was ruined. She was scavenging for food, and he had given her a piece of bread. She broke off and began to cry quietly. Hearing is the last of the five senses to go, and I like to think that he could travel back into the past with us, even though he could no longer see us clearly nor feel which of us was holding his hand. We had been with him then, we were with him now, and the memories we shared were as real as the books on the shelves and the photos on the walls.

My father was seventy-six, which was nearly twenty years more than the lifespan of the average Russian male. Many of his friends were dead, and others were too ill to travel. Some of the neighbours came by to pay their respects, and a few of his former colleagues from the Ministry dropped in. Most of them had forgotten by now about the furore I had caused nine years earlier, but I got a few odd looks, and one or two queries which I guessed they would not have dared put to my father. Their curiosity reminded me how much I owed him for his support throughout that whole messy business. He had guided me in my dealings with the media, the Party, the security organs and the other official bodies who were taking an interest in my affairs. He had encouraged me to take advantage of the book deal offered by a German publishing house to leave the Soviet Union. He had even given me the courage to go back and talk to Katya when I thought I had lost her for good. It was because of him that I had been able to put it all behind me and make a new life. I hoped I would be able to do as much for my own son if he ever needed it.

But I hoped too that my son would not live through times that faced him with the kind of decisions I had had to make, and that he would not find himself at the midpoint of his life looking back on a wilderness of failure and betrayal. Karl was seven, and his ambition was to be a fireman. I was inclined to hope he wouldn't change his mind. Firemen didn't need to make moral choices. They saved everybody, and that way they ran no risk of coming face to face with someone they had wronged, as had happened to me only a few days earlier.

I had run into Stephen Maletius on the plane to Moscow. There were no direct flights from Munich, and I had had to change planes in Frankfurt. It was a tight connection, and I was one of the last passengers to board. I groped my way down the aisle, and found my seat next to a middle-aged man in a grey suit. As I sat down he glanced up from *Der Spiegel*.

'Stephen!' I said.

'Axel!' he said, and we gazed at each other in barely disguised horror.

The plane was full, and there was no chance of either of us changing our seat. I stowed away my hand-luggage and fastened my seat-belt. Stephen stared blankly at the seat-back in front of him. The doors closed, the plane shunted away from the airport building, the flight attendant began to talk about oxygen masks and lifebelts. By the time we had reached the runway, the shock was wearing off, and it was clear that we could not sit side by side in silence for the next few hours. Concealing our emotions, we began to talk. Like all strangers on planes, we steered clear of personal topics, at least to begin with. We told each other we were looking well, and inquired about our respective reasons for travelling to Moscow. Stephen was going to Russia for his paper, of which he was now foreign editor. The tenth anniversary of the opening of the Berlin Wall was coming up in a few days' time, and he was scheduled to interview Gorbachev and one or two of his acolytes for the occasion.

The plane took off, and we were issued with lunch trays and mini-bottles of red wine. The conversation reached cruising altitude. I had always enjoyed Stephen's company, whatever my doubts about Stephen as a man. He was perceptive and sometimes witty, he had unexpected opinions and interesting comments. As long as we stuck to the affairs of the day, we were safe. We discussed the collapse of communism, the rise of the robber capitalists, and the craving sometimes expressed by residents of the former East

Germany to see the Wall go back up five metres higher. We agreed that the East European countries had expected too much too soon, and that disappointment was inevitable. It all happened too fast, said Stephen. The opening of the wall was like a miracle, and people assumed the miracles would keep on coming. Absolutely right, I said, and described people I had met in East Germany who, after forty years of government-sponsored passivity, were bemused by the need to roll up their sleeves and fight for a share of the capitalist spoils, preferring to sag back defeated and reminisce about how much better things had been in their cosy little country behind the barbed wire.

We ate our cheese and attacked our dessert, a kind of Linzertorte made with jam and cardboard. We were somewhere above Poland by then, although nothing could be seen of it but clouds. Yes, I said, it had all seemed so easy back in 1989. Throw out the communists, embrace the free market, say what you want, and get rich. Ten years later, the East Europeans were just beginning to realize that freedom was the starting point, not the finishing line. It was child's play to take down the physical Wall, brick by brick, and throw it away. The hard part was to destroy the wall that was left in people's heads.

'What about Russia?' said Stephen. 'You must be disappointed by the way things have turned out there.'

'Of course I am. Gorbachev had his faults, but he was basically a decent man. Since he resigned, Russia has been sinking into a morass of corruption and self-enrichment. Yeltsin has destroyed the Soviet system, but he's put nothing in its place. He's let the old nomenklatura take charge of the country's assets and line their pockets at the nation's expense. He's turned us into a nation of money-launderers.'

'So in the end, your little trip across Europe with my wife served no useful purpose?'

I looked at him warily. 'What do you mean?'

He gestured impatiently. 'The papers you got hold of.'

'They didn't make any difference. But at least I tried.'

'No regrets then?' said Stephen, raising one eyebrow mockingly. His hair was grey now and his face was lined, but age had given him an undeniable air of distinction. Looking at him now, no one would suspect the missteps of his past.

'Some, yes. I regret what I did to you.'

'I know, I got your letter. You don't have to apologize, Axel. In the end it made no difference. No one ever found out what happened.'

I eyed him curiously. It wasn't the reaction I expected. 'Do you mean that?'

'Of course I do. You have to accept the way life turns out. Regret is pointless.'

Stephen's brand of journalistic pragmatism was rare in Moscow that autumn. Regret was everywhere: the whole of Russia was tainted with it. I saw it in the shame of the old ladies selling family heirlooms by the entrance to the Metro, the defiance of the pensioners marching for the anniversary of the Revolution, the face of a young woman hesitating over the purchase of a single Western yoghurt. I felt it in the air of my father's study, the forgotten faces gazing from the walls, the books on outdated military strategy that would never be read again. Sitting alone the last evening by the bedside, my thoughts drifted back to Raisa Gorbachev's funeral. She had died while I was in Moscow six weeks earlier, and my father and I had watched the funeral on television. They had exhumed some old film footage from the archives, and we had seen for the second time Raisa and Mikhail in their prime, ten years earlier, descending airplane steps, receiving bouquets, bringing hope. So much had seemed possible back then, but it had all gone sour. My father's eyes were full of tears. Not for the Gorbachevs, I suspected, for, like many Russians he took a critical view of the last General Secretary. Some remnant of Party loyalty forbade him from accepting that it was not Gorbachev but seven decades of communist mismanagement that had destroyed the Soviet Union. No, his sadness was for Russia, and perhaps himself. He had lost hope twice in his life: once when the Party failed him, and once when perestroika collapsed. It was regret, not cancer, that was killing him.

My father died late in the evening on the ninth of November. He had been sliding away all day. He had stopped eating several days earlier, and today he had not even drunk his tea. He had not spoken for hours. He was letting go. He had done nothing all day but breathe, and in the course of the evening his breathing became laboured and heavy, each breath an effort for his wasted frame. Listening to him was unbearable. My sister came to relieve me about nine o'clock, and sent me to watch television at the other end of the flat. When she came to fetch me an hour later, I was watching the newscast. Gorbachev and Kohl and Bush were waving to the crowds at the Brandenburg Gate. The Berlin Wall had fallen exactly ten years earlier. In a sense, Stephen was right. Some things defied regret. One was the night the Wall opened. Another was the day when my father rode into Berlin on a tank and found himself nose to nose with an American tank moving in from the West. Or else there was the crust of bread. He had once told me it was the best thing he ever did in his life.

I followed Irina back up the corridor. My mother was already at his bedside. The rattle had stopped, and his breathing was quieter and much slower.

And you, he had asked me slyly, what was the best thing you ever did? I had hesitated before answering. It was the summer of 1995, and we were sitting on the verandah of the dacha drinking beer. Katya was reading a book a few feet away, the children were playing some mysterious game in the birch trees at the end of the garden. The garden shimmered softly under the white northern sky. I wasn't sure what to say. The crust of bread was hallowed family myth. Perhaps because it was not an act of seduction, but of simple human charity. I didn't think I had anything to match up to that. In the end, I said that the best thing I had ever done was to drive to Koenigsberg with Katya in the summer of 1990. My father looked perplexed.

'You mean Kaliningrad?' he said.

Katya looked up and smiled. 'No, Koenigsberg.'

'But we didn't get there anyway,' I added.

'Of course we did,' she said.

Mystified, my father looked from one to the other of us, and we found ourselves telling him the whole story. Some of it he had trouble believing, and if he had been hearing it from me alone, I doubt he would have accepted it as the truth. But Katya was helping me tell the tale, so he went on listening trustfully.

They had always got on well, my father and Katya, and I suddenly wished she was here with him now. But it was too late. My father's life was almost over. For a few minutes longer, he went on breathing, each time more quietly. Once or twice, the breathing seemed to stop, and we glanced at each other questioningly, but then it started up again.

Finally, there was a last long expiration, and that was the end.

One

Katharine

Go, go, go, said the bird: human kind
Cannot bear very much reality.
T.S. Eliot, 'Burnt Norton'

July 1990

In 1990, the Communist Party was still in power in the Soviet Union, and the Cold War was not yet over. If you remember how things were back then, it might make it easier to understand what happened.

When the doorbell rang, it was still quite early in the morning. I was alone in the house. Stephen had been gone all week on assignment abroad, and Jessica had left for school. I opened the door, expecting the postman or a neighbour or an encyclopedia seller. Instead, I found Axel standing in front of me. It had been ten years since I saw him. I recognized him immediately.

'Katharine!' he said. 'Thank God you're home!'

He was breathing fast, as though he had been running. The sleeve of his jacket was torn, there was a button missing from his shirt, his trousers were crumpled and dusty. Behind him, the birds were twittering in the trees, and the garden was cool and hazy with the promise of a hot day to come.

'Axel?' With an effort, I found my voice. 'What are you doing in London? What's happened to you?'

He cast a brief glance over his shoulder. 'May I come in?'

I hesitated a moment, and then I moved aside to let him pass. He closed the door behind him, cast a brief look round, and set off down the hall. He paused at the door to the sitting room, took in the uncurtained windows overlooking the street, and continued towards the kitchen. The windows there looked on to the garden. The previous owner of the house had planted a sturdy barrier of privet round the edge of the property and reinforced it with ten-feet high wooden fences. To keep out the vandals, he had explained proudly. Stephen's phobia was neighbours, not vandals, but the same defence measures were deemed appropriate and had been allowed to remain.

Axel seemed to approve of the arrangements too. 'We will sit here,' he announced, and settled himself at the kitchen table.

I wondered what his phobia was. He looked me in the eye and prepared to tell me about it.

'Katharine, I am sorry to burst in on you like this.' He pushed a lock of hair out of his eyes. He was speaking German, the language we had always used in the past. 'The fact is, my life is in danger. You and Stephen are the only people in London I can trust. I have come to ask you to help me.'

I leant against the kitchen counter and stared at him. 'In danger?'

'Yes. I'm sorry, this sounds melodramatic, but it's true. I have nowhere else to go.'

'But what—?' I looked harder at his dishevelled appearance. 'Do you mean someone's, er . . .'

'Someone is chasing me, yes.'

'Oh. Who—?'

'The KGB.'

'Oh. Why—?'

'Where is Stephen? Has he left for the office?'

'Stephen's not here. He's gone to Lithuania for the paper.'

'Lithuania? Oh God, no.' Axel sagged in his chair and glanced rather desperately round the kitchen. There were dark circles under his eyes, and his face had a battered look that hadn't been there when he came in. Or perhaps I hadn't seen it in the white morning haze. His gaze came to rest on a loaf of bread that was sitting on the table, next to a pile of books on Rilke. 'Would you mind if I ate some of that?'

I shook my head. He pushed aside the books, cut a slice, wolfed it down, and cut another. 'I haven't eaten since breakfast yesterday.'

'What's happening to you? Is there anything I can do?'

'I don't know. I was counting on Stephen being here. I need to think what to do next.'

He reached out to the loaf for the third time. I pulled myself together and offered him some breakfast.

'Thank you,' said Axel, sounding surprised, and I realized that the welcome so far hadn't been rapturous. 'That is very kind of you.'

'Not at all,' I said politely, picking up the frying pan.

'But perhaps you could take a look at the street first? If you wouldn't mind?'

'The street?'

'Just to make sure that everything is normal.' I was staring at him like the village idiot, so after a minute he spelt it out for me. 'To make sure that no one is watching the house. An upstairs window would be better.'

'Oh. Right.' Since leaving Moscow, I had lost the knack of trying to anticipate the KGB. I put down the frying pan and went upstairs. Nothing untoward was happening in the street, at least not that I could see. The birds were still singing, a few late commuters were leaving for work. I went back to the kitchen to report. Axel had poured himself some coffee and was leafing through Rilke's letters to Lou-Andreas Salomé. He watched me as I put the rashers of bacon into the pan and lit the gas.

'I am glad to see you again, Katharine, even though I wish it was not under circumstances like these.'

'Yes,' I said, 'it's been a long time, hasn't it?'

'I didn't know if I was going to see you at all. I found Stephen's name and address in the phone book, but I wasn't sure if you would be there too.'

'Oh, Stephen and I patched things up after leaving Moscow. These days we get on very well.'

'I'm glad to hear it,' said Axel. I looked up, but he was watching me flip over the bacon with a perfectly bland expression.

'One egg or two?' I asked.

'What are all these books on Rilke for? Is Stephen writing a piece?'

I cracked eggs into the pan and didn't answer. Axel ate three eggs, five rashers of bacon, two slices of toast, and drank two more cups of coffee. I finished up the pot to keep him company and work out my next move.

While he ate, we listened to the news on Deutschlandfunk. German economic union, which had taken place a few days earlier, was going well. The replacement of the East German mark by the West German Deutschmark had encountered relatively few hitches. The political union of East and West Germany was expected by the end of the year. Chancellor Kohl was scheduled to meet President Gorbachev in ten days' time to resolve the final obstacles.

I started to make some comment about reunification, but the announcer moved on to the Soviet Union, and I broke off to listen. In Moscow, delegates to the Twenty-Eighth Congress of the CPSU were split between conservatives who wanted the Communist Party to continue to lead the country, and reformers who wanted to see it transformed into a normal political party. The conservatives were not adapting easily to the prospect of change. Gorbachev was coming under fire for betraying Marxism-Leninism, surrendering Eastern Europe, condoning the rise of a liberal press, and attempting to democratize the military.

Axel muttered something about dinosaurs.

The last item concerned Lithuania. The parliament in Vilnius had suspended its declaration of independence, and the Kremlin had lifted its economic blockade of Lithuania. However, negotiations were not expected to get under way for at least another week.

'When will Stephen be back from Vilnius?' said Axel.

'I don't know. If nothing's happening, he may file today or tomorrow for Sunday's edition and then come home.'

'I see.' He pushed his plate away. 'Thank you. That was very nice. May I ask one last favour before I leave?'

'Of course.' I hoped my relief at the news that he planned to leave wasn't too obvious.

'Could I take a bath?'

'Naturally,' I said. 'No trouble at all.' I took him upstairs, showed him how the taps worked and got a clean towel out of the airing cupboard. Then I went down to tackle the mess in the kitchen and wrestle with my conscience. Should I let Axel leave and take his chances on the street? Or should I find out what his problem was and see if I could help? I put the books on Rilke back in their pile, ready to go in the car later on. I knew from experience that, once Stephen joined me, I would need a place to retreat.

I was halfway through the washing up when the doorbell rang. I swore to myself and went to answer it. A man I had never seen before was standing in front of me. He had a receding hair-line and a natty summer suit, and, when he opened his mouth, impeccable English with a pronounced Russian accent.

'Mrs. Maletius? Mrs. Katharine Maletius? My name is Petrov. I am a welfare officer at the Soviet Embassy. Please.' He handed me a plasticized identification card. A cold draught flickered down my spine.

'What can I do for you, Mr. Petrov?' I switched back into the hostess routine I had been using on Axel. Treat the KGB as a purely social predicament, and perhaps they will go away and leave you alone.

'Please. Your neighbours. I would not wish . . . May I come in for a minute?'

I ushered him into the sitting room. He didn't seem to mind uncurtained windows. We sat in the chintz-patterned armchairs on either side of the fireplace. He caught my glance at the clock and got to the point.

'Tell me, Mrs. Maletius, do you remember the name Axel Kanevsky?'

'Of course. He was my husband's assistant in Moscow.'

'I have come to warn you that Axel Alexandrovich is at present in London. We think he may try to get in touch with you.'

I tried to look incredulous. 'Really?'

'I must explain, Mrs. Maletius, that Axel Alexandrovich is a sick man. A few days ago, he suffered an accident, and his mental faculties have been affected. He suffers from periods of amnesia. He cannot remember who he is, where he lives. You understand?'

'I think so.'

'There is something else. He suffers also from paranoia. You understand this clinical term? It means he can be dangerous. If he comes here, Mrs. Maletius, you must be very careful. If he comes to you and says that he is being pursued, that his life is in danger, I suggest you pretend to believe him. Tell him you will help him to hide, do not tell him that I have been here talking to you, try to reassure him. And then please contact me at this number as soon as you can without arousing his suspicions.' He handed me a piece of paper. 'We are very concerned about Axel Alexandrovich, Mrs. Maletius. I hope you will help us.'

It was grotesque. After five years of glasnost and four of perestroika, did they really expect me to swallow a tale like that? In other circumstances, I might have been tempted to laugh. But Petrov had hardly taken his dark brown gaze off my face since he stepped into my house, and it was beginning to have a slightly hypnotic effect. His soft, urgent voice frightened me more than the words he was using. I steeled myself to answer normally.

'If Axel is ill, why is he wandering round on his own?'

'Unfortunately we did not take enough precautions to protect him from himself. Yesterday he was in a car on his way to the airport – we were sending him back to Moscow for medical treatment – and he jumped out at a traffic light and ran away from the person escorting him.'

I got to my feet. I couldn't take any more of this. 'I understand perfectly, Mr. Petrov. If we hear from Axel, we'll certainly get in touch with you, but I should warn you that we're leaving for France this evening.'

My use of the first person plural was instinctive. Maybe these people knew already that Stephen was away, but, if they didn't, I saw no reason to let them know I was a woman living alone with her daughter on a secluded London street.

'I assume your husband is out at the moment?' said Petrov.

'He's at the office,' I agreed.

'But he's going to France with you tonight?'

'Yes.' Impossible to backtrack now.

'Then I wish you both a pleasant holiday, Mrs. Maletius.'

The door closed behind him. I stood in the doorway of the sitting room and watched him walk down the path and turn into the street. He moved with a confident tread and looked neither to right nor left. For a moment, the house was absolutely still. I breathed quietly, in and out, and fought to control my rising panic.

'The Rezident,' said Axel from somewhere above me. 'The top KGB man at the London embassy. Has he gone?'

'Yes.' I looked up. He was leaning over the banister, wrapped in a large pink bath towel. 'Did you hear all that?'

'Yes. I thought you handled him very well.' He started down the stairs. 'Are you really leaving for France today?'

'Yes.'

'Where are you going?'

'Normandy. We have a house there. Jessica and I are driving down to Dover when she gets out of school this afternoon.'

'Jessica?'

'My daughter.'

'You have a daughter? How old is she?'

'Eight,' I said.

'Will you take me to France with you?'

I stared at him.

'I think I should leave England. Since Stephen is not here, there's no point in staying.'

'Why do you want Stephen so badly? Because he's a journalist? I can put you in touch with one of his colleagues, if you like.'

Axel shook his head violently. 'I can't take the risk. I would have trusted Stephen, but . . . England is not safe for me. I must leave as soon as possible. Maybe it was Fate that sent me to your house. I have a much better chance of getting out of the country by sea than by air. Probably they have placed watchers in the airports already, but it's harder to control the ports. How much luggage are you taking with you?'

'A lot,' I said ungraciously. 'Were you planning to hide in the boot?'

'On the floor in the back. Do you have a rug to put over me?'

'Jessica travels in the back. She might give you away.'

Axel frowned. 'Then we will have to think of something else.'

The front door suddenly rattled as something was pushed through the letter box, and made us both jump.

'What is it?' asked Axel in a whisper.

'Only the local paper. But if anyone comes . . . Maybe you should get dressed.'

'Of course. But I was going to ask if you could lend me something of Stephen's. My own clothes, as you saw, are not very presentable.'

'What happened to them?'

'I jumped out of a car at a traffic light. That much was true. Then I slipped when I was running away and tore my jacket.'

'So they really were sending you back to Moscow?'

'No, I was meant to be flying to Ghana. They just wanted me out of the way. But if they get hold of me again, this time it will be Moscow. The Serbsky Institute.'

My eyes widened in disbelief. The Serbsky Institute? The notorious psychiatric clinic where the regime interned its opponents under Brezhnev? For the second time that morning, I felt icy cold. Had Petrov been telling the truth? Was Axel clinically paranoid? 'Let's go and find some clothes,' I said carefully, but Axel had seen my incredulity.

'They still put people in there,' he said curtly. 'Don't believe everything you read in the paper about political liberalization in the Soviet Union.'

I didn't answer. He put out a hand and pulled me round to face him. 'Katya—'

His torso was stronger and more muscled than it had been ten years earlier. I averted my eyes. 'Don't worry. I'm not going to hand you over to them.'

'Don't you believe me?'

'I didn't say that. Do you want some clothes, or don't you?' I pulled away and started up the stairs. He followed me up to the bedroom in silence. While I went through Stephen's cupboards, he stood behind the curtains and surveyed the street. I threw clothes on the bed, ignoring him. T-shirt, socks, underpants, jeans. Holiday wear to blend in with the tourists on the ferry. I had no desire to drive him to France, but I could see no way to refuse his request.

'There you are, Axel. I'll leave you to get dressed.'

'Katya. Come over here.' Something in the way he spoke made me do as he said. 'Look at that.' He took hold of my shoulder and pointed down the street. A black car was parked four doors down to the left. Two men were sitting in it. 'Now look that way,' said Axel, tightening his grasp. I looked. Another black car was manoeuvering into a space over to the right, just in front of the Reynolds' house. John was a stockbroker in the City, and Barbara was a personnel officer in an Oxford Street department store. Neither would be home before seven. The car could stay there all day, with no questions asked. We watched to see if anyone got out of the car. No one did. On a quiet street like this, both sets of watchers could sit there all day and no one would notice.

'It's hard to be sure at this distance,' said Axel, 'but I think the driver of the car that just arrived is the man who drove me to the airport last night.'

For the rest of the day, I did more or less what I had planned to do. I ran the dishwasher, watered the plants, loaded the Volvo and locked the house. I kept my mind on what I was doing and tried not to think of the men sitting waiting in their black cars outside.

Around half past two, Axel, wearing one of Stephen's suits and Stephen's spare pair of glasses, and carrying Stephen's old briefcase, walked down to the end of the garden, pushed aside the loose board in the fence, squeezed into the alleyway which ran between the gardens, and followed it as far as the park. Following my instructions, he made his way between the seesaws and the tennis courts and emerged in the street which led to the station. Swinging the briefcase with the air of a man released from his workaday shackles, he sauntered back down to the traffic lights, crossed the road by the

Baptist church, and wandered up our street, surveying the houses with the detached air of one who is soon to leave all this behind him. The watchers in the first black car sat up straighter as he passed. They stared intently as he turned into our driveway, pausing to nip off the head of one of the roses, opened the door, and entered the house. Once he was out of sight, there was a frantic burst of activity on the car phones, but no one got out of their car. As far as we could tell, their attention was still directed at the street, not the house. They seemed to accept that what they had seen was my husband coming home from the office. When we left the house to drive to Jessica's school, neither car followed us.

'That doesn't mean anything,' said Axel. 'They might have someone else doing that. Keep an eye open for anyone following us to the school.'

He had changed back into T-shirt and jeans, and switched the reading glasses, which he said gave him a headache, for ordinary sunglasses. He had also borrowed an old leather jacket whose pockets bulged oddly, with the contents, I supposed, of the three manila envelopes he had requisitioned earlier in the day. From a distance, it was certainly hard to tell him and my husband apart. Even here in the car at close quarters, the semi-familiarity was unnerving. I couldn't imagine why I had never noticed the physical similarity before – same height, same build, same dark-blond colouring – and then I realized it would have been less marked ten years earlier. Axel was skinnier and sharper then, while Stephen already had the solid self-assertiveness of the professional fact-finder. As to the rest, one could probably just chalk it up to heredity and the fact that their respective ancestors had been born within a few miles of each other. Koenigsberg

Man. I switched on the car radio to hide my unease, and the cassette I had been listening to the previous day came on. The dignified eighteenth-century cadences cascaded into the car. I turned the volume down.

Axel took the cassette out of the machine, looked at it and put it back again.

'You listen to this?'

'No. Stephen must have left it there.'

We turned the last corner and came in sight of Jessica's school. I found a place to park, and put the cassette in its box.

'Get her into the car,' said Axel, 'and I'll turn round and introduce myself. How long before she comes out?'

I looked at my watch. 'Three minutes.'

'Get out and wait for her. I'll read the paper. What are you looking at me like that for?'

'That's exactly the kind of thing that Stephen would do. Hide behind his paper to avoid saying hello to the mothers.'

Axel gave me a bland smile. 'I must have inherited Stephen's behaviour along with his clothes.'

'My God, that's all I need!'

The words were out before I could stop them. Axel raised his eyebrows. From inside the school came the sound of the bell, followed by a crescendo of voices and a rush of feet. Jessica was in the forefront of the stampede across the courtyard.

'There she is,' said Axel.

I turned to stare at him. 'How do you know who she is?'

'Katya, with hair that colour, she couldn't be anyone's child but yours.'

He was right, of course. I slammed the car door harder than was necessary and went to meet her.

'Mummy, Mummy, we played games all afternoon, and I hit a six at rounders, and it was my best hit ever, and Susan Evans was the backstop and she's absolutely useless, and Gillian hit a six too, and can she come and stay with us when we get back from France, Mummy, Mummy, please say yes, and you have to sign this and send it back before the start of the new term, and there's another one too, but I think I put it in my satchel, otherwise I won't be able to—'

'Of course, darling, we'll see about that on the boat. In you get.' I opened the car door, and steered her gently inside. 'Right now we have to drive very fast, or we're going to miss the boat.'

The first thing she saw was the back of Axel's head and the newspaper he was holding in front of his face. 'Daddy!' she cried joyfully. I shut the car door and went slowly round to the other side of the car. I paused to wave to a couple of other mothers. I pretended to adjust the strap of my sandal. I pushed the wing mirror forward and then I put it back where it had been before. This was going to be harder than I thought.

'Yes, your Daddy and I look a bit the same,' Axel was saying as I got into the car. I had forgotten how good his English was. He had put the radio back on and was listening to the news. 'I'm sorry if I disappointed you. I hope you don't mind me coming on the boat with you instead?'

'Oh no,' said Jessica. 'In fact it might be a good thing, because you can come out on deck with me if it's windy, because Mummy won't go out if it's windy, and she won't let me go out on my own because she thinks I'm going to fall overboard, and Daddy's always reading his newspaper, and so I always have a really rotten time on the boat. You will come on deck with me, won't you?'

'Of course I will,' said Axel.

'Brilliant,' said Jessica. 'It's a pity Mummy didn't tell me earlier that you were coming with us, then I might have had something to look forward to all day while we were playing silly rounders. Why didn't you tell me, Mummy?' she added accusingly.

'Because I forgot. Axel called after you were in bed last night, and in the rush to get you off to school this morning, it slipped my mind.'

'It's a good job we had a spare ticket, isn't it? When's Daddy coming?'

'He doesn't know. Some time next week.'

'If that's what he says, it's going to be longer than that. It won't be till the week after next, maybe not even then.'

'Why do you say that?' said Axel.

'Because he always says he's going to do things, and then he doesn't. Mummy, I'm starving.'

'There should be a packet of biscuits somewhere.'

'Brilliant. Can we have some music please? I hope you aren't going to want to listen to the news all the time, Axel. That's another thing my father does. Put on that concerto thing, Mummy – you know, the one you listen to.'

Axel held up the box with the cassette I had just taken out. The Brandenburg Concertos. 'This one?'

'That's right. Did you bring me some clothes? I hope you don't expect me to go to France looking like this.'

'You look very nice,' said Axel, turning to look at her. 'That's a very pretty dress.'

'That's my *school* dress,' said Jessica.

'I'm afraid you'll have to stay like that until Dover,' I said. 'Everything's packed in the suitcase.'

'But you always remember to leave something out for me,' wailed Jessica.

'Today I forgot,' I said. 'Today I had a lot of things on my mind.'

Today, Jessica, I had Moscow on my mind. The city of blank walls and dead faces. You spent your first two years there, but I doubt you remember much about it. As for me, I try to keep it as far from my thoughts as I can. For the past few years, I haven't been doing too badly.

Stephen and I arrived in the USSR in June 1979. To become Moscow correspondent of an up-market Sunday newspaper was no small achievement at the age of thirty-one, and Stephen was in a hurry to prove himself worthy of the task. Before we left London, he had taken a course in Russian, and embarked on an extensive programme of reading. He planned to make his mark on the profession, and was already talking knowledgeably about relations between Brezhnev and the Politburo and the Central Committee, and the definitive study of the Soviet life and system that he intended to write at the end of our three years of field work. As soon as we arrived, he threw himself into his work, attending press conferences, hunting out dissidents, chasing up contacts. I was left pretty much to my own devices.

I hated Moscow on sight. Driving into the city on our first day, I was struck by the frightening lack of connection between the elaborate Stalinist-Gothic skyscrapers on the Ring Road and the wasteland of pot-holed boulevards and broken windows that surrounded them. The city was decaying, and nobody cared. I had seen much the same thing as we left Leningrad a few hours earlier. There was a gap between rulers and ruled, between myth and reality, and life had drained away into that gap. The crowds tramping endlessly down the concrete boulevards walked like zombies, with unfocused expressions and shapeless clothes. Moscow was the city of the living dead. The huge red-lettered Party slogans appalled me with their dehumanised messages about Peace and Glory and Labour. They bore no relationship to anything real or alive. What chilled me the most was the lack of colour, fantasy, idiosyncrasy. Everything was the same, everything was sludge-coloured. There were no advertising posters on the streets, no Western clutter of shops and stalls and restaurants and cafés to break up the terrible monotony of the grey suburban apartment blocks and the immense grey boulevards. There were no display windows, no coloured awnings, no neon shop signs to catch the eye and stimulate the mind. LENIN IS ALWAYS WITH US said the banner hanging from the rooftops at the end of the street.

It took me some months to understand that there was life in Moscow, but that it was lived out of sight. Behind their dead eyes, the people in the streets were alive and well and thinking all manner of non-socialist thoughts. Behind the scabby facades of the buildings, life was going on in the same dishevelled, noisy way as on the rest of the planet. But as foreigners, Stephen and I were on the outside looking in, and the authorities took good care that there was nothing to see. They assigned us an apartment in an eight-storey block for foreigners. It was separated from the adjacent buildings by a ten-foot high wall, and two guards stood sentry by the entrance twenty-four hours a day.

Unlike Stephen, I arrived in the USSR speaking no Russian, unable even to decipher the alphabet. The paper was prepared to pay for lessons for Stephen, but not for me. When they told him this, Stephen decided I didn't need to learn Russian beforehand. I would pick it up once I got there. Since I already knew French and German, he assured me, it wouldn't be a problem.

It was an enormous problem. Even getting around town was an ordeal. Taxis did not understand where I wanted to go, and with no knowledge of Cyrillic it was impossible to find my way in the metro. French and German were no help at all. In other countries I had visited, the sight of a distraught foreigner with a map on a street corner would attract any number of willing rescuers. Not here. The Muscovites' reluctance to help, or even communicate, reduced me to despair. Once, lost in the metro, I approached a woman official standing on the platform. She reeled out a stream of rapid instructions. 'Ya ne ponemayou,' I told her carefully. I don't understand. Out came the same instructions, replayed at the same speed, followed by a glare to indicate that the interview was ended. I slunk off in the direction indicated by her pointing finger, found a sign marked VYKHOD, EXIT, one of the few words I knew, and walked home.

'You don't understand,' said Axel. 'It's not part of her job to help people find their way. She's only paid by the State to stand on the platform. Never ask someone for help in their official capacity. That's not what they're there for.'

Axel was the assistant assigned to Stephen by the Soviet Foreign Ministry. His job was to make calls on Stephen's behalf, read the Soviet press, accompany Stephen on interviews and trips, and do everything that Stephen's still limited Russian prevented him from doing himself. Since Stephen's office was in the same building as our apartment, Axel and I saw a lot of each other. I was twenty-three and he was twenty-five. I had a degree in German and had spent a year in Munich. Axel's mother was German, and he spoke the language fluently. It became natural for me to stop on my way upstairs to say hello, ask Axel's advice on esoteric aspects of Moscow life, recount my latest triumphs and setbacks.

Axel frequently came upstairs to the flat looking for books or papers, requesting a packet of sugar, providing the solution to the problem we had discussed the previous day. Most of the other foreign wives were older than me, and we had little in common. They spent their time chalking up grudges against the system, and planning their next trip to Helsinki. Towards the end of the summer, I met a Russian girl in a bookstore where I was looking for a Russian grammar. I had written down the name of the book, but I was unable to pronounce it correctly. The salesgirl couldn't or wouldn't speak English. Natasha was standing behind me in the queue. She came to my rescue, deciphered the title, and browbeat the assistant into checking the shelves. When it turned out they didn't have the book, she bore me off to another shop. We talked, exchanged addresses, and agreed to meet again. The second meeting never materialized. It took me some time to realize that Natasha had had second thoughts about the wisdom of getting involved with a foreigner. For months, Axel was the only living person I knew.

The journey to France was uneventful. The traffic was fluid and the sea was calm. I kept a watchful eye on the driving mirror, but no one was following us, and no one appeared to suspect that the man sitting beside me was not Mr. S.J. Maletius, British citizen, born in Bristol on January 10, 1948, not even the young passport officer in Dover, whose gaze seemed to go back and forth from Stephen's photograph to Axel's face more times than was necessary for a routine check. But, as Axel pointed out later in the bar, he probably hadn't been on the job long enough to realize that no one looked like their passport photo.

'Drink that up.' He pushed a glass of whisky towards me.

'Frontiers are in the mind, not on the ground. Don't look so guilty.'

'The barbed wire in the mind,' I said, and immediately wished I hadn't. I could see that Axel knew exactly what I was referring to. There was an awkward silence. Despite the heat, Axel was still wearing Stephen's leather jacket.

Jessica came bouncing towards us with a packet of crisps.

'How long have you and Mummy known each other?' she demanded. 'Would you like a crisp? Why haven't I seen you before?'

'Your parents and I met a long time ago. But we haven't seen each other for several years. I don't live in England, you see.'

'Where do you live?'

'Moscow.'

'Are you a Russian?'

'Yes. How did you guess?'

'Well if you live in Moscow, it's obvious, isn't it? Anyway, you don't speak English like we do.'

'You mean I have an accent?'

'Yes. It doesn't matter, though. I have an accent too when I speak French. Everyone knows I'm not French. They can't tell I'm not German though,' she added smugly.

'Du sprichst auch Deutsch?' said Axel.

'Natürlich,' said Jessica disdainfully.

'We lived in Bonn for three years,' I said, 'and Stephen speaks German to her at home.'

'Do you speak French, Axel?' Jessica was intent on establishing her linguistic ascendancy.

'Not very much.'

'Well, never mind. They don't understand English in Morigny, but if you need anything, I can interpret for you.'

'Darling, Axel isn't coming to Morigny. We're just giving him a lift as far as Calais.'

Jessica's face fell. 'Why can't he come with us? Just for a few days, until Daddy comes. Why don't you come with us, Axel? We have a big house, you can sleep in the spare room. You don't have to go back to Moscow right away, do you? Mummy, he can come with us, can't he? Please say yes, please, please!'

'Axel has his own plans, Jess. We mustn't interfere.'

'You don't have plans, do you, Axel? Why can't we be your plans?'

Axel looked from her to me and back again. He was smiling disarmingly, and my heart sank. 'Actually, I do have time to spare. Where exactly is your house?'

La Morosière was on the edge of Normandy, fifty kilometres west of Chartres. It had been the property of my great-aunt, who had moved to France before I was born and stayed there for the rest of her life. By the standards of suburban Leicestershire, this made her a raving eccentric. Christmas cards marked 'Joyeux Noël et Bonne Année' were received every year with bemused reverence, and Aunt Eleanor was regarded as a latter-day Hester Stanhope. She had died five years earlier, leaving the house to me. Although we had never met, the fact that I had lived in Russia and Germany gave me an edge over the rest of the family. My sister, who had done a degree in Russian and was about to spend six months in Leningrad, said it wasn't fair.

'What are you going to do with the money?' said Stephen, when we heard the news.

I looked at him warily. Stephen was a firm believer in state-of-the-art technology, and there had recently been talk of a new computer. 'What money?'

‘The money from the house. When you sell it, I mean.’

‘I don’t know if I am going to sell it. I haven’t decided yet.’

‘You don’t mean you’re going to keep it?’

‘Why not? It looks rather nice.’

He gave me a tolerant smile over the top of his newspaper.

‘Be reasonable, Katie. What will we do with a house in France?’

‘Use it for holidays.’

‘Holidays? You know how difficult it is for me to get away—’

‘Exactly. This is somewhere Jessica and I can go on our own, and you can join us between two world crises. We’ve been posted abroad ever since we were married, and we have no house of our own in England. I’m tired of spending holidays camping in my mother’s spare room.’

My resolve was hardening as I spoke. Until then, I had had no very clear idea what I would do with the house, but Stephen’s opposition was making me determined to hold on to it. I think he realized this. His lips tightened, but he stopped arguing. He decided we would visit the house on our way back to England from Bonn three weeks later, hoping no doubt that damp or dry rot would bring me to my senses. But I fell in love with La Morosière on sight.

It was a traditional farmhouse standing at the end of a quiet lane, miles from anywhere. Tall hedges ran along the side of the property that bordered the road, and on the other side were open fields. Further down the lane, green and impenetrable, rose the forest.

‘Look, Mummy, cows,’ said Jessica.

‘My God, it’s really the back of beyond,’ said Stephen.

We unlocked the door and went inside. There was a big living room with oak beams and a fireplace. A winding staircase led to three sloping-roofed bedrooms. The walls were white, the furniture was oak, the windows looked out over grass and apple trees. In her youth, Aunt Eleanor had inherited a large sum of money from someone alleged to be rich and disreputable, whose role in her life had never been wholly elucidated. She had left me what remained of her nest egg, in the form of an account at the local Caisse d'Epargne, though I had omitted to mention it to Stephen. I had no intention of allowing my great-aunt's savings to wind up in the coffers of Apple Computers. I prowled round the house evaluating what needed doing, and found less than I expected. Aunt Eleanor had been fit and alert until the day she keeled over in the garden picking up the windfalls, victim of a sudden, massive stroke. Everything had been kept in working order up to her dying day. The neglectful patina of old age that I had expected to find over everything, dirty paint, cracked china, was totally absent. The house was not damp, there were no leaks, and the roof had been redone quite recently. I could see that Stephen, in spite of himself, was impressed.

'I like this house,' said Jessica. 'Will we come here next summer?'

'Yes,' I said.

'It would make a superb working environment,' said Stephen.

'Can I have the bedroom at the top of the stairs?'

'There's no telephone, Stephen. No television either, I don't think.'

'Of course not, that's just what I mean.' He too was prowling round, though his attention seemed to be fixed exclusively on the skirting boards. 'If I ever find time to write my book on Moscow . . .'

I refrained from pointing out that if he was serious about writing a book on Moscow, he would have done it a long time ago. We had had enough rows about that in the past. What Stephen liked best was the investigative side of his trade, the gathering of facts that gradually came together to reveal a unsuspected insight or a new theory. Writing up what he had learned was a necessary chore. It had to be done, but he got no pleasure out of it. It was not in his nature to sit down and write a full-length book, taking no phone calls, sending no faxes, meeting no sources.

'What are you looking for?' I said instead, as he peered into the corner behind the rocking chair. 'Dry rot?'

'Dry rot? Lord, no. I'm just looking for a place to plug in the computer.'

It was after midnight when Jessica and I reached La Morosière with our clandestine passenger. The house was waiting for us, crouched among the apple trees. We had passed only three houses since we turned off the main road, all of them dark and shuttered. People went to bed early in the country. The gardener and his wife had been in during the day, but at this hour they would be long gone. The farm next door was uninhabited. There was no one to see us arrive: no one to notice that it was a stranger, not Stephen, sitting in the front seat. La Morosière had its own access road leading off the lane. No one came down it except to see us. We were two kilometres from the nearest village, and seven from the nearest town. I found myself grudgingly thinking that it was the perfect place to hide out.

Jessica had already unlocked the front door and switched

on the house lights. I cut the headlights, got out of the car, yawned and stretched. My back was stiff from the hours of driving. The scent of newly cut grass came sharp and clean on the night breeze.

Axel began to unpack the car and mobilized Jessica to help. He kept his voice low, and made her do the same. By now all three of us were speaking German.

'Sssh. Don't you know that sound travels at night?'

'What does it matter?'

'You'll wake up the neighbours.'

'We don't have any neighbours. Only miles away, up the lane.'

'Yes, I saw them as we came past, but at night they can hear you. They won't be pleased if you wake them up so late. Pretend we've arrived here secretly and we don't want anyone to know, so we mustn't make any noise.'

Jessica, always ready for a new game, began tiptoeing round with exaggerated caution. Axel did the same, and they finished unloading the car in silent hilarity. I watched them, and the breeze raised goose-pimples on my skin. Was the danger still with us? Had it followed us across France and down the familiar lane, and was it lurking behind the gatepost at this very moment, ready to pounce?

Axel saw me shiver and when Jessica had disappeared into the house, staggering under a box of provisions, he came to stand next to me. 'I'm sorry, I didn't want to frighten you. I shouldn't have said that.' He took my hand, and pressed it reassuringly. 'There is of course no danger here. I just like to be careful, you understand?'

'I understand,' I said, and took my hand away. 'It's late. Let's get some of this food into the fridge and then I'm going to bed.'

* * *

The first time I saw Axel was the day after we arrived in Moscow. I was busy unpacking a trunk in our new flat. My hands were dirty, and there was a hole in my jeans. 'Katie,' said Stephen, 'this is Axel, my assistant.' I stared at Axel and Axel stared at me. After a moment, he said it was nice to meet me. He had dark blond hair and a washed-out black T-shirt. Stephen and I had been married for just ten months.

I had met Stephen in my last year at university. He was eight years older than me, and already a successful journalist. He knew where he was going and what he wanted. I was impressed by the spurious media glamour that surrounded him: headlines, cables, front-page articles. I was seduced by the need for the news to get through. At that point, I had no idea what to do with my life, and when he proposed to me I accepted at once. With him, I believed, I would have a more focused and purposeful existence than I could achieve on my own. I couldn't quite convince myself that I was in love, but I managed to make myself believe that love was unnecessary.

When we reached Moscow, I was beginning to lose my illusions. The need for the news to get through seemed less like a moral imperative, and more like an emotional alibi. Stephen didn't need a wife: he was married to his work. His idea of a normal working day was twelve hours' solid toil, and his notion of leisure was to study Russian grammar. Stephen did not need people. He could be a convivial guest or hospitable host with those he regarded as interesting or useful, but he never grew close to anyone, and I knew it wouldn't bother him if he never saw them again. Sometimes I thought it wouldn't bother him if he never saw me again either.

For Stephen too was realizing he had miscalculated. I eventually worked out that he had married me in a moment of self-doubt. His mother had just died, his career was flagging. A few months later, with his career back on track and his emotions returned to cold storage, his need for companionship had vanished. When he married me, he thought I was like him. He had some idea that we would lead parallel lives. Poor Stephen. He thought he was getting an independent woman who would be there when he wanted to talk, and who would pursue her own affairs when he was busy. By the time we got to Moscow, it was becoming clear that I needed him in a way he did not understand and could not reciprocate.

Probably I should have left him in Moscow and gone back to England and found myself a job. In the beginning, I suppose I stayed because of Axel. And then, when Axel went, it was too late.

After lunch the next day, Jessica went off on her bicycle to play with the children at the farm down the road, and Axel and I were left on our own in the garden. We sat on at the table with a bottle of wine and the camembert that Marcel and his wife had left as a welcome-back present.

The fears of the night before had vanished: today I was afraid of no one. I had unpacked the books on Rilke and read a couple of the Duino Elegies, and they had put me back in touch with my own world. '*Höre, mein Herz, wie sonst nur Heilige hörten . . .*' I had inspected cupboards, rearranged ornaments, and made mental notes of copper that needed cleaning and windows that needed painting. I had taken possession of my house again. The landscape that stretched before me was lush and full and peaceful, and the hum of insects filled the air. The summer fell softly around me, the house reared behind me like a bulwark. Nothing could touch me, not the KGB, not Moscow, not even Axel. Here I was safe.

The wind ruffled the fringes of the green and white parasol. Axel and I made conversation. To begin with, we talked about the house. I told him about Great-Aunt Eleanor, described the trials of long-distance dealings with electricians and carpenters, and made us both laugh. He asked after various members of my family, whom he had met when they visited Moscow. Was my father still with the bank? Was my sister still interested in Russia? My father was planning to retire next year, I told him, and my mother was still teaching. Juliet had written a thesis on readers' letters to Soviet newspapers, and then abandoned Russia for Unilever. I was surprised he remembered them so well.

Then he said, 'It's so peaceful here, so far away from everything. It's very different from your house in London. I feel much better today.'

'Yes?' I said. 'I'm so glad.'

'Katya. Don't talk to me as if I were Petrov. You English, you put on this big social act, and underneath one never knows what you're really thinking.'

I looked up and met his eyes. 'You know perfectly well what I'm thinking.'

'Yes,' Axel agreed. 'I promise I will only stay for a day or two. As soon as I have decided what to do, then I will leave.'

We watched each other across the table. The apple trees bent lazily in the wind.

'What have you done?' I said. 'Why are they looking for you?'

He waited for a moment before answering. 'When I told Jessica last night that I lived in Moscow, that wasn't entirely true. At the moment, I live in Germany. I've been working as an information officer in our consulate in Hamburg for the past two years. A few days ago I was given by mistake some papers, highly confidential, with restricted circulation. When I realized what was in them, I decided they ought to be made public. I contacted a German journalist I know, explained what they were, and asked if he was interested. He said he would talk to his editor and call me the next day. But the next morning, I was summoned to the office of my superior and told I was being transferred immediately to Ghana.'

'What? You think the journalist tipped off—'

'Perhaps. Or perhaps I was already under surveillance. It doesn't matter. I was given one hour to pack my things, and then I was driven to the airport to catch a plane to London. There are no direct flights from Hamburg to Ghana, you see. I was collected at Heathrow and driven to the Embassy, and then taken back in the evening for my flight to Accra. That's when I managed to jump out of the car and make my way to your house. I hoped Stephen would print my documents.'

'What are these documents?'

He hesitated. 'I think it's wiser if I don't tell you that.'

Somewhere across the fields, a tractor started up. Axel poured the last of the wine, his attention riveted on the two glasses, a lock of blond hair falling unheeded across his face. I cut myself a triangle of camembert and ate it carefully.

'Axel, if you're thinking of waiting for Stephen to get back from Vilnius, I should warn you that what Jessica said yesterday is true. He doesn't always show up when he's supposed to.'

'Yes, I understand. What I need is to get to Moscow—'

He broke off as Jessica skidded round the corner of the house and dropped her bicycle on the grass. 'Their aunt and uncle have arrived from Évreux. It's not fair. Who's coming for a bike ride with me?'

* * *

What I loved most at La Morosière were the evenings. The heat lingered on in the sheltered garden while the light drained out of the day, and the sounds of the woods and fields and air died slowly all around. The insects fell silent and the tractors too. After a while there were no more cars, even on the main road. The voices from the gardens up the lane could be heard no more. It was at this time of day that the peace of the place was so thick you could almost reach out and touch it.

But tonight everything was different. The cocoon had been ruptured. We were vulnerable. The more I thought about what Axel had told me, the more it alarmed me. If the contents of these papers was sufficiently explosive to get him shipped off to Africa, then the KGB was going to keep looking for him. When he failed to resurface, they would double-check. It would be easy to discover that Stephen was out of the country, easy to guess who had left for France in Stephen's place, and not very much harder to find La Morosière and track us down.

Jessica went to bed without protesting at nine o'clock, worn out from the exertions of the day. We had gone for a long bike ride during the afternoon, while Axel stayed behind, pleading the need for a siesta.

'I thought you said he slept all morning?' Jessica had said suspiciously as we wobbled out of the gate.

'He just wants to laze around in the sun for a bit. With no bossy little eight-year-olds telling him what to do all the time.'

'I hope you don't mean me. I was nine last October.'

'So you were. I was getting mixed up with last summer. Sorry, Jess.'

'I hope you didn't tell Axel I was eight.'

'I don't think I told him anything. He hasn't asked, believe it or not.'

'If he does, then I'll tell him I'm nine.'

'Just wait till he asks, okay?'

When we came back, we found him poking round the empty farmhouse next door, inspecting bags of cement and piles of electric wires. The owner lived thirty kilometres away, and was doing up the place for his son. Renovation plans fuelled the conversation until dinner time. While I made bolognese sauce, Axel and Jessica kicked a ball round the garden, to their great mutual satisfaction. That was something Stephen never did. He was always too absorbed with a book or the computer to engage in such unproductive pastimes.

'Do you have children of your own, Axel?' asked Jessica at dinner.

His mouth was full of spaghetti: he shook his head.

'Why not? Aren't you married?'

'No.'

'Why not?'

'Jessica!'

'I was married once, but it didn't last very long.'

'What was her name?'

'Marusya.'

'That's a weird name. Is it Russian?'

'Yes.'

'What about Katya? Is that a Russian name too?'

'Yes.'

'I've never heard anyone call Mummy that before.'

'No one else does,' I said. My eyes met Axel's: he smiled guardedly.

'Can I have some more spaghetti please? It's a pity you

don't have any children. Then you'd be able to play football more often.'

'You're quite right.'

'Of course, you can come and play with me whenever you want.'

When I came downstairs after putting her to bed, it was still light. Axel was sitting at the table. He had cleared away the remains of dinner, leaving only the bottle of wine and two glasses. He raised the bottle inquiringly.

I shook my head. 'No, I don't want a drink.' The idea of a long evening sitting alone with Axel in the garden was intolerable. 'I'm going for a walk before it gets dark.'

'I'll come with you. There won't be anyone around at this hour, will there?'

Being cooped up all day had clearly made him restless. I wondered how long he thought he could stay here without showing himself. Obviously he could not pass for Stephen at close quarters, and he had vetoed my suggestion that I should introduce him as a visiting friend.

We walked along the lane that led to the forest, and turned on to an unpaved track that led into the trees. Ahead of us, the sun was setting, vast and red and calm. Neither of us spoke. The only sounds to be heard were the noise of our feet on the path, and the distant croaking of frogs. '*O und die Nacht, die Nacht, wenn der Wind voller Weltraum . . .*' The words of the Elegies I had read that morning ran lightly in my head. After about a kilometre, we came to the lake.

It wasn't really a lake, but a large marshy pond. In a clearing to the left of the track stood a cabin with a small verandah. Axel stopped dead when he saw it.

'Who lives there?'

'No one. It's a hunting cabin. They only use it in autumn.'

'Ah.' He walked round it, pulling thoughtfully at the shutters, and I wondered if he was evaluating its possibilities as a refuge, should Petrov and his cohorts mount a full-scale siege of La Morosière. It occurred to me that because of him I would never be able to look on La Morosière with the same innocent pleasure as before, and I was suddenly angry. God damn Axel, what right did he have to force his way into my house, my family, my life? Sowing incertitude, shattering perspectives, in the same unexplained, destructive way as he had done ten years earlier.

'What's that thing?' he asked.

I followed his gaze. 'It's a raft. You can pole out into the lake. Jessica and I took it out once, but there's nothing much to see.'

'How deep is the lake?'

'It's quite shallow. A lot of mud and weeds on the bottom.'

'What's on the other side?'

'I don't know. More woods.'

And if you're thinking of using it as an escape route, you can bloody well check it out yourself, Axel. He was spoiling it all for me, the lake, the woods, the cabin. I should have left him in the garden. I should never have brought him here.

He stopped fiddling with the shutters, and walked back across the clearing towards me. 'What's the matter, Katya?'

The question, no less than the gentleness of his tone, took me aback. In the past, he had had an uncanny gift for sensing my moods. It seemed he had it still.

'Nothing.'

He put a hand on my arm and pulled me gently towards him. I stiffened.

'Katya?' His face was very close to mine.

'Axel, please. Don't.'

'I've missed you, all these years. Until yesterday, I didn't even realize how much.'

I didn't believe a word of it. 'You should have thought of that earlier,' I said, taking a step backwards. 'You were the one who walked out.'

'What?'

'Disappeared, if you prefer.' He didn't answer, and my exasperation increased. 'You know perfectly well what I mean. One day you were making calls to the Central Committee for Stephen, and the next you'd vanished into thin air, some fat girl showed up to take your place, and the Foreign Ministry more or less denied that you'd ever existed. As a way of ending an affair, it was pretty effective.'

'My God,' said Axel, in a very odd tone. 'Didn't Stephen tell you—'

'How could Stephen tell me anything? He didn't know what had happened to you either!'

'Is that what he said? Listen, Katya.' He took hold of my shoulders again, clutching me so hard that it hurt. 'When I left, it had nothing to do with you.'

I stared at him uncertainly. This time, for some reason, I did believe him.

'Really?'

'I was transferred to the provinces. It wasn't my choice. I couldn't tell you what was happening, I thought you'd understand. The last time we talked, I thought—'

He broke off. We were both silent, thinking of that last conversation.

'No,' I said finally, 'I didn't realize that.'

'So all this time you've been thinking—?'

'Yes.' I shook off his hands again, and took a couple of steps towards the track. 'But it doesn't matter. I got over it a long time ago. People change. Both Stephen and I have changed, especially me. We get on much better these days. In fact I would say we have a really good marriage now.'

Axel hadn't moved from where I had left him. In that dim light, I couldn't see his face.

'We should get back, it's going to be dark soon.'

'Yes.' He followed me across the clearing. The air of calculation that had been present in everything he had said and done for the past two days had gone, and he seemed genuinely at a loss. We started up the track in silence.

After a while, I said, 'I'm sorry I doubted you. I should have known better.'

'The last thing I wanted was to cause you pain.'

'Don't let it worry you. I really don't think about it any more.'

'Don't you?' said Axel.

'It all seems so remote. I was so young. One takes things much more to heart at that age.'

'If I'd known you spent ten years thinking I walked out on you, I don't know if I'd have dared to come knocking on your door yesterday.'

'Oh that's quite all right,' I realized that I had slipped back into my Petrov voice again. 'I'm glad I was able to help. For old times' sake, you understand.'

'Oh yes,' said Axel dryly, 'I understand. Don't worry, Katya, you make yourself very clear.'

The KGB found us the next day.

In the morning, I drove into Morigny, leaving Axel and Jessica playing cards. Morigny was two kilometres away. It had two hundred and ninety inhabitants, a church, three cafés, a school inaugurated in 1833 by Louis-Philippe, and a general store selling everything from postcards to anchovies. I slunk in like a thief, purchased eggs and milk and salt, and told everyone who asked that Stephen had caught a chill and was taking it easy for a few days. Don't let people know he's not here, Axel had said. If anyone comes making inquiries, we don't want them to think you're on your own.

After lunch, I was pressganged into the card game. We sat in the shade of the green and white parasol and played Cheat. The heat flowed down in waves from a cloudless blue sky. Even the hum of the insects sounded limp. We were nearing the end of the second game when I heard the sound of a car coming down the lane.

'Spades,' said Axel.

'Cheat,' said Jessica.

Axel turned the card over. The Ace of Spades.

'Oh no!' moaned Jessica. She had three-quarters of the pack, I had one quarter, and Axel, with only two cards left, was set to win the game.

The noise of the engine grew louder. The car had turned off the lane into the access road. It was coming to La Morosière.

'Hearts,' said Jessica, throwing a card face downward on the table.

'Hearts,' said Axel. The car turned through the open gateway and drove into the courtyard in front of the house.

'Cheat,' said Jessica.

'Excuse me a minute.' Axel disappeared into the kitchen with his remaining card. Thirty seconds later, Marcel, the gardener, appeared round the corner of the house.

'Bonjour, Madame! Quelle chaleur!' He sat down in Axel's chair and mopped his brow. 'Bonjour, petite. Ça va bien?'

I fled into the kitchen to get him a beer. Axel seemed to have taken refuge upstairs. 'Where's your father?' I heard Marcel saying, and I stopped dead in the middle of the room.

'Daddy? Oh, he, er, he's not here just now.' The hesitation was slight enough to be put down to her uncertain French.

I went back outside and put a glass and a bottle of beer in front of Marcel. Ignoring the glass, he raised the bottle to his lips.

'That's better. Did your friend show up then?'

'Friend? What friend?'

'There was someone asking for you in Morigny this morning.'

'In Morigny? This morning?'

'In the shop. Wanted to know where your house was.'

He looked at me expectantly. I pulled myself together. 'That's odd, we're not expecting anyone.'

'Asked if you already had any visitors staying.'

'I wonder who that could be.'

'Madame Boutigny said he had a foreign accent.'

'Did she tell him where we lived?'

'Ah non,' said Marcel, horrified, and launched into a complicated rural explanation of the impropriety of intruding on other people's privacy without authorization.

'Well, we'll just wait and see if he shows up,' I said, when he had finished. 'In the meantime, Marcel, maybe we should settle our accounts. How much do we owe you for the garden and the cleaning?'

'I'm going for a bike ride,' said Jessica. 'Is that all right?' I looked up and her eyes met mine. The picture of innocence.

'Don't go too far,' I said automatically.

* * *

Marcel left ten minutes later. I had paid him what we owed, and arranged for his wife to come in and clean for a couple of hours the following day. In the afternoon. That way Axel would have plenty of time to pack his things and go. Because Axel, I had decided, was going to have to leave. It was hard enough hiding him from the neighbours. If the KGB was about to come calling, it was time to admit defeat.

Jessica had not yet returned. I sat under the parasol and waited for Axel to come downstairs.

He caught the expression on my face right away. 'Something wrong?'

'They've picked up your trail.' I told him what Marcel had said. 'Today is Sunday, everyone will be at the fête in the next village, and they're unlikely to find us. But tomorrow, when the Mairie opens, all they have to do is ask for directions to La Morosière. By tomorrow morning, you must be gone.'

Axel picked up the cards that were lying scattered on the table and began stacking them tidily together. 'I see.'

'They can't do anything to Jessica and me if you're not here. No one's seen you: we can deny the whole thing.'

'Can you trust Jessica not to—'

'It seems I can. Marcel asked her where Stephen was: she said he wasn't here. Not that he hadn't come, but that he wasn't here. As if he'd gone for a walk or something.'

'I'm afraid that was my idea,' said Axel, with no trace of regret. 'I suggested she should say that if anyone wanted to know where her father was.'

'Damn it, Axel, you've got a hell of a nerve!'

'I explained that people might think it odd if they found out I was here alone with you while her father was away.'

'Did she understand why they would think it odd?'

'She seemed to. Eight-year-olds know a lot these days. What will you say if anyone asks where Stephen is?'

'I'll tell them he had to go to Paris, and that I drove him to the station in Verneuil to take the train. That will be easy enough to corroborate because that's where I propose to drive you first thing tomorrow morning. There are no more trains today, or I'd take you there now. There's one around six tomorrow morning, you'll be in Paris by eight, and from there you can head straight for the airport to get a plane to Moscow.'

'I don't like the idea of you staying here on your own.'

'We'll be fine.'

'You're really throwing me out.'

'Yes I am.'

'I guess I'd do the same in your position,' he said unexpectedly. 'You've done a lot for me already, and I'm very grateful. I have no business putting you and Jessica at risk any longer. What time did you say the train was?'

Jessica came back shortly afterwards, and the card game resumed. I left them to it, and decamped to the far end of the garden with a blanket. Deception was exhausting: I could hardly keep my eyes open. I spread the blanket on the ground under a tree and lay down. The hum of insects muted and died. Through a blur of sleep, I saw Axel and Jessica talking earnestly. Her enthusiasm for him was growing by the hour, and he seemed to enjoy her company too. My last thought as I fell asleep was relief that he would soon be gone.

When I woke up, Axel was sitting a few yards away, watching me. Sometimes the mind plays strange tricks. The heat had lessened, there was no sign of Jessica. For a moment, I thought I was in Moscow, in the bedroom of our old flat,

Stephen was away on a trip somewhere, and Axel had spent the night with me.

'Axel? Darling? What day is it?'

'What?'

My mind snapped back into place and the garden came into focus. I saw the trunk of the tree Axel was leaning on, the check pattern of the blanket, and I remembered where I was and what I was doing there.

'What did you say?' repeated Axel.

'I don't know. Nothing. I was dreaming.'

I sat up and pushed the hair off my face. Axel didn't take his eyes off me. I had the strange feeling he knew exactly what I had been thinking.

'What happened to you?' I said.

'What do you mean?'

'Why did they send you to the provinces?'

'Stephen really didn't tell you?'

'No.'

Axel sighed. 'Then I suppose I will. Do you remember that Stephen and I made a trip to Lithuania? A few days before I left?'

'I remember.'

'From there we went to Koenigsberg.'

'Koenigsberg!' I stared at him blankly. 'But it was closed to foreigners! How did you get in?'

'We took a train from Vilnius. They don't check passes on the trains. I lent Stephen some clothes so he wouldn't stand out. He kept his mouth shut and I did all the talking. The Russians took him for a Lithuanian and the Lithuanians took him for a Russian.'

'Stephen never told me he'd been to Koenigsberg!'

'I think he was disappointed by what he saw. The city was

badly bombed during the war. The cathedral is still in ruins. A lot of restoration work is needed. He found it a melancholy place. He wanted to find the house where his father had been born. He had an address, we searched for a long time, but there was nothing to be found. They'd built a football pitch on the place where the house used to be.'

'So the lilac tree had gone,' I said, remembering an old photo Stephen used to carry round with him.

'Yes, that's right. He said there was a lilac tree.'

'I can't believe it! He'd been talking about Koenigsberg for years.'

'I'm sorry, Katya.'

'But they found out anyway?'

'Yes. They withdrew my Moscow residence permit and declared me unfit for further contact with foreigners. Effective immediately. I couldn't even let you know.'

'Why didn't they do anything to Stephen? An American we knew in Moscow made an unauthorized trip somewhere and he got deported.'

Axel shrugged. 'How would I know? Something to do with the international political situation maybe.' Jessica came out of the house with a ball and he got to his feet. 'Probably they didn't want to jeopardize relations with the UK at that particular time.'

At Yalta, when Churchill, Roosevelt and Stalin divided up the world between them, the old East Prussian capital of Koenigsberg was claimed by the Soviet Union. The city had once been a member of the Hanseatic League, and its position near the Baltic Sea appealed to a country in need of ice-free harbours. It was formally awarded to the USSR at the Potsdam Conference in 1945. The following year, it was renamed Kaliningrad, in honour of Mikhail Kalinin, one of Stalin's old comrades-in-arms, whose achievements included sending his wife to the camps, and authorizing the execution of children caught stealing bread during the 1930s famine. The German population of the city was deported en masse after the end of the war, the area was repopulated with Russians, and Kaliningrad became a military base off-limits to foreigners.

By then, Friedrich Maletius was long gone. Koenigsberg had been bombarded by the Allies in 1944, and the city centre almost completely destroyed. Friedrich's mother and sister were killed in the bombing. His father was missing on the Russian front. There was no reason to stay. Friedrich made his way across Poland to Berlin. In 1946, he met an Englishwoman stationed there, married her and moved to England. Their son Stephen was born two years later.

Friedrich never set foot in Germany again, but Stephen was brought up with a strong sense of his cultural roots. The Maletius family had lived in East Prussia since the sixteenth century. Johannes Maletius and his son Hieronymus had set up a printing works in the town of Lyck and helped to found a school. A century later, the renowned Latin scholar Jacob Maletius became Rector of the University of Koenigsberg. Later, the family had turned to medicine, and both Stephen's father and grandfather had been doctors. One of my husband's most treasured possessions was a photograph of the old family home in Koenigsberg, taken before the war, with young Friedrich and his sister Sophie grinning awkwardly into the camera in front of a blooming lilac tree. Stephen used to say, only half-jokingly, that his life's ambition was to pick a branch off that tree, 'my lilac tree – they can't stop me taking it.' This was one of the reasons he had been so enthusiastic about his posting to the Soviet Union. Moscow was not just the prestige and challenge of a coveted assignment, but the gateway to Koenigsberg and the family heritage.

And Axel, in Stephen's eyes, was the key that would open the gate. Axel's mother had married a Russian army officer stationed in Kaliningrad. She was one of the few Germans who had managed to stay on in the city. Axel and his elder brother and sister had grown up speaking both German and Russian. Otto, the brother, still lived in Kaliningrad, though their parents had long been posted elsewhere, and Axel occasionally visited him. When he heard that, Stephen was convinced his chance had come. With Axel's help, he would get into Koenigsberg and pick that branch of lilac. But then Axel disappeared. And round about then, the references to Koenigsberg petered out.

At the time, I assumed Stephen's silence was pragmatic. It seemed I had been wrong. Stephen had not renounced his ambition; he had achieved it. Not only that, he had been lying about it for years. Remembering the weeks we had spent speculating what had happened to Axel, I was shocked and baffled. Stephen must have known exactly why Axel had been replaced by fat Nina. Why then had he said nothing to me?

Later that evening, the phone rang. Stephen had insisted on getting it put in, though I had so far resisted the invasion of a fax machine. I was putting Jessica to bed, and Axel had gone for a walk on his own. We had had our share of phone harassment in Moscow, and I hesitated a moment before picking up the receiver. But it was only my husband.

'Katie? Is everything all right?'

'Fine,' I said. 'How are you?'

'You managed to drive down all right? No problems on the ferry?'

'Plain sailing. Stephen—'

'Is the house all right? Have you seen Marcel?'

'Yes, he was here today. I paid him what we owed. Everything's in order. Stephen, there's something—'

'That's good, because there's a spot of bother here. I'm trying to get a visa for Estonia, but it'll take a while to come through. I won't be joining you for at least a week.'

'Another week! Oh God, no! Can't you get here sooner?'

I sat down abruptly on the chair by the telephone. As soon as Axel got on the train tomorrow morning, the ghosts of Moscow would come crowding out of their hiding place. I did not want to be on my own for another week. The books I had brought from London would not defend me. Rilke and his elegies would not hold the ghosts at bay. I needed protection. From myself, from the past, and possibly, it occurred to me, from Petrov too.

'I'll try, but don't count on it. What's the weather like down there?'

'Wonderful, but—'

'I envy you. It's raining here.'

'Then cut and run for it. What do you need to go to Estonia for?'

'Look, I can't go into that now. I don't decide where events are breaking, do I?'

'But if they won't give you a visa?'

'They will in the end.'

'How long is it going to take?'

'How the hell do I know?' said Stephen irritably. 'A week,

ten days. For God's sake, Katie, you're not going to make a scene, are you?'

In June 1979, Stephen and I travelled to the Soviet Union by sea, bringing a car we had bought in England. The ship docked in Leningrad and we spent one night there before embarking on the drive to Moscow. Inturist had billeted us in the Hotel Pribaltiskaya, a depressing concrete monstrosity at the mouth of the Neva, set in a wilderness of tower blocks and empty spaces. It was raining, and there was a cold wind blowing in from the Baltic. We walked across the vast empty square in front of the hotel towards the seashore. Neither of us spoke. It was early evening: there was no one about. We stood on the seafront and looked out across the Gulf of Finland. Beyond the cranes of the port of Leningrad, islands rose dimly in the mist. I was disappointed: there was not a palace nor a golden dome in sight. This was not how I had imagined our first evening in Russia.

'How far are we from the city centre, Stephen? Is it close enough to walk?'

'Lord, no, we're miles out of town. I doubt they have public transport out here.'

'I saw some taxis parked by the entrance to the hotel.'

My husband gave me a wary glance. 'I'm not sure my Russian's up to handling taxis yet. We'll only get ripped off. In any case, this is hardly sight-seeing weather.'

He had a point. 'Maybe it'll have cleared up by morning,' I said hopefully.

Stephen sighed. 'Katie, you don't seem to realize I've come here to work. We won't have time to go wandering round Leningrad tomorrow morning. I have to get to Moscow as soon as possible. I'd have set out tonight if they'd let us.'

'And slept at some picturesque little inn along the way?'

'I grant you that's a bit of a problem,' he admitted. 'If you've seen all you want to see, let's go and get something to eat. I want to watch *Vremya* at nine o'clock.'

'Watch what?'

'*Vremya. Time.* The main evening newscast. Poor Katie, you've got a lot to learn, haven't you?'

I stared at him sourly, and didn't answer. So his Russian was good enough to follow the newscast, was it? But not to tell a taxi driver to take us into town. I pulled my coat around me and said nothing. Even then, I knew better than to argue the merits of sightseeing over television. I knew already that Stephen would not go out of his way for other people, unless, of course, there was a story in it. That evening, we stayed at the Pribaltiskaya.

'We'll come back another time,' Stephen promised. 'We're here for three years. We have plenty of time to see Leningrad.'

He was right: he made several trips to Leningrad during our stay, but I was never invited to accompany him, neither there nor anywhere else. There was always a good reason for me to stay in Moscow. He was only going to be a few hours, I wouldn't have time to see anything, it would cost too much. To this day, I have never seen Leningrad.

I was nearly asleep when I heard the noise. It was very faint, but I knew immediately what it was. The creak of the gate. Someone had entered the courtyard in front of the house. Suddenly wide awake, I sat up in bed. The front door was on the latch: we never locked it. There was nothing to stop anyone from entering the house. I listened, but I could hear nothing. The intruder's feet made no sound on the grass. I felt my way to the door and opened it soundlessly. Axel had got there before me. He had left his room without my hearing, and was halfway down the stairs. In the faint light that filtered through the skylight, I saw that he was wearing jeans and a T-shirt. He was holding something in his right hand. With his left, he put a finger to his lips, gesturing to me to stay where I was.

He disappeared round the bend in the stairs. The silence seemed to go on for ever. At last, I heard the door handle turning. There was a creak as it opened. After a minute, I caught a couple of soft footfalls, followed by a muffled exclamation. Finally came the sounds of a scuffle. Thuds, bumps, panting, a stifled cry. I hung over the banister, straining to make sense of what was happening, too scared to move. Then came the chink of breaking china, followed by a much louder crash. After that, the sound of a chair overturning, and then silence again. I clung to the banister and waited to see who would appear in the faint light at the foot of the stairs. Axel or the intruder? After what seemed an eternity, I heard the scrape of a match and Axel whispered softly, 'Katya. You can come down now.'

The man was lying slumped on the floor at an odd angle, with a chair half overturned against his legs, and the fragments of Aunt Eleanor's best vase scattered over the tiled floor. Axel was kneeling beside him, examining his face by the light of a match. The moon shone in through the unshuttered windows, and there was enough light for me to see a gun lying on the table and a knife a few yards away on the floor.

'Is he dead?'I said fearfully. 'I'll put the light on.'

'No!' Axel's fierce whisper stopped me in my tracks. 'There may be someone else outside. Hold this.'

He gave me the match to hold while he felt for a pulse. I went on lighting matches, one after the other. I had gone through five before Axel finally looked up and said, 'Yes, he's dead.'

His face was grey and strained in the flickering light.

'What happened?' I said.

'I'm not sure. I think he lost his balance and went down on the edge of the table.'

The match went out and left us in the dark.

'Oh God,' said Axel, 'what am I going to do now?' His voice was ragged and unsteady. Instinctively I moved towards him and put my arms round him. He grabbed at me like a drowning man and buried his face in my shoulder. I could feel his heart pounding. He was clutching me so tightly that it hurt. Dimly I sensed that he was reacting to more than the aftermath of the fight. He was afraid, and this was an emotion he hadn't shown so far. He had been tense, especially the first day in London, but that was all. I went on holding him until his heartbeat steadied and he stopped trembling.

'I suppose we ought to call the police,' I said at last. 'Do you really think there's another man outside?'

Axel dropped his arms and took a step backwards.

'Katya, let's get one thing straight. Calling the police is the last thing we can do.'

'Why? What do you mean?'

'Think about it. The police come, they start asking questions, they want to know what happened.'

'He was trying to break in!'

'And then he fell down all by himself?'

'Oh,' I said. 'I see what you mean.'

'You'll have to say you were alone here with Jessica. Which

is going to cause problems because you've been telling people that Stephen's here too.'

'Oh.'

'They'll find out who he is and where he comes from. Then they'll discover that Stephen is in the Soviet Union at this very moment. They'll start putting two and two together and making God knows how many.'

'All right,' I said, 'you've proved your point. What do you want to do instead? Throw the body in the lake?'

It wasn't a serious suggestion, but to my surprise he appeared to take it seriously.

'Why not? It's as good a solution as any. I could weight the body with a couple of bags of cement from next door. The Soviet Embassy is unlikely to report him missing, there's no reason for anyone to drag the lake. Even if he were found eventually, there's a good chance that the water would have made him unrecognizable—'

'Axel, for God's sake!'

'I'm sorry. I shouldn't have said that. I didn't want to upset you.' He put his arms round me again. I remembered reading somewhere that hot sweet tea was good for shock, and proposed making some. Axel shook his head.

'Not until we know if anyone else is out there. I'll go and take a look. Wait here, and don't put any lights on. I'll be as quick as I can.'

He eased open the door and slipped out into the night. Rather than stay in the dark with the corpse, I groped my way back upstairs and went to check on Jessica. She was fast asleep, breathing evenly, undisturbed by the fracas. I sat on the bed and watched her sleep, in the thin ray of moonlight that fell through a gap in the shutters. Gradually her tranquillity got through to me and I began to feel calmer. This was real, the soft rise and fall of the child's body, the warmth of her skin, the clean shampoo smell of her hair. What had happened downstairs was not. It belonged to another world, it had nothing to do with me. Sitting there quietly, I could almost believe that when I went back downstairs I would find the chairs back in their place, the broken vase whole on the shelf, the space where the body lay empty and innocent.

Then I heard the creak of the gate again, followed by a series of soft thuds. Axel was closing the shutters. Realizing that I was still in my nightdress, I went into my own room, pulled on some clothes and went back downstairs. Axel opened the front door and put on the light. The body was still on the floor. I got a blurred impression of a dark sweater and brown hair, and hastily averted my eyes.

'Why don't you make us that tea now?' said Axel. His face was pale, but he seemed calmer.

I made the tea and we huddled like conspirators over the kitchen table to drink it, talking in whispers so as not to wake Jessica.

'I found a car parked at the top of the access road, but there's no one in it. He must have come alone.'

'I thought they always worked in pairs.'

'In the Soviet Union they do. They might not here. Two men combing the countryside would attract attention. Even one on his own raised eyebrows. We're going to have to get out of here, Katya. Not just me. You too.' He took my hand. 'You can't stay here on your own now. When he doesn't come back, they'll send someone to find out what's happened.'

'I know.'

'We ought to leave as soon as possible. Preferably before daybreak.'

'Yes,' I said, and I think my lack of hesitation surprised him as much as it did me. 'As soon as you like.'

One third of it was Stephen. The resentment sparked off by his phone call, combined with Axel's revelations, and the discovery that I wasn't the only one with ten-year-old unconfided secrets, had pushed any loyalty I might still have felt towards him into some inaccessible corner of my mind.

One third of it was fear. Out here in an isolated house, in a country that wasn't mine, with a body on my conscience, I felt much less confident of my ability to bluff my way through an encounter with the KGB. By now I was skating on ice nearly as thin as Axel himself. I had ignored a polite request to inform them of Axel's presence, smuggled him out of England under their noses, and hidden him for three days. In London, we had still been treading on civilized ground. The terrain here was a good deal rougher, and the ground rules non-existent.

The final third, of course, was Axel himself. At twenty-three, in Moscow, I would have done anything for Axel: smuggle samizdat to the West, Bibles to the East, defect to the USSR, betray my husband, my country and myself. Age, motherhood and creeping disillusion with the ways of the world made it improbable that I would ever again let any man rip my life apart to such an extent. Unless, of course, the man was Axel himself. His disappearance had left me with a sense of things unfinished, accounts unsettled, a journey of discovery uncompleted. I was being offered the chance to put an end to a decade of frustration and speculation. Answers and explanations were suddenly within my reach. While I had no illusions that they would be easy to obtain, for Axel was as full of silences and evasions and forbidden zones as ever, I knew if I let pass the opportunity, I would regret it for the rest of my life.

Two

Axel

Once the decision was made, we worked quickly. We were out of La Morosière in less than an hour. While I hauled Pavel out of the house and into his car, Katya put the sitting room to rights, packed some clothes, and wrote a note for Marcel, telling him she and Jessica had left early to go to the sea, and might stay with friends for a few days. Then I went to wake Jessica, who was fortunately too sleepy to ask many questions, and carried her out to the car. We checked the shutters and locked the door. Jessica flopped down in the back seat of the Volvo and went straight back to sleep. Katya drove up the access road to the lane, and I followed in Pavel's Renault. At the intersection, I waited until I saw her taillights turn on to the main road and accelerate towards the village. Contrary to what I had told her, I could not be sure that Pavel was alone. When I was certain she had got safely away, I turned in the other direction and drove deeper into the forest.

The night was black and my nerves were on edge. I was alert for a movement in the trees, a glint of metal in the shadows, traps, attacks, ambushes. It was not standard procedure to send operatives out unaccompanied. My guess was that there had been some kind of delay. I could think of no other reason why Pavel would enter the house alone. But it was unthinkable that he would not have back-up on the way, and there was no telling when it might arrive. The moon had gone behind a cloud and the forest was in darkness. Anyone could be waiting out there. I didn't start to relax until the trees were behind me and I was driving through open fields. Here and there, farmhouses slumbered peacefully. A sign told me there was a village two kilometres away. It was reassuring to feel the presence of other people, even though I knew that in an emergency they would be no help at all. The fact was, my life was in danger. The KGB had found out what I had done, and were hunting me in earnest. How they had discovered the loss of the papers was a mystery, for I had covered my tracks well, but evidently they had done so. And now I was on the run. If they found me they would not hesitate to kill me. I had had the proof of that already.

Despite the danger, I felt an odd kind of relief that everything was out in the open at last. Driving along the empty lanes, my spirits rose at the idea that I would not have to go back to my desk in Hamburg and take up where I had left off, routing money transfers from the Moscow Narodny Bank to the Crédit Suisse, ploughing through files in bureaucratic German, safeguarding the assets of the foundering communist empire. It had been years since I had been able to take pride in my country, the Party, or the organization I worked for. I had seen too many abuses, and been responsible for too many of them myself.

Since the Berlin Wall came down, the pressure had been building. I had been sleeping badly for months, and getting odd pains in my chest. Like the rest of the world, I had not foreseen the East German people's revolt against the walled-in, spied-on existence that had been imposed on them for decades. When I saw them flooding through Checkpoint Charlie, saluting the world from the top of the Wall, weeping for joy in the arms of strangers, I was astonished to find myself weeping too. Less from joy, perhaps, than from shame. That night I was obliged to confront the evil that had been done in the name of justice and equality. I was ashamed to think that I was part of it.

My only consolation was that the unbelievable had come to pass. The opening of the Wall was a miracle for our times. The triumph of freedom, the victory of the people – for once, all the clichés were true. *Wir* sind das Volk. The euphoria was justified, and so was the champagne. Unfortunately, it didn't last. The politicians took over almost at once. Chancellor Kohl began to draw up ten-point plans for reunification, and East German intellectuals demanded the preservation of their country's socialist destiny and superior moral values. Meanwhile, orders began to arrive from Moscow. My masters had not foreseen the opening of the Wall, and they were powerless to prevent what followed – the open-air meetings, the candlelit processions, the citizen round-tables, the inexorable dismantling of the police state – but they were determined to salvage as much from the shipwreck as they could. I found myself helping to evacuate files, debrief agents, transfer funds. It was perfectly plain what my masters were hoping to achieve, especially as they were attempting to do the same thing in the Soviet Union too. The Communist Party had held power for forty years in Eastern Europe, and for seventy in Russia. They weren't going to bow out gracefully now. The Party and the Stasi might not be in a position to exercise power openly any more, but they had ways of making sure they kept control.

I had spent nearly all my working life in Germany. In

a sense, it was as much my country as Russia. Still, it was events in Russia that finally moved me to take action. In February 1990, the Central Committee voted to modify the Constitution and abolish what Marxist jargon called the 'leading role' of the Party. What this meant was that the Soviet Union could now develop into a democratic multiparty state. The Communist Party would become an ordinary political party with no special privileges – and its leaders stood a chance of escaping the indignities that had befallen certain of their colleagues in Eastern Europe, including imprisonment, trial and summary execution. The element of self-interest was too blatant to be overlooked, but the vote was encouraging. It looked as though the Party was on the way out.

Three days later, I received a copy of an order from our Chairman, Vladimir Kryuchkov. Top secret, restricted circulation. As well it might be. My colleagues and myself were requested to take all necessary measures to prevent the formation of a political opposition in the Soviet Union, and to maintain the 'leading role' of the Party, constitutionally or otherwise. There was to be no change in the established order.

Their cynicism sickened me. The same night I began to work out ways to copy the papers crossing my desk and take them out of the building. I would hide them in my apartment and wait for the chance to pass them to a Western journalist. At the time, I was thinking in terms of the West German press. It was only by the purest of chances that my journalist turned out to be Stephen.

We had arranged to meet at six o'clock in Chartres, in the station café. Katya and Jessica were to drive there directly, while I disposed of the body. Since I had to go a lot further than the lake, it took longer than I thought.

During the last few kilometres, I began to worry whether they would still be there. Back at the house, Katya had done everything I told her, but she might have had second thoughts along the way. I had expected her to put up more resistance when I told her we had to leave, and I wasn't sure why she had agreed so readily to my suggestions. I had caught her surveying me once or twice during the weekend with a long cool look that suggested she knew there was more to me and my tales than met the eye. The spire of the cathedral rose serenely into the pale dawn sky, and the cornfields shivered in the thin morning breeze. I put my foot on the accelerator and drove as fast as I dared towards the town.

I left the Renault on the Boulevard de la Résistance, hoping it would go unremarked for a few days among the other parked cars. Grabbing the canvas bag that contained three plain manila envelopes and a change of clothes, I went down the hill to the station at a run.

There were three cafés side by side on the square in front of the station. I hesitated, momentarily at a loss, and then I saw them through the window of the middle one. With that amazing red-gold hair, they were hard to miss. They were sitting hunched together in a corner of the room, heads bent, Katya staring into her coffee cup, Jessica picking at a croissant.

They looked up as I came in, and an identical look of relief swept over their faces. Jessica leapt to her feet and hugged me. Katya gave me the first real smile I had had from her in three days. I gave Jessica a kiss on the cheek and then, after a moment's hesitation, I kissed Katya too.

'Everything went all right?' she asked. 'You didn't have any problems?'

I shook my head, her smile broadened, and she kissed me back. My spirits rose. I had not been expecting such a warm reception. Katya had every reason to distrust me. When I walked up to her house and rang the bell, my one concern was to get the papers to safety. I had given barely any thought as to who I was going to find standing in front of me. On first sight, in her shapeless T-shirt, with her hair pinned untidily on her head, she seemed like an older, more faded version of the girl I had known in Moscow. Ten years with Stephen had taken their toll. I was surprised she had stayed with him so long.

When I had thought of her during those years, it was with a kind of vague tenderness, and I had assumed she felt the same for me. I was shocked to discover I was wrong. It had never occurred to me that Stephen would not tell her about the trip to Koenigsberg.

For ten years she had been thinking of me, not with the nostalgia befitting a lost lover, but with the bitterness reserved for a man who had abandoned her. The idea made me uncomfortable. I really hadn't wanted that. Three days earlier, I had walked up the path without a qualm, yet now I was wishing I had never done so. Or, more accurately, that I could have done so under circumstances that did not oblige me to lie to her.

When Pavel broke into her house, I could have told her part of the truth. There were a number of reasons why I didn't. If I had told her the truth about the body on the floor, I would have had to explain what had really happened in London three days earlier. That in turn would have led us back to Moscow. So much of our relationship was founded on lies that it would be hard to disentangle. I didn't want her to think worse of me than she did already.

That was part of it, but there were other considerations too. Operational necessity, for one thing. We had to get away as fast as possible. In that moment when Pavel entered the house with the knife in his hand, my life had changed forever. I wasn't playing games with reality any more, I was an outlaw on the run from my own organization. It was not a pleasant thought.

We had a hurried breakfast and left. The newsstand in the station was just opening, and Katya paused to buy the previous day's edition of Stephen's paper. I reckoned we had a head start of about three hours.

'Where are we going?' Jessica asked, as we got into the car. 'Are we really going to the sea?'

'No, darling,' said Katya, dropping the bundle of newsprint on the back seat, 'we're going the other way. We're going east.'

I looked at her in surprise. We hadn't made any plans beyond the rendezvous in Chartres.

'You said you had to go to Moscow,' she said, catching my look. 'That's the right direction, isn't it?'

'Are you offering to drive me to Moscow?'

'I'm not offering anything. For the time being, we'll just drive. See how far we get. Maybe we'll go to Estonia and pick up my husband.'

We made our way through ugly car showrooms and box-like hotels towards the edge of the town. Automatically, I switched on the radio. In Berlin, the economy was collapsing, factories were closing, and workers were striking for fear of losing their jobs. In Bonn, Kohl had called on West Germans to accept financial sacrifices in the name of a common German future. I glanced round for the bag with the manila envelopes, but it was locked away in the boot.

'There's a map of France in the glove compartment,' said Katya briskly. 'Tell me which way to go.'

I did as I was told. 'We'll take the routes nationales, I think, rather than the motorway. Tell me when you've had enough, and I'll take over the wheel.'

She glanced at me dubiously. 'Do you have a licence?'

'No.'

'Then I'll drive. Besides, the insurance only covers Stephen and me.'

'You don't mind?'

'I like driving. Not necessarily this car, mind you. This is Stephen's baby.'

'You had a Volvo in Moscow, didn't you?'

She slowed for a red light. 'We always have Volvos.'

'Katya,' I said impulsively, 'I'm glad you're here with me. Both of you.'

'I'm glad too,' she said, and I looked at her curiously. It wasn't something she'd have said the previous day. Ever since Friday, she'd been keeping herself on a tight rein. Hair tied back, feelings buttoned down. Very English. I wasn't sure if she treated everyone in that arm's-length, hands-off way, or if it was only me. She watched the traffic flowing past in front of us. Two days in the sun had brought a glow to her cheeks. Contrary to what I had thought in London, she was as beautiful as ever, but in a different way. In Moscow, when she was twenty-three, it shone out of her like a beacon. These days, it was subtler, one would have to dig deeper.

'Katya, I—'

'Don't say anything, Axel. Let's just drive.'

The light went from red to green. The road stretched flat and straight before us. She smiled at me, and flicked her hair out of her eyes. She was wearing it loose for the first time since Friday. The gesture shot me back into the past. I remembered the first time I saw her. She was wearing a grubby blue T-shirt, and jeans with a hole in the knee. She had a scarf round her head and a smudge on her face. Stephen frowned at her: catching his look, she pulled off the scarf and let her hair fall in a burnished cloud around her face.

When I first met them, I spent a lot of time speculating about Stephen and Katharine and the reasons which had induced them to get married. I didn't dislike Stephen initially. He was agreeable enough in a cool sort of way, and I respected his competence as a journalist. But as a husband for Katya, he was no good at all. He was too reserved and unemotional: she was too naive and unsure of herself. In the beginning, I was merely amazed that he could treat her with such lack of understanding. Later, I began to hate him for it.

The other thing I spent a lot of time thinking about was Katya's hair. It was an amazing colour, or rather it was a whole spectrum of colours, from russet to auburn to copper to gold: so many different lights and tints that I couldn't even put names to them. Admittedly, it wasn't all I thought about. Katya and I were a classic case of lust at first sight. But for several months, we did nothing about it. We never even acknowledged it. I suppose we both developed scruples: it dawned on Katya that she was newly married, and on me that I had a job to do. Lack of opportunity was also a deterrent, for Stephen was constantly present. So we waited. We all got to know each other better. I behaved the way I had been told to behave, to put them at their ease and gain their confidence.

To begin with, this made me uneasy. It troubled me to refer to the Party in the same offhand, faintly contemptuous way as they did, but after a while, it began to come naturally, and in the end I ceased to notice it.

After three months, Stephen's paper summoned him home for consultations. Katya was in the office when the telex came through, and at the thought of London her face lit up like a child seeing a Christmas tree for the first time. Though she never complained outright, I knew how lonely she was in Moscow. She was trying to make friends with a Russian girl she had met in a bookstore, and sometimes got me to make phone calls, which were never returned. Clearly the girl was too scared to pursue the relationship, but Katya hadn't realized that yet. I was glad she would have the chance to go home for a few days.

'When do they want us to go?' she asked.

'As soon as possible,' said Stephen. 'But Katie, I'm going on my own. I can't take you with me.'

It was as though all the lights on the Christmas tree had gone out. 'Why not?'

'Because the paper isn't going to pay your fare too. In any case, I'll only be gone three days. It isn't worth it.'

'It's worth it to me.'

'Don't be silly. We've only been here since June. Your parents were here last month, and so was your sister. You can't be homesick yet.'

'I've been homesick every day since we got here.'

Stephen sighed in exasperation. 'If you made more of an effort to get acclimatized, it would help. You should go out more, visit Moscow, go to museums and exhibitions, instead of sitting moping in the flat all day.'

'There's no point going to museums. It's all in Russian, I never know what I'm looking at.'

'If you worked harder at your Russian maybe you'd understand.'

'I am working at my Russian. It's a difficult language.'

'I can get around on my own. All you need is perseverance.'

She didn't answer.

'But perseverance has never been your strong suit, has it?' said Stephen nastily. 'You don't know what you want and you never will.'

I was startled by the vicious edge to his tone. For a minute, Katya was too stunned to answer, and then she rounded on him. I had been standing there mesmerized: I realized belatedly that it was time to get out and leave them to it, but I was too slow.

'If I'm so useless, why did you marry me in the first place? You made a mistake, Stephen, didn't you? For once in your perfectly calculated life you slipped up. Or did you? Perhaps what you really wanted was someone like me? Someone you could put down all the time and who wouldn't answer back?'

'There's no need to get hysterical.'

'I am not hysterical. I'm just telling you a few unpleasant truths. Is that your definition of hysteria? When someone tells you something you don't want to hear?'

'I certainly don't want to hear this. In any case, the discussion is closed. You can't go with me to London. And now, Axel and I have work to do.'

He sat down at his desk, turning his back to her, and began to read a pile of dispatches. She was left high and dry in the middle of the room. She hesitated for a few seconds, staring at Stephen. She didn't look in my direction. I think she had forgotten I was there. Then she picked up a mug from a table a few feet away and hurled it at the wall. It broke into fragments. Coffee slid down the wall in a pale brown flood. The door of the office slammed behind her.

Stephen was pale but unmoved. 'I do apologise for my wife's behaviour. Would you get me the Foreign Ministry, please?'

I didn't see Katya again until after Stephen had left. She came down to the office to apologize for what she called the "scene" (Stephen's word, I guessed), and to ask me to call Natasha yet again. She looked white and tired and vulnerable.

'What are you doing married to that man?' I said.

She stared at me. 'What did you say?'

'You and he are totally wrong for each other. Why did you marry him? Didn't you realize how different you are?'

'Of course I did,' she said, with the glimmer of a smile. 'That was the point.'

I didn't understand what she meant, but it didn't matter.

'Were you in love with him?'

'Oh no,' she said, matter-of-factly. 'I've never been in love with anyone. I don't think I'm capable of it.'

'What?'

'Don't look so horrified. One can get by quite well without it. It wouldn't matter if Stephen weren't so—'

'Then you admit that marrying Stephen was a mistake?'

'Of course it was,' she said, still smiling, 'but not for the reasons you think. I miscalculated, that's all. Could you make that call to Natasha, please?'

Resignedly I dialled the number. By now, I knew it by heart. Usually it was Natasha's mother who took the call. Natasha herself was invariably out. Shopping, at the university, visiting her grandmother. They were never short of excuses. Today, however, she picked up the phone in person.

'Natalia Vasilevna? Please hold on. I have someone who wishes to speak to you.' I held out the receiver to Katya.

'Natasha? It's Katharine.' Her face fell. 'Damn, we've been cut off.'

'No,' I said, 'she hung up on you.' I took the receiver from her and replaced it on its stand. 'Katharine, you must stop calling her. She doesn't want to speak to you.'

'I don't understand.'

'That's the way we live in this country. We don't just have barbed wire surrounding our concentration camps, we also have barbed wire in the mind.' I was getting quite good at remarks like that by now. Sometimes Stephen would look at me curiously, but Katya took my ideological nonchalance for granted.

'I don't believe it. I really liked her, and I thought she liked me too.'

'I expect she did. But meeting foreigners is risky. She agreed to meet you again, and then she thought better of it. She tried to let you down lightly, Katya. You shouldn't have gone to her flat, where all the neighbours can see she's being visited by a foreigner, and you shouldn't keep calling her.'

She walked over to the window and stared down at the street below. The guards, the fence, the concrete walls, the foreigners' ghetto: I knew exactly what was going through her mind. 'How am I ever going to make any friends in this bloody country?'

I moved across the room to stand behind her. 'You have

to find Russians who are authorized to have contacts with foreigners. It's more convenient for everyone.'

'Is that what I should do?' The taut line of her shoulders relaxed, and the tension went out of her body. She turned round and looked at me. We were very close together. I put my hand on her shoulder and drew her back into the room.

It took us all day to drive across France. We stayed on secondary roads and avoided towns. The sun shone down, there were no signs of pursuit. The spectres of the previous night receded. Combine harvesters breasted the fields in a cloud of dust, and the smell of the cut corn came in sweet and clean through the car windows. Jessica chattered cheerfully and taught me to play 'I Spy'.

At noon, we stopped to buy food, and picnicked in a field out of sight of the road. It was very hot. Katya read the paper for a while, and then went to sleep, curled up on her side with her skirt rucked up round her knees and her hair spread over her shoulders. Jessica and I played cards, and I watched Katya sleep. I wasn't sure what she was doing in the middle of France with me. There was a lot about Katya that I didn't understand. How could Stephen, who had made her so miserable in Moscow, make her happy now? Especially as his behaviour didn't seem to have improved much over the past decade.

'Hearts,' said Jessica, putting down a card. Why had he never told her about the trip to Koenigsberg, if they got on as well as she claimed? Why had she been so upset after he called the previous night? I didn't know what she was hiding. I just knew she was hiding something.

'Cheat,' I said, and turned over the card. The Jack of

Spades. After all, the answer was obvious. She must have another man. It was the only explanation. I turned the idea over in my mind, and could find no evidence to disprove it. But I didn't care for it at all.

About three, we got back in the car and set off again. The rolling agricultural country of the Île de France began to give way to hillier, wooded land, and the forests had a look of Germany about them. I listened with half an ear to the newscast. Forebodings in Germany, resentment in Moscow. The conservative Politburo member Yegor Ligachev had been loudly applauded when he told the Party Congress that West Germany was 'swallowing up' the East. He was right, of course. Unfortunately, the East couldn't wait to be swallowed, and the Volkskammer had just voted to merge with the Federal Republic as fast as possible. I thought about crossing the border that night, but decided to wait. It was getting late, Katya had been driving all day, and there might be trouble at the frontier.

'Have they gone now?' said Jessica, breaking into my thoughts.

'Has who gone?' said Katya.

'The spies, of course. The ones that Axel saw last night. When he came to wake me up.'

'Spies?' said Katya, glaring at me.

'They aren't around just now,' I said, 'but that doesn't mean to say they won't come back.'

'What will we do if we see them again?'

'We'll have to run away.'

'Why are they spying on you, Axel?'

'They're looking for some papers I have.'

'What papers?'

'I don't know if I can tell you that.'

'Do you mean they're confi— confidential?' She brought out the word with an air of triumph. 'That's all right. I've seen papers like that already. Daddy shows them to me sometimes.'

'Does he?' said Katya, catching Jessica's eye in the driving mirror.

'Once he did,' Jessica amended.

'Did he warn you not to tell anyone what was in them?' I asked.

'Of course,' she said superciliously. 'That's what "confidential" means, you see.'

'Well if you know that, then perhaps it's all right for me to tell you a little bit about them. But you must swear never to talk about them. You mustn't even talk about them to your mother or me, unless you're absolutely sure that no one can hear what we're saying.'

'I swear.' Her eyes shone with excitement.

'The papers are about Germany,' I said.

'Germany?' She was clearly disappointed.

'Do you know what happened in Germany last November?'

'Of course I do. The Berlin Wall came down. My friend Birgit wrote and told me about it. And I saw it on television too.'

'Good. Now do you know what's going to happen in Germany now there isn't a wall any more?'

Jessica thought. 'It's not going to be two countries any more? It's only going to be one country?'

'That's right. But some people don't think this is a good idea. They want to stop it happening. They want Germany to stay as two countries, not one. And the papers explain all that.' Jessica was listening, round-eyed, and I sensed I had Katya's attention too. 'The papers are the proof of what they're trying to do. That's why I had to get them away from the spies and that's why we're driving to Germany now. Germany is on the way to Moscow, and I have to go to Moscow and show the papers to someone who'll be able to stop them.'

We found a hotel a few kilometres from the frontier. It was late, and the patronne made it plain that people who showed up at this hour did not deserve a place to stay. She had just one room left, she informed us with a challenging stare. Katya looked as though she was about to demur.

'That's fine,' I said, pulling out the two British passports.

'You're lucky to have it. We're booked solid all week.'

Katya saw the passports and got the point. I was travelling on Stephen's passport: Jessica was on hers. We were a family. One room was all we could take without attracting comment.

The patronne registered us as Mr. and Mrs. Maletius, gave us the key to our room, and warned us with unconcealed satisfaction that the restaurant stopped serving in half an hour. We summoned Jessica, who had been instructed to check the parking lot for spies while I was masquerading as her father, and clattered thankfully upstairs.

The room had one double bed, one single bed, a huge oak wardrobe, and a great deal of flowery wallpaper.

'Are we all sleeping together?' said Jessica, surprised.

'This was the only room they had left. You and your mother can take the double bed, and I'll sleep in the single bed.'

'Where'll we get dressed?'

'In the bathroom. Look, over there.'

These arrangements suited Jessica's notions of propriety. Her brow cleared. 'I'm hungry,' she said.

When Jessica was in bed, Katya and I went for a walk. I wore Stephen's leather jacket, with the three manila envelopes distributed carefully round the inside pockets. I didn't want to risk leaving the papers in the hotel. The village was small but picturesque, with cobbled streets and half-timbered houses. The sun had set and it was nearly dark. At one end of the main square was a mediaeval tower, all that was left of the ancient walls. I took Katya's hand, and we wandered slowly towards it.

'Will Jessica be all right?'

'She's already fast asleep.'

'It's been a long day.'

'She's been very good. KGB bogeymen seem to be a good way to get her cooperation.'

'She's wonderful. It's not always easy to talk to children, but I don't have any problems with her.'

'You wouldn't,' said Katya dryly. 'Jessica talks enough for two.'

'The odd thing is, she reminds me of someone, but I can't think who.'

'Probably another talkative child you came across some time. Listen, Axel, were you telling Jessica the truth about those papers this afternoon? Is there some kind of plot to prevent German reunification?'

'Sssh, not so loud.' I glanced around, but there was no one in sight. 'Let's go this way.' I steered her past the tower and into a street leading towards the outskirts of the village. The street lamps had flickered on: it was nearly dark.

'It's not a plot. I was simplifying for Jessica's benefit.'

'What is it then?'

'It's an attempt to make reunification as long and difficult as possible. The aim is to make sure that in ten years' time there are still two Germanies in people's minds.'

'Oh. But what—? Who's behind it?'

'Ultimately, the hardliners in Moscow. They won't let go of East Germany without a struggle. And of course there are elements in East German society that are only too happy to cooperate. Old Party and Stasi people, for instance.'

'I thought the Stasi had been disbanded.'

'Nominally it has, but that's not the point. After the Wall came down, a lot of personnel files were removed from Stasi headquarters, taken to Soviet military bases, and transferred to Moscow. The KGB knows where to find practically every Stasi officer in the country.'

She digested this in silence. We had come to the edge of the village. A vine-covered hillside rose dimly out of the dusk.

'And now some of them are being taken over by Moscow and retrained in active measures.'

She looked at me blankly. 'Active measures?'

'That's a KGB term. It means spreading disinformation. The idea is that the old Stasi loyalists should do everything they can to give people in both parts of Germany false ideas about each other, and make it harder for them to fuse into a single nation.'

'How will they do that?'

'One way is through the press. If you read the papers carefully, you'll see that attempts are being made to stir up bad feelings on both sides.'

She looked up, startled. 'You mean it's already under way?'

'It's been going on for some time. In East Germany, you

say that West Germany is going to take over the East. You call it an Anschluss and compare it to Hitler's annexation of Austria. You say that "we" East Germans are going to lose our national identity, and it's the end of the socialist ideals our country once had. You whip up anxiety about whether people are going to find jobs in a free market.'

'All of which is at least partly true.'

'Of course. That's how disinformation works. The art of the plausible. In West Germany, you complain about the high costs of reunification, you emphasize that taxes are going to sky-rocket, and you claim that everything "we" West Germans have gained by dint of hard work since the war will have to be sacrificed.'

She thought about it. 'Wasn't there something on the radio this morning about East Germans going on strike because people were worried about losing their jobs?'

'That's right. There's been no unemployment in East Germany for forty years. The idea of it scares them to death.'

'Are you saying the strike was the result of deliberate manipulation?'

'Disinformation is a very grey area. You can never know for sure.' I sensed her impatience. 'But, yes, I would assume there's a connection.'

We were walking along the edge of the vineyard. Some misshapen lumps of stone rose out of the earth beside us: perhaps the overgrown remains of the old town wall. I climbed on one of them, and pulled her up beside me. The stone was still warm from the heat of the day.

'You have to understand that East Germany is in a highly vulnerable state right now. Communism fell apart too fast, the system collapsed too rapidly. Everything is changing, and no one knows where they stand any more. People were used to having everything mapped out for them: school, training, work, career. They aren't equipped to take charge of themselves and decide their own future. Added to which, the economy is in crisis, unprofitable factories are closing, and unemployment is going to get worse and worse. It's not what they expected when they breached the Wall.'

'So it's easy to play on their fears. But what's going to happen when Germany actually reunifies?'

'At that stage, there's a good chance they'll start looking for a scapegoat.'

'You mean they're going to turn against the West Germans?'

'Not only them. There's a lot more racism around since the Wall came down. Right-wing groups have been emerging all over the place, and there've been attacks on foreign contract workers living in East Germany. The West Germans despise the Easterners, and the Easterners will need someone to despise in their turn.'

She frowned. 'That doesn't mean they're going to turn into racists overnight.'

'East Germany is not a tolerant society, Katya. They're used to having enemies. That's the way you define your identity in a Communist system. In the Soviet Union, we had the warmongering Western imperialists, and in East Germany, they had the wicked West German capitalists. It doesn't matter who the enemy is. There just has to be one.'

'So the underlying tendency is already there, and the Stasi is just going to help it along?'

'That's right.'

'But surely people will realize what's happening?'

'If active measures are carried out well, you have virtually no chance of tracing them.'

'My God.'

'Do you understand now why I didn't want to tell you about it?'

She looked at me narrowly. 'Why did you change your mind?'

I didn't answer. Mainly because I didn't really know. I had several reasons, all so jumbled up together that I no longer knew which were important and which were not. I had known from the beginning that I would have to reveal part of the truth. It was the only way I could be certain of her cooperation. A few crumbs in Normandy, a few crumbs today. What I hadn't foreseen was that I would feel impelled to divulge practically everything I had been working on for the past six months. I wasn't sure where this confessional urge had come from. Perhaps my anger had reached the point where I could no longer keep it to myself. Perhaps the knowledge was a burden that I had been carrying for too long. Or perhaps it had come from the same place as the impulse to take her in my arms by the lake two nights earlier: not love, not lust, only the need for human closeness to comfort the loneliness and ward off the dark.

'I suppose because you have a right to know,' I said lamely. 'I've disrupted your holiday, got you entangled with the KGB, driven you out of your home.'

'Very considerate,' she said, and smiled at me in a way I didn't altogether like.

'It's getting late. We ought to go back to the hotel.'

'Yes.'

Neither of us moved. It was quite dark now. A few lights glimmered here and there, but for the most part the village was asleep. I put out a hand and caressed the back of her neck, under her hair. She didn't resist.

'Katya?'

'Mm?'

'The other night, you told me you were happy with Stephen. You said you had a good marriage. Is that true?'

This time she made no attempt to prevaricate. 'I'm not unhappy, put it like that. Neither is he, as far as I know.'

'Do you still sleep with him?'

She gave me a curious little smile. 'From time to time.'

I stared at her, but she went on smiling. I had seen that smile before, ten years ago in Moscow, when I asked her if marrying Stephen wasn't a mistake. It made me uneasy. Whatever was amusing her, it was something I couldn't see.

'But not all that often. He has his life, I have mine. We live in the same house, sometimes we eat meals together, sometimes we take holidays together. More often we don't. He goes to Estonia, I look after Jessica. Jessica is the glue that holds us together. Without her, it would fall apart in a week.'

'Does she know how things are between you?'

'I don't think so. There are never any scenes. I don't throw coffee cups at the wall any more. Jessica's never said anything. I think she accepts that it's the way things are. I try to make sure she doesn't suffer from it – well, that's not the right word. Nobody suffers in our house. We're all in emotional hibernation.'

'Poor Katya,' I said.

Without warning, she turned on me.

'Don't say that. I don't want your pity, Axel. I'm all right. My life may not be very exciting, but I can handle it. In fact, it's all I can handle. I had all the ecstasy and passion and excitement with you ten years ago. And the suffering too, my God, I had that. And I don't want to go through any of it again. I'm burned out, Axel.'

Three

Katharine

By that stage, I wanted one thing and one thing only, and that was to sleep. My undignified little outpouring to Axel had been the last straw in a long and tiring day. I wanted to forget about everything, wipe it all out of my mind. We walked back to the hotel, two feet apart, in total silence. I was struggling to stop myself sobbing out loud with exhaustion and humiliation. I had one idea in my mind: to pull up the covers, put out the light and sink into oblivion. *Human kind cannot bear very much reality*. I had been reading T.S. Eliot lately, trying to draw parallels with Rilke, and the lines flickered mockingly at the edge of my mind.

But when we got back to the hotel, Jessica was awake.

'And about bloody time too,' she said, leaping up in bed like a jack-in-the-box. 'Where the hell have you two been? I thought you were never coming to bed!'

'It's none of your business where we've been,' I snapped. 'You're supposed to be asleep. And watch your language, young lady. You're not in the school playground now!'

The tone was sharper than I intended: both she and Axel gaped at me.

'Don't scold her,' said Axel. 'At her age, all alone in a

strange hotel, it's not surprising she can't sleep. We're coming to bed now, Jess, it's all right.'

'What do you mean, at my age? I'm nine years old, I'm perfectly capable of looking after myself. I just happened to wake up and wonder where you were, that's all.'

'Nine? But I thought—' Axel began, and stopped. I didn't look at him. I grabbed my nightdress off the bed and fled into the bathroom to get changed. I spent as long in there as I dared, rubbing cream on my face and taking it off again, staring at myself in the mirror and trying to convince myself that it didn't necessarily mean anything, he might not put two and two together and realize what it meant, it might not cross his mind that I had lied to him deliberately.

When I went back into the bedroom, Axel and Jessica were lying sedately in their respective beds. Axel was recounting a Russian fairy story in a low voice and Jessica was on the point of falling asleep. The room was lit only by the bedside lamp. The shadows were deep and comforting. Axel put a finger to his lips. I got into bed, switched out the lamp, and lay listening to the end of the story. By the time Grey Wolf had carried Tsarevich Ivan home to marry Yelena the Beautiful, Jessica was breathing evenly and deeply. I heard the bedsprings creak as Axel changed position, and felt his hand groping for mine. We lay silently in the dark, and after a while I began to feel a strange kind of peace seeping through me. His hand against mine was warm and dry and reassuring. After a while, I forgot about the enemies lurking outside, and the perils awaiting us tomorrow. I slept.

They were waiting for us next morning when we crossed the border.

The weather had changed in the night. When we left the

hotel, the sky was grey and overcast, and it was much cooler. We drove through Forbach, an ugly frontier town lined with cut-price stores, and picked up the motorway. Axel fiddled with the car radio, trying to get the news. I noticed that his hands were shaking slightly. He had decided to take the motorway, on the grounds that it would be easier to slip through unnoticed. At first, it seemed that he had calculated correctly. The traffic was heavy, and there was no sign of life in either the French or the German police checkpoints. A row of trucks was lined up awaiting inspection, but nobody seemed to care about passenger cars. The sign ahead said Koblenz, Trier, Kaiserslautern. We were in Germany.

'We've made it!' I said. 'Should we stop and change some money?'

'No,' said Axel, 'keep going.' His eyes were glued to the window. There was a filling station to the right of the frontier post. A black Mercedes slid out of the forecourt behind us.

'What's the matter?'

'I don't know. Just drive. As fast as you can.'

'This is a diesel engine. It's not built for speed.'

'Try to lose that car. The one right behind us.'

'The Mercedes?'

'Do you think you can do it?'

I doubted it, but didn't say so. I pulled into the left hand lane and pushed my foot to the floor. Almost immediately, I was obliged to give way to a BMW with flashing lights demanding the road. I dropped back into the right lane, and found the Mercedes immediately behind me.

'Are there spies in that car?' demanded Jessica.

'Are you sure they're following us, Axel? Couldn't it be a coincidence?'

'I don't think so. There's something about them.'

I tried to pull out again, and the same thing happened.

'You see?' said Axel. 'I'm pretty sure they're following.'

'I don't think I can lose them. The Germans drive too fast, and there's too much traffic. In any case, there's not much chance of outdistancing a Mercedes. Not in this car.'

'Just keep going then. Drive normally. We'll see if they stay behind us.'

I drove normally for twenty kilometers. Perhaps slightly faster than usual. The industrial chimneys of Saarbrücken disappeared behind us and the road struck through the forest. The black Mercedes stuck to us like glue, overtaking when I did, changing lanes when I did. Axel's hands had stopped shaking. He watched the car and its occupants in the courtesy mirror, and his face got steadily grimmer. After a while, he took the gun out of his pocket and put it on his knees. Jessica's excitement vanished and she began to sob.

'Mummy, I'm scared!'

'We have to leave the motorway,' said Axel.

'If we do that we'll stand no chance at all.'

'On the contrary, it's our only chance. We have to drive into a city and try to lose them.'

'Where?'

'Kaiserslautern.'

'How far is that?'

'Fifty-six kilometres,' said Axel, reading off a sign by the roadside.

'There's nothing sooner?'

'No town big enough. We can't be sure of losing them in a small place.' He turned round and rubbed Jessica's knee comfortingly. 'Don't cry, Jess, it's only me they want. They won't do anything to you and your mother.'

The sobs became a flood. 'But I don't want them to do anything to you either!'

'They won't,' said Axel. 'All I have to do is give them the papers I told you about and they'll leave me alone. But since I don't want to do that, we'll just see if we can't get away from them first.'

We drove on towards Kaiserslautern. I stayed mostly in the outside lane, and the Mercedes stayed behind me. In the end, I ceased to notice it. The traffic was still heavy. Cars, a few caravans, a lot of trucks. Axel was trying to divert Jessica with a detailed account of all the nice things we were going to do when we got rid of the 'spies', starting out with swimming pools and ice creams and building up to helicopter trips and visits to Disneyworld. I stopped listening and concentrated on the road signs. Kaiserslautern forty-nine, Kaiserslautern thirty-seven, Kaiserslautern fifteen. A creeping feeling of unreality stole over me, and I began to feel light-headed. None of this was really happening. Watchers in broad daylight on a quiet surburban street, a body at midnight in a remote Norman farmhouse, and now a car chasing us on a German Autobahn. I tried to tell myself I should be scared. I should at the very least be worried. My daughter was in the car with me, she was only nine years old, I should be taking a more responsible attitude. But I was undaunted, I was even faintly euphoric. I had crossed my own frontier several hours earlier, lying in the dark with Axel's hand in mine, and was already wandering in another country where no border guards or KGB men could find me. I was flying, not driving. The feelings that had been lying dormant all these years were reawakening. Nothing the men in the black Mercedes did could touch me.

'Kaiserslautern-West,' said Axel. 'Exit here.'

We left the motorway and drove towards the town centre.

The streets went past in a blur. A residential area with smooth, manicured lawns and well-dressed people waiting patiently at bus stops. An industrial zone with factories. A row of pink houses and a church tower. People walking calmly down the street, going shopping, on their way to work. An ordinary day. And always the black Mercedes in the rear-view mirror. We reached the centre: a couple of department stores, Kaufhalle and Karstadt, a fountain, pedestrian precincts, the town hall. No different from hundreds of other German towns. We drove stubbornly round the one-way system, stopping at traffic lights, turning left, turning right, past the Rathaus, past the department stores, out towards the Autobahn, back towards the Stadtmitte. And the Mercedes followed. Without being able to see the driver's face clearly in the rear-view mirror, I could sense from the way he drove that he was beginning to relax. We had failed to shake them on the motorway, we had failed to shake them here. They thought they had won. They were waiting for us to get tired and give up the game.

When we drove past the pink houses for the third time, I knew we were beaten.

'It's no good, Axel, I can't get rid of them. You'll have to jump out at a traffic light and make a run for it. Maybe you can lose them in the pedestrian street, or in Karstadt.'

'No!' wailed Jessica. 'We can't do that, we can't just leave him.'

'Of course not. We'll pick him up later.'

'How?' said Axel. 'That's the first thing they'll think of. There are two of them in the car. One will jump out and follow me, the other will stick on your tail to see what you do.'

'The police,' I said. 'It's our only chance. We have to find a police station—'

The traffic light at the intersection ahead turned orange. I slowed automatically.

'Accelerate!' yelled Axel. 'Quick! Before the lights change! That's it, never mind that car.' I swerved violently to avoid a car pulling out from a parking place and nearly rammed an Audi in the next lane. Horns blared, but I ignored them. 'Turn right, round this corner, that's it! Keep going.'

He turned to look behind. The lights had changed and the traffic was moving in the other direction across the intersection. 'We've done it! They couldn't follow, they're stuck. Now, quick, turn right again here before they get round the corner. And then right again.'

We were in a part of town we hadn't been through before. Our pursuers were nowhere in sight. I burst into tears.

We left the Volvo in a suburban shopping street on the outskirts of Kaiserslautern.

'It's too distinctive,' said Axel. 'A grey Volvo with British plates, driven by a beautiful redhead, with another beautiful redhead in the back,' he turned to grin at Jessica, 'what more could they want?'

'Maybe we should dye our hair,' said Jessica hopefully.

'What will we do without the car?' I asked.

'Steal one,' said Jessica.

'Rent one,' said Axel.

There was a large garage with an AVIS sign a couple of streets away. We rented a dark blue Volkswagen Polo, using my driving licence and credit card, drove out of Kaiserslautern and found a Gaststätte in a nearby village. As soon as we were out of sight of the car rental firm, Axel took over the wheel. He had neither licence nor insurance, but I was in no state to drive. My crying fit had subsided, but my legs would barely hold me up. My head was spinning, and I felt as weak as a kitten. Jessica, meanwhile, had got over her fright and was taking it all in her stride. 'Delayed shock,' said Axel, 'I was surprised you managed to stay so calm back there.'

It was early for lunch, but the Gaststätte obliged with schnitzel and chips and generous helpings of Schwarzwaldtorte.

'We should get to Berlin by this evening,' said Axel, as we were finishing our coffee. 'It's motorway all the way.'

'We're not going to Berlin.'

The look Axel gave me would have frozen ice in midsummer. 'What?'

'We're going to Munich.'

'What for?'

'We're going to see Birgit!' chanted Jessica, bouncing up and down gleefully.

'We're going to spend the night with some friends of mine. Tomorrow I'll drive you to Berlin or wherever else you want to go, but first we're going to leave Jessica with them.'

He gave in more easily than I expected. I didn't pause to examine the reasons why. After the Volvo, which handled like a tank, the Polo was light and amazingly easy to drive. I felt as if we were barely touching the ground.

'At least no one will be expecting us to go in this direction,' he said resignedly, as we drove south to pick up the motorway at Karlsruhe.

'Just as well. You've changed cars, but not drivers. What are you going to do about me?'

'Nothing. I like you the way you are.'

'Sure you don't want me to dye my hair?'

Axel threaded his fingers through my hair caressingly. 'God forbid.' His hand slid down to my neck and stayed there.

'Axel—'

'It's all right, she's asleep. Flat out. She had a tough time this morning.'

We all did, I thought. Signs of strain were apparent on his own face too. The lock of hair flopping over his forehead was a shade lighter after a weekend in the sun, but the battered look I had noticed that first morning in London was back beneath his tan. He had turned on the radio and Mozart's Requiem was playing in the background.

'Tell me something,' I said abruptly. 'Why are you risking your life to get these damn papers to Moscow? Is it really worth it?'

'I think so, yes.'

'Whatever these people do, Germany will work things out sooner or later.'

'I'm not doing it for Germany, I'm doing it for Russia. It's the same there too, the Party won't let go. For seventy years, our country has been plundered and mismanaged. Our people have been deceived, abused, exploited. Since 1985, things have taken a turn for the better. Eastern Europe has gonc its own way, Lithuania and the other Soviet republics are trying to go theirs. We have a parliament where things are debated openly, we have newspapers that tell the truth. Exiled writers are returning home, their books are being published. It's the second chance we thought we'd never have. But the hardliners want to turn back the clock, clamp down on free speech, put the dissidents back in jail, bring back the barbed wire. We have to stop them before it's too late.'

We drove through a well-tended village, gleaming with geraniums and fresh paint. I was taken aback by the passion in Axel's speech. In Moscow, he and I had never discussed political topics. He used to refer to the Party with a casual disrespect that Stephen claimed was designed to lull us into a false sense of ease. My own impression had been that he was simply not interested in politics.

'What's more,' he went on, 'they aren't just blinkered, they're corrupt. They've started taking money out of the country and stashing it away in Swiss numbered accounts. We need that money to rebuild Russia, but all they can think of is their own well-being. It's disgusting, Katya. Russia needs a new start, and so does Germany, but it's impossible to build anything with the Party and the KGB still pulling the strings and lining their pockets. We have to get rid of them, sweep them right away. We need to eradicate the old system once and for all. If we don't do that, it'll just go on for years, the same mistakes, the same corruption.'

The Requiem reached a sonorous conclusion, and the news came on. Axel turned up the volume. The Soviet hardliner Yegor Ligachev had announced his retirement from the Central Committee. The Party Congress had passed a resolution stating that the Soviet Union was under military threat, and that the armed forces should be prepared to protect the borders and repel aggression.

'You see,' said Axel. 'They think they're still in 1945. They can't accept the loss of Eastern Europe, they can't accept what's happening in Germany . . .'

'Why are they so upset at the idea of Germany reunifying?'

'How much do you know about the Great Patriotic War?'

'You mean World War Two? Well, of course I know about it!'

Axel looked at me uncertainly, and said he doubted that very much. It was hard for foreigners, he explained, to grasp the importance of the Great Patriotic War in Soviet mythology. In many ways, it was even more important than the October Revolution. It wasn't just a major event in the history of the Soviet Union, it was the one event that everyone in the country could be proud of. The Soviet army had driven back the Fascists, reclaimed their own country, and saved Europe too. All this had given the communist regime a legitimacy it had lacked before. The victory over Fascism justified every one of the sacrifices that had been made in the Twenties and Thirties. It made everything worthwhile: the brutality of collectivization, the ruthlessness of Stalin's industrialization drive, the deaths, the suffering, the hunger . . .

'What you have to understand is that it's not just Germany they're losing, it's a whole set of beliefs, a whole way of life. The conservatives see German reunification as the loss of everything they and their fathers fought for, a betrayal of the millions who died in the war, and a humiliation for the Red Army. East Germany was Moscow's creation, and it had closer links to Moscow than any of the other East European countries. Walter Ulbricht, the first Party leader, spent the war in the Soviet Union. Markus Wolf, the head of foreign intelligence, grew up there. They were Moscow's men, and East Germany was Moscow's country. It's hard for them to let go.'

The news ended and a programme about world trends in art collecting began. Axel switched the radio off. We drove past a sign that said Karlsruhe, Stuttgart, München. We had nearly reached the Autobahn.

'What did you tell your friends on the phone?' said Axel.

'I just asked if we could stay the night. I said we'd explain when we got there.'

'Who are they? What do they do?'

'Volker is a journalist with the *Süddeutsche Zeitung*. Gudrun translates Harlequin Romance into German.'

'What is Harlequin Romance?'

'Love stories. They publish several books a month, all with pretty much the same plot. The hero is dynamic, virile and impossibly handsome. He sweeps the heroine off her feet in the first ten pages. After that all kinds of obstacles crop up. This goes on for two hundred pages, and then they live happily ever after.'

'Oh,' said Axel, clearly baffled.

'Gudrun says they're read mainly by housewives who need a break from scrubbing floors and wiping noses. Some people get through a new one every day. I did myself at one point. Soviet housewives will take to them like a fish to water once someone gets around to setting up a joint venture.'

'You think so?' said Axel. His tone implied that Soviet housewives were a cultural cut above their Western counterparts.

'Never underestimate the human desire to escape.'

'So we can leave Jessica with your friends for a day or two?'

'Yes, they won't mind. They have two children her age. She was terrified this morning.'

'I suppose it's best.' He threw a glance towards the back seat, and there was so much affection on his face that I had to look away. He knows, I thought, oh God, he knows.

He turned back to me. 'And you read those books too?'

'I used to read them.'

'Is it so bad with Stephen?'

'The first year in Bonn was terrible. Since then, things have improved.'

'But, Katya, the life you described last night. How do

you bear it?' He paused for an instant. 'Do you have someone else?'

'You mean another man?'

'Yes.'

'You could say that.' I smiled to myself. 'It's a habit I picked up in Bonn.'

We had moved to Bonn in 1983. Straight from Moscow. My relations with Stephen plunged from a bad patch into a worse one. I'd convinced myself that things would improve once we left Russia, but they didn't. The move was unexpectedly hard to cope with. I had finally got used to Moscow, and made a few friends. Jessica was two and a half, and neither of us enjoyed being uprooted from our familiar routine and adapting to new surroundings. She took to throwing tantrums, I sank into depression, Stephen stayed long hours in his new office. Then, at a dinner party, we met Gudrun and Volker Heisler and I started reading Harlequin Romance. It began as a joke: Gudrun lent me a couple of books to broaden my cultural horizons, as she put it, and before I knew it, I was getting through three or four a week. Gudrun, whose other main activity was a doctoral thesis on Kant, was disconcerted. Stephen was scathing. At that point, I decided I needed a job. In Moscow I had been unable to work, but in Germany it was different.

'I started off doing translation work. Not because I enjoyed it, but because it was something I could combine with looking after Jessica. Then I got the idea of writing biographies. German writers aren't very well known in England, and German literature is one of the few things I know about. I talked to my old tutor at university and then contacted the publishers of a series called "The Writer In His Own Words". Basic biographical information plus a bit of literary analysis, all in two hundred pages. So far I've done Kleist and Hölderlin, and right now I'm working on Rilke.'

'Rilke In His Own Words?' said Axel. For some reason, he was smiling broadly. 'So that was what all those books were for. And you've been doing this for five years? I had no idea.'

'How could you have known? I publish under my maiden name, Katharine Mortimer.'

A Mercedes with Munich plates swept by in the outside lane. I watched it go. Our pursuers of the morning had been registered in Frankfurt.

'Now I understand,' said Axel, still smiling. 'You escape your own life by becoming immersed in someone else's. What does Stephen think of your books?'

I didn't answer right away. The book on the nineteenth-century playwright Heinrich von Kleist had sold quite well, and the one on the poet Friedrich Hölderlin was also doing nicely. But my achievements lay in an area which Stephen had earmarked as his own, even though he had not yet had the leisure to commence construction. When the book on Kleist was accepted, he expressed regret that I had not chosen someone more relevant to present-day concerns. Recently, at a dinner party, he had observed that at least writing kept me in pocket money.

'He doesn't take them very seriously,' I said, 'but then he doesn't think literature is serious either. He doesn't think it's necessary. Not like news is.'

Axel laughed. 'It doesn't sound as though he's changed much since Moscow. What was it you used to say? The news must get through? Mind you,' he added pointedly, 'it had its advantages.'

'Yes,' I said, after a pause, 'I suppose it did.'

* * *

Of my affair with Axel, Stephen never had an inkling. He came back from his trip to London with instructions to get out of Moscow, visit the republics, and 'take the pulse of the national minorities.' The foreign editor had read a book by a French Sovietologist forecasting the rise of nationalism and the break-up of the Soviet empire, and had concluded that this was what was needed to sell Sunday papers to the thinking masses that autumn. Stephen threw himself into the project with enthusiasm. Within half an hour of his return, Axel was telexing the Foreign Ministry for permission to visit Kiev and Tbilisi. I was not invited to go along, and neither was Axel. On learning that he could procure the services of a local guide from the republican foreign ministries (whose sole function, despite their imposing title, was to receive foreign visitors), Stephen decided that Axel would be better employed staying in Moscow, holding the fort and keeping down expenses.

With Stephen out cross-examining the country from Tashkent to Riga, Axel and I were able to pursue our affair with relative facility. Axel would leave the office around five and return late in the evening, when the dezhurnaya had gone to bed and the guards at the gate had changed shifts. His pass allowed him to enter the building at all hours of the day or night: he said they never challenged him. I didn't ask him how he spent his evenings: contending, I supposed, with the time-consuming business of Soviet daily life, standing in line to buy food, commuting out to wherever he lived. He never told me the exact location of his flat, which he shared with his uncle, sister and grandmother, but I gathered it was somewhere on the outskirts of Moscow. Visualizing a war-torn housing development like the one Natasha lived in, I did not press the point. I wasn't interested in Axel's family. All I wanted was Axel himself. Waiting for his return, I spent my evenings in a frenzy of expectation, wandering from the kitchen to the living room to the bedroom and back again, unable to eat, unable to read, unable to think. When he arrived, we lost little time in preliminaries. We didn't talk much at all those first weeks. I emerged with terror and excitement into a sexual no man's land whose existence I had long suspected, but never attained. It was in despair of ever finding it that I had married Stephen. All the insignificant events of daily life seemed intensified, and my time, instead of flowing formlessly past, became coloured and punctuated with activity, broken up into a chiaroscuro pattern of presence and absence, utilized instead of endured. For the first time ever, I could feel myself existing.

After a couple of months, the inadequacies of the system began to make themselves felt. What I had originally intended as a passing sexual fling was developing into far more than that. At the outset, I had told myself that it was Stephen's intolerant behaviour which was driving me into the affair. If he would only treat me as an adult with normal emotional needs, instead of a tantrum-throwing child, I wouldn't need Axel any more. But, as the weeks passed, it became increasingly clear that Axel was not an emotional substitute – Axel was the real thing. I wanted him as a permanent part of my life, and I wanted to be part of his life as well.

So I began to ask questions, but I got no answers. Axel was happy to talk for hours about his childhood in Koenigsberg, his schooldays, his studies at the Philology Faculty (which was what the Russians called the place they went to study foreign languages), but questions about the present came up against a blank wall. I went underground: I became a master of the innocent question and the loaded hint, but he anticipated all my moves, and I learned nothing. Around this time we began to play a silly make-believe game that Axel invented, partly, I later realized, as a way of turning aside my questions, partly because he too knew that make-believe was all we had.

It occurred, to me, of course, that his reticence might be due to the presence of unseen listeners. I knew that both our flat and Stephen's office were theoretically under electronic surveillance. We had been briefed on the dangers of this before leaving England, and Stephen was continually breaking off harmless discussions in mid-sentence and warning me to watch my tongue. Lest anyone should remain in doubt, an ambulance with a full team of medical orderlies arrived in the courtyard of the apartment building twice a day, the 'orderlies' walked quickly over to the special lift that was kept permanently locked and guarded, and five minutes later the team they had relieved emerged from the lift, got into the ambulance and drove off. The special lift went only to the sixteenth and top floor of the building, where the surveillance equipment was housed. The regular lifts stopped at the fifteenth floor. The superior quality of Soviet medical care was a standing joke among the residents of the building.

After watching this performance every day for several months, I was prepared to assume that every room in the apartment was bugged, including the kitchen, the bathroom, and the bedroom. Axel, however, showed no such apprehension. The first time he came to the flat at night, I broached the topic. 'Don't worry about that,' he said, taking me in his arms, and so I didn't. Reasoning that he would be laying himself open to sanctions if his affair with me became known, I concluded that the microphones were less numerous and less effective than I had supposed, and gradually forgot about them.

So it wasn't fear that lay at the root of his discretion.

In the end, I confronted him pointblank. It was half past one in the morning of a freezing December day. Stephen was away in Baku, and we were lying in bed after making love. There was a radio beside the bed. Sometimes we put it on, sometimes we didn't. I leaned over and turned it on.

'Why don't you want to talk about yourself, Axel?'

He ran a finger down my cheek. 'In our country, one keeps one's life in separate compartments, Katya. The public compartment, the private compartment. But in my case, I have two private compartments. One is my life at home, my friends, my family. The other is you. You're a foreigner, and you're a married woman. If I tried to tell my friends about you, they wouldn't understand. They'd be afraid, they'd disapprove, they'd tell me to break it off and find a nice Russian girl. So it's best that they don't know anything about you, and you don't know anything about them.'

'It's not quite the same.'

'No it's not. But if you've never met my friend Sasha or my grandmother, and you don't know anything about them, there's less danger that you'll drop something about them in front of Stephen.'

'Stephen's so busy thinking about his Uzbeks and Latvians that he wouldn't even notice.'

'Stephen is very absorbed in his work,' conceded Axel. 'But one day he will begin to be suspicious. And then I don't know what we will do.'

I lay back on the pillow, suddenly overcome with depression.

'Maybe you should go out and find yourself a nice Russian girl right away. Before Stephen figures out what's going on and complains about you to the Foreign Ministry, or we get posted somewhere else . . . Let's face it, there's no future for us anywhere.'

I was unprepared for the vehemence of his reaction.

'Don't say that!' He rolled on top of me and started kissing me, smothering my face with fierce, desperate little kisses. 'Don't think of it that way! Who knows what may happen? Who knows what the future holds?'

'Axel—'

'It's all right for you, you can leave Moscow, go wherever you want, divorce Stephen, find someone else—'

'I don't want anyone else—'

'Then neither do I! Don't tell me to find myself a Russian girl, I don't want one. I only want you.'

That night was the last we spent together. The next day Stephen came back from Baku, and we left one week later for Christmas in England. Axel helped us to carry our luggage down to the taxi, and gave me a chaste, farewell kiss on the cheek. The words and caresses of that last night echoed in my mind the whole time I was away. I found later, when he disappeared from my life, that they were imprinted on my memory for good.

Gudrun and Volker Heisler lived in Schwabing, in a large sunny flat overlooking the Elisabethplatz. I knew Munich well. I had lived there for a year as a student, and Stephen and I had visited the Heislers several times before. The sun was shining, the square was bright with coloured parasols, the city felt relaxed and cheerful. It was like coming home. At Axel's insistence, I parked two streets away from the flat. The Heislers greeted Jessica and myself with affection, and Axel with polite reserve. Christoph and Birgit bore Jessica off to one of the children's rooms with a lot of shrieking and squealing.

Gudrun closed the door on the noise, gave me a glass of white wine, and quizzed me discreetly on Stephen's whereabouts and Axel's credentials while we dealt with the food. I guessed that Volker was bringing his interviewing skills to bear on Axel as the men drank their beer in the living room. We had decided in advance what we were going to say: the truth, up to a point. Axel was Russian, working in the Soviet Consulate in Hamburg, Stephen and I had known him in Moscow ten years ago, Jessica and I had decided to take a trip with him while Stephen was in the Baltic States.

'Jessica's getting tired of all this driving, though. I wondered if you'd let us leave her here for a few days,' I said casually. I was slicing bread with my back turned towards her. There was a pause before she answered.

'You know we're always happy to have Jessica. But where will you be?'

'Axel has to get to Hamburg by tomorrow night. I thought I might drive him up there.' Gudrun said nothing, apparently absorbed in arranging different kinds of ham and sausage in an elaborate pattern on a serving dish. 'I haven't seen him for so long, and it'll give us a chance to talk.'

'So you're going to drive up to Hamburg and then drive straight back again.'

'Well maybe not directly. I thought I might stay up there a couple of days. Take a look around. I've never been to Hamburg, believe it or not.'

Another pause. This time she was dealing with the cheese.

'Won't Jessica mind being left behind?'

'Not in the least. You know how well she gets on with your two. She was delighted when she heard we were coming here. Of course, if it's putting you out, then I'll come back sooner.'

'As far as Jessica is concerned, you're not putting us out. We're very fond of Jessica, it's a pleasure to have her. As for the rest of it . . .'

'Gudrun. Please. Try to understand.'

It was a lot to ask of her, I knew, especially as I didn't understand too well myself. When I started this conversation I had not intended to let her think Axel and I were driving up to Hamburg for a couple of nights of illicit passion. But with no car chases and confidential papers to distract her, perhaps she was seeing things more clearly than I was.

'Oh I understand,' she said dryly. 'I know that you and Stephen – I know he doesn't always give you an easy time. But he's a friend of ours too. It's difficult to know what to say.'

'Oh.' That aspect of the situation hadn't even occurred to me. 'I'm sorry, Gudrun, I hadn't thought. I shouldn't have asked. Maybe we—'

'Just make sure you get back before Stephen returns from Estonia. I suppose he doesn't know about any of this?'

I shook my head.

'Then make sure it stays that way,' said Gudrun tartly. 'The less men know about things, the better it is for everyone.'

That summer, if you found yourself in the company of Germans, it was inevitable that sooner or later the talk would turn to reunification. While the children were with us, there were other things to say, but when the meal was winding down, and the children had wandered off to pursue their own concerns, and we were on our third bottle of Frankenwein, the conversation moved naturally towards the future. I don't remember if it was I who asked them what they thought, or

Axel. What I do remember is that their opinions contrasted sharply. Volker was strongly in favour of it. Gudrun was a lot more reticent.

'For four decades,' said Volker, 'we've had only half a country. Now we have the chance to construct something whole, something permanent. Something better.'

Gudrun sniffed dubiously.

'It's a chance we never expected to have. Twelve months ago, who would have believed that we could be sitting here having this conversation today? Who could have believed that the Wall could come down? How can we justify throwing that chance away?'

'Come down to earth, Volker. Just look at what we're getting into. They have six decades of totalitarianism behind them. East Germany is the only country in Europe to undergo first Fascism, then Communism. It's left them with a completely different mentality. You heard what my cousin in Kassel said.' Her cousin, she explained, had a small engineering works in a town near the East German border. 'He hired two or three East Germans when they started coming over last year. It was a total disaster. They weren't used to putting in a full day's work, they got tired, they were slow. They had to be completely retrained: they'd never seen anything like the machinery he was using. They had no sense of initiative: they never did anything they weren't told to do.'

Volker brushed away her objections with confident briskness. 'Obviously, they need time to adapt. They aren't used to the way we do things. Everything was so different in their system. But they'll learn in the end.'

'It's going to cost billions to teach them.'

'It's true that we'll have to make some sacrifices, but it's our duty to make them.'

'Duty!'

'Yes, duty. They've been deprived of all this by an accident of geography. If the Red Army had arranged to advance further West, we might have been in the same boat. Your cousin in Kassel certainly would! They have the right to material prosperity and spiritual freedom just the same as we do. We have no right to say, No, we aren't going to help you, it's your problem, not ours, figure it out on your own. Don't you remember all that stuff about "our brothers and sisters in the East" that we used to hear? People may not think in those terms any more, but the fact is they are still our brothers and sisters.'

'They're our distant cousins, Volker. We've been looking at each other over the barbed wire for forty years. We don't understand each other any more.'

'That's certainly true,' said Axel, looking up from his glass. 'You think they're deprived country cousins who need to learn the right way to do things—'

'I didn't say that, I just said they needed to learn modern working methods.'

'– and they think you're obsessed with material wealth and consumer goods—'

'Which doesn't stop them coming over here and hauling back washing machines on top of their Trabis,' said Gudrun.

'– and, of course, both of you are wrong,' finished Axel, and they all glowered at each other.

I tried to distract them. 'I can't help thinking it's all going too fast. Why not preserve two German states as an interim measure, and work towards some kind of union in a few years' time?'

'We can't do that,' said Volker. 'For one thing, the East

German state has no legal reason to exist if it's not communist any more. For another, the East German economy is unravelling so fast that reunification is the only way to stop it collapsing. Unemployment is rising, two thousand people a day are moving West, and they'll keep on doing so as long as East and West Germany remain separate countries. We can't find jobs for them here, and their hospitals and schools and public services can't function properly any more because there's no one left to run them.'

'Reunification is unavoidable,' said Axel, draining his glass, 'but it isn't going to be the panacea everyone seems to think.'

'Yes, well, I have yet to meet a Russian who's in favour of reunification,' said Volker irritably.

'I'm not Russian.'

'But Katharine said—'

'I'm half Russian. And half German. My mother is German. So you see,' he added maliciously, 'I can move here too if I want.'

'Then you'd better hurry up,' said Gudrun. 'It's getting crowded.'

'Try Dresden,' said Volker, picking up the wine bottle. 'They have plenty of room. You can run a hospital if you like.' He refilled Axel's glass. 'So reunification isn't going to solve things?'

'How can it? East German expectations are far too high. They think they're going to go from socialism to capitalism overnight.'

'Obviously, that's unrealistic. More wine, Katharine? Ten years is what they're saying in Bonn.'

'More like twenty. It takes a long time to change the way people think.'

'A lot depends on the economy. The faster we get their economy going, the faster they'll adapt to a new way of thinking.'

Axel smiled sceptically. 'The East German state encouraged its citizens to remain passive, stay out of sight, and take no initiatives. That's not good training for the market economy.'

Out in the hall, the phone began to ring. Gudrun got up to answer it.

'And of course there are people who have a vested interest in making sure that the process is as painful as possible.'

Volker looked at him narrowly. 'Do you think they're going to succeed?'

'With the weapons they have at their disposal, yes, of course they will. They have the money, they have the property, they have the assets. They have people who've travelled, who know how things work, who understand foreigners. They have the contacts, they have the experience. The rest of the population doesn't have a clue.' He paused significantly. 'Best of all, they have the files.'

He looked at Volker. Volker nodded gloomily.

'The files?' I said.

'The Stasi files. Half the population of East Germany spied on the other half and reported on them to the secret police. And now the chance has come to find out who did what, and who betrayed whom, and who worked for the Stasi as an unofficial collaborator. The Stasi maintained files on one citizen in three, and they coopted literally thousands of inoffizielle Mitarbeiter. In other words, Informers. Some of them were fairly prominent people. Churchmen, politicians, writers, dissidents – if I gave you their names you wouldn't believe me. Practically everyone who was anyone was involved with the Stasi in some way. It was impossible not to be. It was the only way you could function. But people who suffered because they were informed on aren't going to be any less resentful because of that.'

Gudrun came back into the room. Axel glanced up as she passed, but went on talking. 'As for Westerners, you don't understand it at all, you don't realize the pressures to inform that exist in a totalitarian society, and you condemn it outright. So if they choose their moment and let these revelations trickle out one by one, they can destroy public figures who might be able to play a valuable role in the new reunified Germany. Party leaders, ministers, members of parliament – a lot of people are vulnerable. Revealing this will undermine West Germany's confidence in the East, and destroy East Germans' confidence in themselves. Not to mention what will happen when people look in their files and discover that their friend or their child or their husband informed on them. Germany is sitting on a time bomb. Those files are going to poison the climate for years to come.'

For a moment, no one said anything. Then Christoph sidled into the room and whispered something in his mother's ear.

'No,' said Gudrun, 'it's too late. It's time you were all in bed.'

'This isn't just your personal opinion, is it?' said Volker.

Axel reached for the bottle and poured what remained of the wine into his own glass.

'May I ask what your source is?' said Volker.

'I can't tell you that,' said Axel.

'No?' said Volker.

Axel shook his head. His eyes met mine. I guessed what was going through his mind. He didn't know Volker, he had had a problem with a German journalist already . . . 'You'll see,' he said. 'You'll find out. You West Germans don't know what you're getting into. You think you're reclaiming the lost half of your country, but you're in for a surprise. What you're going to find yourselves dealing with is Lenin's ghost.'

'Lenin's *ghost*?' said Gudrun.

'Who was that on the phone?' said Volker.

'Rachel. She wanted Günther's new phone number.'

'Rachel your sister-in-law?' I said, surprised.

'She and Günther split up,' said Gudrun. 'She's living with a Russian now,' she added, and her gaze slid distrustfully from me to Axel.

Axel wasn't listening. He was somewhere else, wrestling with other demons. 'The Communists have ruined us. The things they made us do, to ourselves, to other people . . . It doesn't bear thinking about. It's going to take decades to cut ourselves loose. If we ever do. They were there for over half a century, and it'll take at least that long to get rid of what they left behind. We'll be dealing with their legacy for years to come.'

Gudrun looked at her watch, and got to her feet. 'Let's go and make up the beds, Katharine. I thought I'd put you and Jessica in the spare room, and make up a bed for Axel on the sitting room couch.'

'Fine,' I said, following her obediently out of the room. She wanted to be able to confront Stephen with a clear conscience next time they met, and I couldn't say I blamed her. Rachel, the errant sister-in-law, was English too. I could see she would want to be careful. Jessica, however, was oblivious to such considerations.

'Why can't I sleep with Birgit?'

'Yes, Mama, why can't she?'

'Tomorrow, maybe,' said Gudrun, and remained deaf to

all their pleas. Axel was allowed briefly into the bedroom to say goodnight, and that was all.

'It would be nice,' said Jessica after he had gone, wriggling sleepily under the covers, 'if Axel was my Daddy. But of course I already have a Daddy. Can one have two fathers, ever?'

It took me a moment to reply. I felt as if she had punched me in the stomach. 'No, darling,' I said, pulling the duvet round her shoulders. 'One can't really do that. Sleep well, Jess.'

I switched off the light and left the room. The corridor outside was in darkness. Christoph and Birgit were both in bed, and I could hear voices coming from the sitting room at the other end of the flat. Still talking about Lenin's ghost, no doubt. I leaned on the door and closed my eyes. Oh God, now what? There was a movement in the shadows, I opened my eyes, and saw Axel beside me. He must have heard and seen everything. Our eyes met. There was no way he could have misinterpreted the guilt and confusion written all over my face. I steeled myself for questions, recriminations, reproaches. Axel didn't say anything. He pulled me into a corner partially screened from view by two tall bookcases, and began to kiss me. This time, I had no thought of resisting. I found myself moving into his arms as if we had last done this ten minutes, not ten years ago. Nothing had changed. The way he held me, the feel of his body against mine.

We were interrupted by Gudrun's voice behind us:

'*The kiss lasted only a few seconds, but it was enough to set her pulse racing and her senses tingling. His lips moved – was it her name he spoke? – and then his arms were around her and he was kissing her with a passionate hungry frenzy that was like nothing she had ever experienced before.*'

Axel released me. I laughed nervously. 'Is that an excerpt from your work in progress?'

Axel held out his hand for the book, and examined it gingerly. '*Desperate Yearning*. Is this what you plan to use to corrupt our Soviet housewives? Perhaps I have misjudged Comrade Ligachev when he urges us to stay with the old ways. I shall petition the Central Committee to restore him to his former position.'

In December 1979, the Soviet Union invaded Afghanistan. When Stephen and I returned to Moscow after Christmas in Leicestershire, nothing was the same. Stephen's trips to the national republics were cancelled. He and Axel were worked off their feet. Axel was cool and guarded, avoiding my eyes when Stephen was in the room, keeping the conversation on neutral subjects when we were alone together.

One morning, when Stephen was at a briefing at the Foreign Ministry, I screwed up my courage and went down to the office to ask Axel what was wrong. It was a bitterly cold day. The sky was like iron. A few snowflakes floated past the window. The office was messy and stuffy. Axel had turned on the radio and the Brandenburg Concertos were chugging away in the background on Moscow radio's classical program.

At first, Axel pretended not to understand what I was talking about. When I persisted, he announced that he had complications in his private life, frowning meaningfully to remind me that there was a veto on further investigation of the subject.

'What does that have to do with us? I thought I was in a separate compartment from everyone else.'

'I thought so too,' said Axel, in a tone of such sadness that

I walked straight across the room – he was doing something at Stephen's desk and I was loitering uneasily in the doorway – and put my arms around him.

'Axel, what's wrong? Can't you tell me?'

But he only shook his head and unhooked my arms and pretended to be searching for something in Stephen's papers.

'All I can tell you is that the situation has become very complicated. It would be better if you stopped coming down here. Stay away from me, it will make things easier in the end.'

'Are you trying to tell me you've found a nice Russian girl, after all?'

Axel shook his head bleakly.

'Please, Katya, you must go now. The Minister will soon have finished explaining to the foreign correspondents why it is necessary for us to lend fraternal assistance to our threatened little southern neighbour and Stephen will be back. My God, this war. I can't believe—'

'Surely the war in Afghanistan doesn't have anything to do with us?'

'The events in Afghanistan have changed many things.'

'But not for us! Why should they change things for us?'

'We have to stop seeing each other.'

'I don't want to stop seeing you!'

'Katya, my little love, you must be reasonable. It's better for both of us.'

'I don't want to be reasonable. I love you, Axel!'

'We have no future, you said so yourself. Now or later—'

'And you said one never knew what life might bring.'

We stood there, glaring at each other across the desk, and then Axel opened his arms and I fell into them. We made love then, on the lumpy office couch, with the springs sticking into us, slowly and tenderly, with nothing like the fierceness and thirst of that night in December, slowly, savouring every moment, knowing that this time might really be the last.

When it was over, and we were putting our clothes to rights, he said, 'I love you, Katya. Whatever happens, I want you to remember that.'

For the next two weeks, I stayed away from the office. I saw Axel only once, when Stephen brought him upstairs for a drink after work. We talked about the Moscow Olympics and the American hostages in Iran. Axel didn't stay long. After he left, Stephen said that relations had been strained since we came back from England. According to him, Axel disapproved profoundly of the invasion of Afghanistan, but couldn't bring himself to say so to a foreigner.

'I've decided to take him to Lithuania next week,' he went on. 'A few days away from Moscow might help get things back to normal.'

'Axel's going to Lithuania with you?'

'Yes. What are you looking like that for?'

'Nothing, I'm just surprised. You always take trips on your own.'

'Usually there's no point running up extra expense. They always give you a guide who knows about local conditions. But Lithuania's different. Axel grew up just a few miles away, and he knows it well.'

'I see.' I maintained my composure with difficulty. I too had been planning to take advantage of Stephen's trip to Lithuania to try and get relations with Axel back on the old footing. Fortunately, Stephen wasn't looking at me. He was fiddling with the radio trying to pick up the BBC World Service, though without much success. Since the invasion of

Afghanistan, the Soviets had started jamming foreign radio stations.

The whine of the jamming irritated me. I picked up my book and left the room. The memories of our last love-making, the knowledge that he loved me had kept me going for the past two weeks. I would just have to wait a bit longer. The chance would come: it was merely a matter of patience.

But one week after the trip to Lithuania, Axel disappeared from our lives for good. He was replaced by a fat lady called Nina in a pink knitted cardigan. The Foreign Ministry refused to tell us what had happened to Axel, and practically denied that he had ever existed. Stephen was irritated by Soviet high-handedness and annoyed by the change in his routine, but after a couple of weeks he got used to working with Nina, stopped comparing her unfavourably with Axel, and behaved as if she had been there for ever. Axel dropped out of our conversation, for I could not trust myself to mention his name without bursting into tears. He occupied my thoughts completely. I woke every morning in a state of depression: conscious, as soon as I opened my eyes, of his absence and my despair.

Stephen realized that something was wrong, but by the greatest of ironies, he never found out what. I had the perfect alibi. The day Axel disappeared was the day I discovered I was pregnant. Jessica was conceived on the lumpy office couch on a bitter Moscow day with so much love and tenderness that, whatever has happened to me since, whatever lies I have told, whatever regrets I have, I cannot bring myself to feel remorse for the way she was brought into being. It is a gift that not all parents can offer their children.

Four

Axel

I had never had children of my own. My marriage to Marusya had only lasted a short time, and she had made it clear from the outset that child-bearing was not part of her plans. Marusya was a lecturer in Marxism-Leninism at Moscow State University, and a professional believer in Five-Year Plans. Looking back, that was partly what drew me to her. My affair with Katya had been spontaneous, uncontrolled and dangerous. My relationship with Marusya functioned within clearly defined parameters. She would not accompany me on postings abroad, she would not sacrifice her career to mine. She would stay in Moscow, and we would see each other as often as possible. I found these stipulations oddly reassuring. With Marusya, there was no risk of falling off a precipice into the unknown.

Our marriage came to grief on an obstacle that neither of us had foreseen: the Party. Marusya's ambition was to help steer our country towards the Radiant Future. She was capable, methodical, and possessed one hundred percent blinkered vision. I believed that with her at my side I would be able to stifle my growing doubts and share in her commitment. But it didn't work that way. During the years that followed the invasion of Afghanistan, I lost my faith in communism. The war dragged on, a boyhood friend was killed, and the rightness of the socialist choice came to seem increasingly in doubt. The old men at the top, gasping for breath, hung obstinately on to power: first Brezhnev, then Andropov, then Chernenko. The spectacle disgusted me. Because of my job, I had access to information that most people did not. It was plain to me that our system was in danger of collapse. I tried to explain this to Marusya, but she refused to believe me. My disillusion and her conviction raised barriers between us. One day I told her that Marxism was not a viable economic theory but an ephemeral system of thought which had been created by an overrated German philosopher in reaction to the industrial excesses of Victorian England. It was a line I had read in *Der Spiegel*. After that, communication was impossible. Our marriage had lasted just three years. We separated on relatively good terms and she remarried two weeks after our divorce was pronounced. Her new husband was a clean-cut, sharp-suited young man whose meteoric rise through the Komsomol hierarchy suggested that he spoke the same language as she did. They invited me to the wedding, but I didn't go. I never married again. I had resigned myself a long time ago to spending the rest of my life as a childless bachelor.

When I began to suspect that I might not be childless after all, I was filled with awe and confusion. Mainly confusion, since I had nothing on which to base my assumption but the fact that Katya had lied to me about Jessica's age, and that her behaviour whenever the subject arose was distinctly strange. I could have been jumping to conclusions, although Jessica's birthdate implied that I was not. Sooner or later, I was going to have to put the question to Katya directly, but something was holding me back: perhaps the fear of her producing cast-iron proof that Stephen, not I, was Jessica's father.

My feelings as we drove out of Munich were hopelessly embroiled, oscillating between tenderness for Katya and the secret she had kept from Stephen for so many years, resentment at the fact that she had lied to me, and understanding of why she had felt it necessary to do so. With all this going on inside me, I didn't feel inclined to talk, and I could feel Katya's puzzlement increasing as we wove our way through the morning traffic and her attempts at conversation were systematically rebuffed. Finally, she gave up and switched on the radio.

The day was not getting off to a good start. The conversation last night had reassured no one, and neither had my decision to change our rental car. Fearing that our pursuers might have located the Volvo and checked with the local car rental agencies, I had confided part of our problems to Volker. He had agreed to rent us a car in his own name in Munich, and to drop off yesterday's Polo in Augsburg, seventy kilometres away. I didn't want them to trace us to Munich and find Jessica. I was pretty sure that they intended no harm to either Katya or Jessica – it was me they wanted – but there was no point taking chances. Volker looked grave as we made our farewells, while Gudrun, who would have viewed a couple of nights' adultery quite favourably by now, embraced Katya with fervour and instructed me to look after her. And look after myself too, she added grudgingly. But then Jessica threw herself tearfully into my arms and made me promise to write to her and to come back and see her as soon as possible. Hugging her close to me, breathing in the childish scent of her body, I felt all sorts of things I had never felt before. Was this what it was like to be a father?

At least this morning no one was chasing us. After leaving the apartment, I had made Katya sit and wait for five minutes in our new black Opel Corsa before pulling out. I had watched the pavements and the traffic and the parked cars and the people going in and out of the nearby apartment blocks. Seeing nothing alarming, I had told her to drive as far as Dachauerstrasse and park again. How did I know the street name, she had inquired, giving me one of her long cool looks. She thought I'd never been to Munich before. The remark brought me up short. This was not the Katya I had known ten years ago. If she had noticed inconsistencies in the tales I used to tell her in Moscow, she had never said as much. A decade of emotional hibernation had sharpened her vision and loosened her tongue. I glanced at her cautiously, and told her I had looked at the street plan before leaving the flat. She started the engine, and I reflected that I had only myself to blame for her new-found acuity. When I walked out of the foreigners' ghetto into the falling snow ten years earlier, I had been too wrapped up in my own misery and regret to wonder what would become of her.

Katya's voice broke into my thoughts. 'Which direction should I take?'

'Nuremberg.'

She looked pale and tired this morning, and there were shadows under her eyes. I suspected she had slept no better than I had. 'We're not really heading for Hamburg are we?'

I hesitated. Then I said, 'No. The route is Berlin and then Warsaw.' At some point I would have to tell her where we were really going, but I didn't need to do it yet. When you were driving, you had no need to deal with reality. You were enclosed in a glass and metal world of make-believe. Your destination could be any of the places on your map.

'I can't drive you all the way to Moscow, you know.'

'I know. We'll work out what to do when we get to Poland.'

The signs for Nuremberg were coming nearer. For a few moments, we both listened to the radio.

Then she said, very softly, 'Why don't we go to Koenigsberg instead?'

I turned my head sharply. 'What did you say?'

'I'm sorry. I was being silly. I was thinking of that game we used to play.'

'The Running Away Game.'

'That's right.'

'Oh, God, Katya, you still remember.'

'Of course I do. Let's run away for real. They've just opened Kaliningrad to foreigners.'

'I haven't been back there for years.'

'Don't you visit your brother any more?'

'My brother? No, he – er, moved to Moscow.'

The answer seemed to satisfy her. We drove in silence for a while, leaving Munich behind, heading for Nuremberg and Bayreuth and the old East German border. We were listening to a Munich station called Charivari, which was playing old hits from the Sixties. Where did our love go, I can't stop loving you, the carnival is over, you were always on my mind. It took me straight back to the time when my sister and I used to listen to the BBC and Voice of America under the bedclothes, when our father, who disapproved of Western radio stations and Western music, was safely in bed.

'You know what you told me about the Party transferring funds out of the USSR?' said Katya suddenly.

I was dragged back to earth with a bump. The confessional urge that had surfaced in Alsace was proving hard to control. I had said far too much to far too many people yesterday.

'Actually, I shouldn't have told you that. It's highly confidential.'

'That's odd, because I read something about it in the paper last night.'

I gazed at her blankly. 'Which paper?'

'Stephen's paper. The one I bought in Chartres.'

My skin suddenly felt cold and clammy. 'What did it say?'

'The same thing you told me. The Party is making sure of its assets. It's transferring funds to numbered accounts in Switzerland, setting up off-shore accounts in Jersey, moving gold reserves out of the USSR—'

'I don't believe it!' The pain was back in my chest for the first time in days. 'Who wrote this?'

'Stephen, of course.'

'There was a piece under Stephen's by-line?'

'Stephen and someone else.'

I swallowed and tried to concentrate. 'What exactly did they write? Have you got it there?'

'No, I left the paper at Gudrun's. They said that the transactions were being made, but gave no detail. Apparently there are more revelations to come.'

I swore to myself in Russian. Someone must have screwed up in Stephen's absence. It was the only explanation. Katya looked up, surprised, and took in my physical state.

'Axel, what on earth's the matter? You're as white as a sheet.'

For a moment, I thought of telling her everything. No more lies, no more hiding places, just letting it all spill out. Then I got a grip on myself. 'Don't worry, it's nothing.

Too much to drink last night. I get heartburn from time to time.'

She glanced at me dubiously. 'Maybe I should pull over.'

I opened the window. 'All I need is some air.'

'Are you sure you're all right?'

'I'm fine. What were we talking about?'

'Stephen's piece on Party funds.'

'Did he say what his source was?'

'No. I wondered if it might be you.'

'How could it be me? He must have got it off someone in Moscow.'

'Ah,' she said. I wasn't sure she believed me, but she couldn't ask any more questions. There were motorways merging all over the place, and she had to pay attention to the road. At least now I knew how they had found me out. As soon as she was entangled with the traffic, I changed the subject.

'Jessica made me promise to write to her, by the way. I hope you don't mind.'

There was a pause before she answered. 'Of course I don't mind, Axel. Just don't be surprised if you don't get a letter back. She's not an awfully good correspondent.'

'Well, at her *age*' – I stressed the word deliberately – 'I wouldn't expect her to be. She'll improve with time.'

Out of the corner of my eye, I could see that she had gone bright red. Yes, she had grown up, my little Katya, she knew enough to tell when people were lying, at least some of the time, but she couldn't keep her own feelings hidden. Oh, my love, my darling . . . The music rose to a crescendo, I forgot about Stephen, I was on the point of making a declaration of some kind – of regret, longing, maybe even love – when the song ended and the news came on. Nine former terrorists from the Red Army Faction, wanted in West Germany for assassination and kidnapping, had been arrested in the East, where they had been living quietly as ordinary citizens for several years. Boris Yeltsin had resigned from the Communist Party. A bomb had gone off in a parked car in a suburb of Kaiserslautern, killing one person and injuring two others. No one had claimed responsibility for the attack, but since the car had British plates, it was thought that the IRA might be involved.

Well what did I expect? While I was wandering round Bavaria, building sentimental castles in the air on the strength of a false date and some odd behaviour, my employers were weighing their options, plotting their counter-measures and putting their plans into action. If I had been concentrating a bit harder, I would have realized something like this was going to happen.

'Do you suppose that might be the Volvo?' said Katya nervously.

'Of course it's the Volvo!'

'We can't be sure of that. All they said was "British plates". They didn't mention the make.'

'Don't try and swallow a coincidence that big, Katya, it'll only give you indigestion.'

'What's the matter with you? I'm the one who ought to be upset. It's my car, after all. Stephen's going to be livid.'

'If you cared what Stephen thought you wouldn't be sitting here now.'

She didn't answer. I took a deep breath and got myself under control. There was no point taking my fear out on her.

'I'm sorry, Katya. I shouldn't have said that. But you must

see that it's a little naive to think the IRA had anything to do with this.'

'But the radio said—'

'The IRA is a smokescreen. If IRA militants passing through Germany take the opportunity to destroy a little British property, no one's going to be unduly surprised. Only you and I and the people who exploded the bomb know better.'

She thought about it. The border drew closer, the signs marked Berlin became more frequent, the flow of traffic grew denser. Trucks bent on business, tourists eager to investigate the mysterious East, a fair number of foreign cars. There was an enormous Rasthof just before the frontier where Western explorers could fill up their tanks and their stomachs before venturing into the wilderness on the other side of the wire.

'But why blow up the car?' said Katya. 'I don't see the point.'

'To let us know they haven't forgotten us. They were giving us a warning.'

The border between West and East Germany had only been open for a fortnight, and they hadn't had time to dismantle the barbed wire. But you could see right away that you were entering another country. The houses were shabbier, the road surface deteriorated abruptly. We stopped in a small town a few kilometres from the border, and it was like going back in time. Rundown pre-war buildings, rundown modern ones, and everything tinted to a uniform murky beige by the spiritual grime of the police state and the Braunkohle they used for heating. The streets were almost empty. There were no cafés and hardly any shops. After the pristine, prosperous villages of West Germany, it was like looking at a sepia photograph of bygone days.

'Why didn't we stop to buy food before crossing the border?' said Katya, looking distastefully at the seedy facades.

'They've been shipping in truckloads of West German goods for the past two weeks. It comes to the same thing.'

She drove round the town, looking for a grocery store, muttering about paint and pollution and oil-fired central heating. The car rattled on the cobbled streets. There were no food shops to be seen. Was it a crime against the state to sell food in East Germany? said Katya irritably, and I said, Yes, it was, because it obliged the citizens to communicate with each other. I felt no compulsion to defend it, any of it. I couldn't understand how I could ever have believed in it, even when I was young, and we had it thrust down our throats the whole time, in school, the Pioneers, the Komsomol. I had been in the West on and off for seven years now, in Munich, in Bonn, and then in Hamburg, and that was at least six too many. I had become too used to light and colour, shop windows and advertising billboards, and the dangerous freedom to think for oneself.

Eventually, we found a grocery store. On the outside, it was grubby and gloomy. Inside, it was like the garden of Tsar Demyan. Shelf upon shelf of golden apples. Gleaming, cellophane-wrapped, made in West Germany. We went round the shop, selecting mineral water, bread, cheese and fruit, and joined the queue at the cash desk. The radio was on in the background, and I listened to see if there was any more information on the Kaiserslautern car bomb, tuning out the two middle-aged ladies in front of us who were complaining about the high prices of the new Western goods. The cashier took their money and began to tell them how hard it was for her eighty-year-old grandmother to choose for the first time in her life between six different brands of washing powder.

'The police are anxious to question two suspects in connection with this morning's car bomb in Kaiserslautern,' said the radio announcer.

'It's too much at her age,' said the cashier, tapping out our purchases on the brand-new cash register. 'Why do you need so many brands of washing powder anyway?'

'It's better quality than the stuff we used to have,' said one of the middle-aged ladies.

'. . . *a man and woman in their early thirties. The man has blond hair and was last seen wearing a black leather jacket.*'

'Yes, that's true, Frau Sprenger, but why do you need so many of them? Ten marks thirty, please,' she added to Katya.

'. . . *the woman has red-gold hair and is of medium height. The couple are believed to be travelling on British passports. Will anyone who has any information* . . .'

'That's the way it is in the West. Those Westerners—'

'. . . *please contact their local police station immediately, or call* . . .'

'Is something wrong?' said the cashier.

'No, I'm sorry, I was just wondering if I needed apples.' Katya had been listening to the radio too. She flashed the cashier a brilliant smile. 'I'll get them tomorrow. How much did you say?'

'Ten marks thirty.'

'. . . *believed to have links to the IRA and are likely to be dangerous* . . .'

She took the money out of her purse and paid. Her hands didn't tremble. She asked calmly for a bag, the cashier gave her one, she packed it without undue haste. 'Tschüss,' she said blithely, including all three women in her smile. 'Tschüss,' I echoed. 'Tschüss,' they said, resuming their discussion. I was proud of her. We walked out of the shop as if we didn't have a care in the world.

The car was parked on the other side of the road. I put an arm round Katya's shoulders. Now that we were out of the shop, I could feel her shaking. I ushered her into the passenger seat. She got in without a word. As I walked round to the driver's seat, I noticed a man further down the street staring at us. Not just any man. He had a dark, clever face and an air of authority. The police, or, more likely, the Stasi. The old state security service, which had tentacles everywhere and files on one citizen in three, disbanded now but still prepared for action, its officers gone to earth, biding their time, awaiting their chance to strike back. Or maybe the KGB, which had had over four hundred officers in East Berlin before the Change, and dozens more scattered around the country. The man watched as I opened the door, taking in every detail of Stephen's old black leather jacket, and then his gaze flickered on to Katya, sitting shivering in the car, with her hair glowing like a halo round her face. I put the groceries on the back seat, started the engine and drove off. I had a clear view of the man in the rear-view mirror. He watched us all the way down the street.

I should have known better. Even before I learnt about the article in Stephen's paper, I should have realized that we had eluded them yesterday through sheer good luck, and that they would do their utmost to find me again. I should have remembered the look on Pavel's face as he came at me with the knife in his hand. I should have left Katya in Munich, taken the car, and set out on my own.

Ignoring the signs for Berlin and the Autobahn, we drove out into the country. After a few miles, the road began to rise steeply, and the trees closed in around us. The Thuringian Forest. I saw a track leading off into the woods, and bumped the car a couple of hundred yards off the road, out of sight of anyone passing by. There was a bench a little farther up the track, offering a protective view down to the road and a panoramic view over the valley. We sat there and pretended to eat our picnic. A few cars went past on the road below but none slowed down, and none turned up the forest track. No one had followed us. So far, we were safe.

I thought regretfully of the nine wanted Red Army terrorists who, with the help of the Stasi, had dropped out of sight as completely as if they had never existed. They had been given refuge, false identities, police protection. One had worked in a Magdeburg steel plant, another had been a housewife in a Berlin suburb. If I had the Stasi on my side now, my troubles would be at an end. They had the means to give me what I needed, even now. A hideout, false papers, transport across Germany. But six days ago I had changed allegiance, and now they were fighting against me. I began to tell Katya that we had to change our plans.

'I'm going to drop you in Leipzig. You can get a train back to Munich from there. I'll keep the car and go on alone.'

'You want us to split up?'

'Yes.'

'But you don't have a driving licence.'

'It doesn't matter.'

'How will you get across Germany?'

'I'll work that out later. First, I want to get you to safety.'

'What makes you think I'll be safe in Leipzig? They're as likely to arrest me on a train as anywhere else.'

'No one's looking for you. I told you, all that IRA stuff is a blind. It isn't you they want, it's me.'

'Are you sure? I've been driving you across Europe for the past six days. They probably figure I'm in it up to the neck. Why else would I be doing this for you?'

Why indeed? Why are you doing this for me, Katya? I got up off the bench and walked up the track into the woods, leaving her sitting there. I emptied my mind of everything but the smell of the pines, the warmth of the sun, the enchanted forest, and the fairy tales, not the Russian stories like the one I had told Jessica the other night, but the old German Märchen my mother used to tell me. Snow White fleeing through the forest from her wicked stepmother, Hansel and Gretel dropping pieces of bread to avoid losing their way – I rounded a bend in the track and stopped dead, for there in front of me was the Little Gingerbread House. A solitary wooden hut standing a little way back from the path in a small sunlit clearing. The grass around was high and untrodden. No one had been near it for weeks, if not months. The witch was not in residence.

I wandered towards it to take a closer look, and an idea began to take shape in my mind. Even if I convinced Katya we had to separate, what then? Leipzig was at least a hundred kilometres off. The Opel had been spotted. We would have to ditch it and find another car. With her British papers, Katya couldn't rent one: without a driving licence, neither could I. Stealing one was possible but dangerous. Even if we found a car, driving to Leipzig was a risky operation. Half the population of East Germany would have heard that radio message, ten percent of them would have paid attention to it, one member of the ten percent had already spotted us. They knew roughly where we were and in which direction we were likely to travel. It was by no means certain we could reach Leipzig unhindered. On the other hand, if we lay low for a day or two, the scent would have cooled, the radio announcement would have been taken off the air, and we stood a better chance of getting away.

The hut, after three days on the road, looked like paradise regained. No noise, no concrete, no metal, only grass and sun and the birds twittering in the trees. I walked round it, inspecting its possibilities, taking care to stay at a distance so as not to leave footprints in the long grass. The door had a solid padlock and was visible to anyone coming up the track. The window at the back looked a better bet. With the aid of a stout branch, I forced open the shutters, broke a window pane, and released the catch. The window swung open. I climbed inside.

The hut was sparsely but adequately furnished. Two wide wooden shelves served as seating space in the daytime and beds at night. Each had a mattress and cushions in cheap, brightly coloured cotton. Between them stood a solid wooden table. Next to the door, another large shelf, with a camping gas and a large plastic washing up bowl standing neatly side by side. A few basic cooking utensils hanging from nails on the wall, and two or three tins of food stacked in a corner. A heavy layer of dust over everything. No one had been there for some time. There was no electricity and no running water, but a cupboard in the corner behind the door revealed a gas lamp and two serious looking buckets. There must be a source of water somewhere nearby. The cupboard also housed two plates, two cups, two sets of cutlery and two quilts. I didn't have to be in Prague till Saturday. Today was Wednesday. We had three whole days. I climbed back through the window and went down the hill to find her.

She was still sitting where I had left her. The picnic had been tidied up and put away. She got to her feet as I approached. Very pale and serious.

'I'm sorry, Axel, I wasn't thinking clearly just now. Obviously you have more chance of getting to Moscow on your own. We can leave for Leipzig as soon as you like.'

'Tell me the truth,' I said. 'She's my daughter, isn't she, not Stephen's?'

She didn't answer right away. Instead she looked me in the eyes, apparently searching for something. What she saw must have reassured her. She nodded wordlessly. It occurred to me, as I took her in my arms, that I was probably engaging in yet more self-deception. The KGB couldn't have road-blocks on every road in East Germany. It might be much easier to get to Leipzig than I thought. But I didn't want to go to Leipzig. I wanted to run away to Koenigsberg with Katya.

The breeze blew in through the open window, and the trees around the cabin rustled peacefully. We had moved the table out of the way, and put the mattresses on the floor side by side.

'We used to have a children's encyclopedia with a picture of somebody being crowned in Koenigsberg Cathedral. I think it was Frederick the Great.'

'If we'd been living in Koenigsberg then, we could have gone to the coronation.'

'Standing outside in the rain to get a glimpse of the king and his court?'

'Certainly not. Sitting inside, in the pews, in our best brocade. My mother's family was noble, remember.'

'But Stephen's ancestor was Rector of the University—'

'No, he wasn't, Katya! It wasn't the same period.'

'– and they wouldn't have let us attend a coronation if we were living in sin.'

'In Koenigsberg, you'd have met me before you met Stephen. We'd have been married.'

'Would we?'

'Of course we would.'

'But what if you'd been a Teutonic Knight?'

'That would have been tricky. I'd have been too busy conquering people and converting them to Christianity to bother about you. I think I'd probably have been celibate too.'

'Then I'd have led you astray.'

'How would you have done that?'

'If you like, I'll show you.'

'Katya? Did you really think I'd walked out on you in Moscow?'

'No. Yes. I don't know. I didn't know what to think. It was too much, all at once, you going, and then realizing I was pregnant. I couldn't think straight for months.'

'I wish it hadn't happened like that.'

'Even if you'd been there, what would it have changed? I could have got a divorce, but you might not have got permission to marry me. We never had a future together, Axel, you know that.'

'Would you divorce Stephen now?'

'Yes.'

'But you've stayed with him all this time.'

'There was nowhere I wanted to go. After I lost you, there didn't seem any point.'

'Is that the only reason you stayed?'

'No. I stayed for material reasons. We have a nice lifestyle, you saw the house. He's away a lot, and when he's there he's busy with his books and his computer. He leads his life, I lead mine.'

'But you still sleep with him?'

'Yes.'

'Why?'

'Why do you think?'

'It's more than that. The way you looked—'

'It can be quite exciting making love to a man who doesn't care about you at all.'

'My God.'

'Don't look like that. You don't need to be jealous of Stephen. It's true, I wouldn't hesitate to divorce him. But I have to think of Jessica. My books don't make enough money to support both of us.'

'Does he know about Jessica?'

'Of course not.'

'He's never suspected anything?'

'I doubt it's ever occurred to him. When he found out I was pregnant, first he was furious, and then he tried to pretend it wasn't happening. He did his best to shut it out of his mind – why would he go looking for more complications?'

'He was furious? But then maybe—'

'That was because he didn't want to have children. He thought they'd distract him. Not that he bothered to tell me beforehand. But when Jessica was born, he changed his mind. Now he's devoted to her.'

'Do you remember the other night I told you I'd gone on loving you the whole time?'

'You didn't mean a word of it.'

'No, I didn't, but it was true anyway. You've been

buried deep inside me, all these years, without my realizing it.'

'What happened with your wife? Why didn't that work out?'

'I only married her because she had red hair.'

'She was me, but Russian?'

'Not exactly. She was a lecturer in Marxism-Leninism. Katya, I really don't want to talk about Marusya.'

'You never want to tell me about your other women. It's not fair.'

'Here we are in the witch's cottage in the depths of the forest. Just you and me. Like in the fairy tales. No husbands, no wives, no children, no Stasi. Let's keep it that way.'

'What do you want to talk about then?'

'Coronations. Tell me about your picture of Koenigsberg.'

'I'm tired of coronations. Are there forests in Koenigsberg?'

'There are, if you want there to be.'

'Seriously.'

'It's marshier up there. Flatter. But there are witches too, of course.'

'Maybe the witch's hut could be on the edge of the sea.'

'Maybe we could get my mother's castle back from the Bolsheviks.'

'What do you want a castle for? Think how draughty it would be. All the gales sweeping in from the Baltic. We're fine here, aren't we?'

'Running water wouldn't be bad. Carrying those buckets will be a pain when there's snow on the ground.'

'Maybe this will just be our summer cottage then. We'll move into your Schloss for the winter. You do have servants, I suppose?'

'Faithful old family retainers, yes, of course we do.'

'And heating?'

'Blazing log fires in every room, Gräfin. And a fur-lined carriage to take you to the coronation.'

'We could wear masks so the Rector wouldn't know who we were.'

'Like the carnival in Venice.'

'Dancing with mysterious masked strangers . . .'

'No, with me. Only with me.'

'How will I know who you are?'

'I'll be dressed in white with a big black cross on my surcoat, and there'll be a serf holding my noble steed outside in the courtyard.'

'It's the same as it was in Moscow. You haven't changed.'

'Yes I have, Axel.'

'Except that you're thinner. Too thin. It's living with Stephen that's done it to you. It's stressful, whatever you say.'

'Stephen and I just ignore each other. That's not stressful.'

'Of course it is.'

'Compared to the way he behaved when I was pregnant, nothing is stressful. It's been downhill ever since—'

'What do you mean? How did he behave?'

'For the whole nine months, he hardly spoke to me. He behaved as if I wasn't there. Sometimes he used to look at me as if he hated me. It was horrible, really horrible. Once or twice I didn't think I was going to make it.'

'What does that mean?'

'Nothing. I shouldn't have said that.'

'Tell me.'

'It doesn't matter, Axel.'

'Tell me. I want to know.'

'When I was seven months pregnant, we were invited to a

reception at the British Embassy. I didn't feel well, I wanted him to go on his own, but he insisted I should go with him. It was stuffy in there, too hot, too many people. Somebody gave me a glass of champagne, I took a couple of sips, and then I blacked out. That's never happened to me before. It was like falling into a bottomless pit. I can still remember how frightening it was. Somebody caught me, but the glass smashed, and the champagne went all over everywhere, and Stephen was furious.'

'But it wasn't your fault.'

'He drove me home. In the car, he said, "If you're going to faint, you should do so in private." He dropped me in front of the apartment block, and went back to the reception. I went up to the flat, and into the bathroom. I unscrewed Stephen's razor and took the blade out. Then I looked at my wrists and poked around and felt the veins and worked out exactly what I was going to have to do.'

'Katyusha—'

'I couldn't see any other way out. I felt as if I was in a trap. Stephen didn't care about me, you were gone. I was so unhappy that night, I believe I would have done it.'

'Why didn't you?'

'I had a photo of you that I used to carry round with me. It was one that I'd taken at a party some time. I'd cut everyone else out of the picture and just kept you. While the water was running, I took it out for one last look, and then I realized that the baby was your baby, it was all I had left, that and the photo . . .'

After a long while, I said, 'What would you have done if it had been Stephen's child?'

'I don't know. I sometimes think about it. I just don't know.'

When it began to get dark, we stopped playing games. We got up and got dressed and ate Gulaschsuppe out of one of the tins on the shelf. Afterwards, Katya took the quilts out of the cupboard ready for the night, and I went down the hill to check on the car and fetch the backpacks we had borrowed from Gudrun's children.

The car was where we had left it, and there was no sign that anyone had been near it. Staying in the shadow of the trees, I made my way cautiously down to the road, and walked a couple of hundred yards in both directions. I saw nothing. No cars parked on the side of the road, no watchers waiting for us to emerge from the woods. For the time being, we were safe. I would be able to spend the night with Katya, fending off questions about the past, telling her lies about the future, using her, deceiving her, betraying her with every word I spoke. I walked back to the car and sat down in the driver's seat. Maybe I should start the engine and drive away out of her life to take my chances with the KGB. She had suffered enough because of me. In Moscow, I had abandoned her, even if that wasn't how I saw it at the time. Because of me, she had nearly died. If it was because of me that she had finally lived, that was no consolation. And now I had come marching heedlessly back into her life, with no thought for what I might find, nor what I might leave behind me. It was true, I still loved her. But I had nothing to give her. Playing at make-believe in a fairy tale forest was as good as it would get. When we came out of the forest, there was nowhere to go.

I locked the car and picked up the backpacks. I had been gone too long. Soon she would start to worry, and I had enough on my conscience already.

When I got back to the hut, she was waiting for me with a saucepan full of hot water, a box marked Clairol and a set face. She took a pair of scissors off the table and held them out to me.

'If I remember rightly your sister is a hairdresser. Do you know how to cut hair too?'

I stared at her blankly. My sister was a pediatrician. Then I remembered that my Moscow legend had me living in a two-room flat on the edge of town with my sister, my uncle and my grandmother (not the German grandmother from Koenigsberg, whom Stephen would certainly have insisted on meeting, but the Russian one from Tambov). Lies were all around me. I would never get free of them.

Katya misinterpreted my confusion. 'I'm too conspicuous with hair like this. You said so yourself.'

'What's in that box?'

'Hair dye. I pinched it from Gudrun's bathroom this morning. It's light brown. Gudrun's colour.'

'Gudrun dyes her hair?'

'Gudrun's hair has been grey since she was twenty. It runs in her family.'

I took the scissors from her and tested the cutting edge with my finger. It cut. Then I took a lock of hair and smoothed it gently back from her face. It gleamed in the obscurity of the hut.

'It'll grow again,' said Katya.

Yes, I thought, but when? When would I see it like this again? When would I see Katya again? I had a meeting in Prague on Saturday. After that, the future was a blank. In the land of make-believe, you don't have to think about things like that. You can drive to Koenigsberg and dance at the coronation, all at the same time. I began to cut, and a lock of hair fell softly to the floor. Katya drew her breath in sharply. I went on cutting. I remembered the Institute at Yurlovo where they had sent me after I lost her. I remembered the bedroom with the pale grey walls and the two narrow beds, where I used to lie awake at night, thinking of her, remembering the way her hair fanned out over the pillow like a curtain of gold. And while I was lying there fantasizing, she was awake too, on the other side of Moscow, running the bath water and looking at old photographs. By the time I had finished cutting, I had made up my mind. Tonight, we would play our games for the last time, and tomorrow I would tell her the truth.

In the land of make-believe, sooner or later you have to stop pretending.

As it turned out, I didn't get the chance. They caught up with us early the next morning.

The day broke cold and misty. Katya kept putting her hand to her hair, as if wondering where it was. Halfway through our breakfast tin of Gulaschsuppe, I said, 'Katya, there's something I need to tell you,' but she wasn't listening to me. She had put down her bowl and her attention was fixed on something outside the hut.

'What's the matter?' My reactions were slow that morning. I had slept badly, and my dreams had been punctuated with images of water running, black pits opening, falling, drowning, dying.

'Listen,' she said, and then I heard it too. The sound of a car engine coming up the track.

My brain snapped back in place. 'Quick! Grab your things and into the woods!'

She snatched up the articles of clothing lying on the floor, I grabbed the leather jacket with the envelopes in the pocket. She scrambled through the window and ran for the trees. I followed her out and cast a final glance back through the window. The bedding was in disorder on the floor, there were unwashed bowls and saucepans on the table. The owners of the hut would know someone had been there, but they wouldn't know who.

Two minutes later, we were crouched out of sight in the shelter of the pines. The car engine had stopped, but the path was still empty. A couple of minutes went by, and I began to wonder if it was a false alarm. Maybe someone had driven up the hill with the intention of going walking in the woods. Maybe it wasn't the owners of the hut after all.

Then a twig snapped, close at hand. Someone was coming up the hill on foot. We waited, hardly daring to breathe. A man appeared round the bend in the path. We both recognized him immediately. Katya turned an appalled face to me: I put a finger to my lips. It was the man from yesterday, the man with the clever face and commanding air. One of East Germany's immense hidden layer of Stasi officers who had been alerted in the past twenty-four hours by the KGB. I let my breath out slowly. We were going to have to be very careful. The net was closing in on us.

We watched as the man made his way towards the hut and circled it cautiously, just as I had done the previous day. He got to the back, saw the open window and stopped dead. Then he reached inside his jacket and took out a gun. Katya gasped. Staying close to the wall of the hut, he slithered up to the window, looked inside, and saw the hut was empty.

He put the gun back where it came from, and swung himself agilely inside. With extreme caution, I transferred the three manila envelopes from Stephen's jacket into my backpack. My gun was in there already, and so was everything else I had brought with me. Then I laid a hand on Katya's arm, and signalled that it was time to move off.

As soon as we were a safe distance from the hut, we stopped for a brief whispered conference.

'Is it safe to take the car?'

'No, we'll have to abandon it.'

'Do you think he found it?'

'Why else would he have come up the hill looking for us?'

'Can't we get down and drive away before he leaves the hut?'

'He won't be there for long. He'll see the bowls are still warm. He'll know we can't be far off.'

We heard him coming almost before I had finished speaking. He was already looking for us. We couldn't see him, but we could tell where he was from the sound of his feet crackling in the undergrowth. He might be clever, but he didn't know how to move noiselessly in the forest. I pushed Katya behind a clump of bushes and crouched down beside her. The crackling came closer. Katya leaned against me, rigid with fright. I hoped she wasn't going to move and give us away. The crackling stopped. He couldn't have been more than twenty yards away. I could feel him peering through the trees. A couple more steps and he was bound to see us. And then we heard a sigh, a muffled oath, and the sound of footsteps retreating towards the edge of the forest. He had decided it was hopeless trying to follow us through the forest on his own. He had gone to summon reinforcements.

As soon as it was quiet, I pulled her to her feet. She was shaking and hollow-eyed.

'Oh my God, Axel, what are we going to do?'

I brushed away the leaves and twigs that had stuck to her clothes. 'We're going to have to walk for a bit. We'll work our way through the woods and pick up the road further down the valley.'

'If we walk along the road they're going to spot us right away.'

'No, they aren't,' I said, with as much firmness as I could muster. 'The description they broadcast yesterday said that I had a leather jacket and you had red hair. But you don't have red hair any more, and I'm going to leave this jacket somewhere in the woods. Once we're away from the hut, they'll have no means of knowing who we are.'

'But on the road, we'll be so obvious, all they have to do is stop us and search us. They'll find the passports, oh my God—'

'They have no right to stop us and search us, Katya. They can stop us and ask questions, but that's all. And since we can both pass for German they won't look any further. They'll let us go.'

She wasn't entirely convinced, but she allowed herself to be persuaded. In any case, there was no choice. The car was out of reach. At some point, we were going to have to come out of the woods and start walking. We shouldered our backpacks and began to make our way towards the road, cutting through the forest in a wide arc.

After about forty minutes, we emerged at the top of a steep bank running down to the road. A truck rumbled by beneath us.

'Why don't we hitch a lift?' said Katya.

I looked at her without enthusiasm. 'We could try, I suppose.'

'It's better than walking along that road. We'd be far less exposed.'

'That's true.'

'And in any case, we need to get to a decent-sized town. We'll stick out like a sore thumb in one of those villages.'

She had a point. We began to make our way down the bank.

'Listen,' said Katya, and I heard the noise of a car climbing the slope towards us. 'Quick, before it goes past.'

'No, wait. Get back up the bank, Katya!'

She obeyed without asking questions. We scrambled up the way we had come, and shrank back into the shadow of the trees. The car was nearly upon us. I wasn't sure why my instincts were telling me to keep out of sight. Judging by the sound of the engine, it was something big and powerful. More likely West German tourists in their Mercedes than the man from the Stasi in his little East German Trabant. The car came in sight, and I saw that it was indeed a Mercedes. With the Stasi officer at the wheel. There was another man sitting beside him, and a third in the back. I caught a glimpse of his dark, clever face, intent on the road, and then the car swept beneath us and he was gone.

'Oh my God,' she said, 'how did you know it was him?'

'I didn't, I just . . . Did you see his number plates?'

'No.'

'They were Berlin plates. *West* Berlin, Katya.'

She looked at me, and decided not to ask what that meant.

'Let's start hitching,' I said, 'before he comes back.'

We clambered down the bank and stood on the edge of

the road. Katya looked round nervously. We were visible for several hundred yards on both sides, and there was nowhere to take cover.

'If the worst comes to the worst,' I said, 'run for it. Downhill. That way you'll go faster. If you can get into the woods, you stand a good chance of losing anyone who comes after you.'

'What about you?'

'Uphill. Our best chance is to separate.'

She looked at me and I put my arm round her. The mist had thickened and it had begun to drizzle. A lime-green Trabant came in view at the bottom of the hill. I put out my hand to signal. The car drew up beside us.

The driver was a cheerful young man who was delighted to meet what he took to be a couple of West Germans. He asked where we were going. I said Weimar, which seemed the nearest plausible destination for West German tourists, and mumbled something about car repairs and missed buses to explain our unlikely means of transport. He accepted the explanation without difficulty. He was going there himself, he added, and could take us all the way.

Katya's eyes had lit up at the mention of Weimar, and I remembered that it had been the home of both Goethe and Schiller, who had been visited there by practically all the other men of letters of the time. I wondered if we were going to spend the afternoon in the footsteps of Hölderlin. It was a pity I hadn't had time to do a more thorough investigation of Katya before embarking on this assignment. If I had known she was a successful author, not a ground-down housewife, I would have handled things differently those first few days. The interesting thing was that Stephen himself had never so much as hinted at her new career – though it was easy to guess why. A name on a book jacket implied a solidity and permanence that a byline, however eminent, could never match.

I switched my thoughts back to the matter in hand. Our driver was busy explaining that he himself had not yet visited the West, except for West Berlin, just once, on the night the Wall came down. He had driven up as soon as the news came on the radio, just dropped everything and left. Wahnsinn, he said, einfach unglaublich. It was crazy, there were people laughing and crying and embracing, hugging complete strangers, climbing on top of the Wall, shaking hands with the border guards, taking photos, opening champagne. So eine schöne Nacht, he said, shaking his head reminiscently, the most beautiful night of my life. His mother didn't think so: she wished the Wall were still there. She didn't want reunification, she thought East Germans should be allowed to solve their own problems in their own way. But what can you expect at her age? he said indulgently. His name was Heinz, and ours? Dieter and Magda, I said, and Heinz left the wheel to fend dangerously for itself and shook hands with both of us.

'I wish I'd seen it,' said Katya wistfully.

'Me too,' I agreed, although I had in fact been in the thick of it, embracing strangers with the best of them, quite possibly even Heinz himself.

When we arrived in Weimar, Heinz dropped us in the town center and asked if we needed a place to stay the night. His mother, he explained, had a room to rent. 'Maybe,' I said nonchalantly, 'we're not sure yet.' Heinz took a pile of neatly lettered squares of paper from his wallet, gave us one and put the others carefully away. I noticed that his mother, the lady who thought East Germany should have stayed behind its barbed wire, had a Russian first name. Ludmilla Stoltenberg. 'Call before you go,' he yelled as he drove away, 'and she'll tell you how to get there.'

Weimar was a pleasant little town, with a cosy literary atmosphere, and an enthusiastic band of cultural pilgrims flowing round the Schillerhaus, the Liszthaus and the other great men's shrines. In deference to the tourists, there were even shops: a whole street of them. We purchased a couple of anoraks in egalitarian grey-beige, acquired a town map and blended in with the pilgrims. Hölderlin had not lived here, it seemed, only visited, and Goethe had not been at home that day.

'They did meet later, though, at Charlotte von Kalb's house,' said Katya, eyeing the Schillerstrasse thoughtfully. 'I wonder where that would have been.'

But the map didn't say, and we had other things to think about. We strolled through the Goethepark, admiring the scenery and reviewing our options, which were limited. Renting a car was impossible, and the idea of public transport made me nervous. Until the previous November, the Stasi had had ninety thousand full time staff. A good many of them were probably combing hotels, airports, bus and train stations all over East Germany. Since I had originally intended to stay in the hut all day, we were in no hurry to move on, and Weimar offered ample camouflage. As far as I could see, the best thing was to wait until dark and try to steal a car. I had never done such a thing in my life before, but theoretically I knew how. Katya had regained her sangfroid since we got out of the woods: she agreed to the plan without hesitation.

The park undulated gracefully down to the River Ilm. On the far bank we caught sight of Goethe's Gartenhaus, where the writer had lived for several years in pastoral seclusion. There was a knot of people gathered on the grass in front of the house.

'What are all those people doing down there?' said Katya.

'Maybe it's for us. The local Stasi reception committee.'

'With an orchestra too?'

It was an open air concert. The orchestra started playing just as we came within earshot, and the grey air was suddenly filled with the bright, limpid grace of a vanished age. The Brandenburg Concertos. It might not be the Stasi, but it was definitely for us. We sat on the grass apart from the rest of the audience and held hands. About halfway through, I became aware that her face was wet with tears. I pulled her against me and put my arms round her.

'Don't cry, Katya. We've lost ten years, but it's not too late. There has to be a way. We'll think of something.'

After the concert, we walked back into town, hand in hand. Neither of us paid any attention to where we were going. Neither of us spoke. Tourists swarmed all around us, calling to each other in a variety of languages, but we were conscious of no one but ourselves. We were back in Moscow on that iron-grey January morning, while the telex clattered in the background and the Sixth Concerto rose to a crescendo and the snowflakes fell faster and faster outside the window. And then a child bounced a ball across the path, and we were once more in Weimar, on a dull July afternoon ten years later. I had Katya's red-gold hair in the bottom of my backpack, and Katya's unhappy marriage on my conscience. Somewhere at the back of my mind I could hear bath taps running. I tightened my grip on her hand, and she looked at me and smiled. Weimar faded again. We were lovers, not fugitives;

we had shed our spurious existence as criminals, stars of the IRA, enemies of the people. The KGB, if it existed, had nothing to do with us.

Which was why we nearly walked straight into the man from the Stasi. He was standing in the middle of the Frauenplan, plunged in discussion with another man, fortunately too intent on his conversation to notice us. We both saw him at the same time, stopped dead, and dived instinctively into the Goethehaus, the entrance to which was less than two feet away.

We spent a long time walking through the elegant Baroque house, studying the writer's personal letters and possessions, moving at an awed pace through the succession of rooms, inhaling the atmosphere of the great man's study, admiring at length his china, sculptures, library, and mineral collection, the inlaid wooden floors and the pictures on the walls. When there was really nothing left to see, we took refuge at the bottom of the garden. At five to five, a buxom lady informed us politely but firmly that the museum was closing. We slunk obediently out into the street. We had planned to wait till dusk and then try to get our hands on a car, but dusk meant nine o'clock at the earliest. That left four hours to kill. And meanwhile, our pursuers had followed us right here to Weimar. Luck or instinct? Or did someone tip them off?

Outside, there was no sign of the man from the Stasi or his companion.

'There's a good chance he won't recognize us,' I said. 'Without the leather jacket there's nothing much to identify me, and you look completely different with your hair like that.'

Katya suddenly clapped a hand to her mouth. 'Oh my God! My hair!' She had gone white.

'What's the matter?'

'The packet of dye! I put it to one side meaning to burn it this morning.' She looked at me with stricken eyes.

'You mean you left the packet in the hut? Oh, for God's sake, Katya!'

'Then when we had to run for it—'

'How could you be so careless? That's our last trump card gone!'

'They don't know my hair is short,' she pointed out, but I refused to be pacified. I had walked back into her life as unthinkingly as I had left it ten years earlier. Now, as then, I had nothing to offer, and nowhere to take her. What was more, it looked as though I had a good chance of getting her arrested too. The museums and shops were closing, and the town was emptying. The clouds had thickened, and rain appeared imminent. We tagged on to the end of a group of tourists who looked as though they were going towards the park, but after a few hundred yards it became evident that they were only heading for their bus. As the first of them started to climb in, Katya put her hand on my arm and I saw the second man from the Frauenplan standing on the other side of the road, his gaze roaming purposefully over the group.

'Damn,' I said.

'What are we going to do?'

'We'll have to get on the bus.'

'But they'll know we aren't part of the group.'

'It doesn't matter, we—'

I became aware of a car hooting, and turned to look. It was the young man we had met earlier, in his sickly green Trabant. I rushed across the pavement, dragging Katya behind me, and leant familiarly on the roof while I bent down to talk to him. With our indigenous anoraks and casual stance, we might just pass for locals talking to a friend.

'So,' Heinz was saying, 'have you had a good day? Do you still need a room? I am going to my mother's now, if you need a lift.'

Heinz' mother lived in a vast high-rise housing development on the edge of town, with twelve-storey blocks rising in every direction as far as the eye could see.

'My God,' said Katya, struggling out from the back of the Trabi. 'It looks just like Moscow.'

'Well and so it was until recently,' I said. Heinz was poking around under the bonnet, the engine was still going, and he couldn't hear us.

'If this was London, the kids would be out painting graffiti on the stairs and breaking old ladies' windows.'

I put my arm round her and kissed the side of her head. Our narrow escape had calmed my nerves. 'But this is a socialist country and such behaviour is not considered cultured.'

'Is your flat in Moscow in a place like this?'

I looked at her in despair. My father was a general, though she didn't know that, and he and his family lived in a style commensurate with his rank. My own flat in Moscow was centrally located and certainly not in a place like this. I was, moreover, its sole occupant. Both my grandmothers were dead, I had no uncles, and my sister lived in Leningrad. Lies were a labyrinth there was no way out of.

'Yes, it's similar, I suppose.'

'So,' said Heinz, closing the bonnet and turning off the engine, 'everything is in order. Let's go and find my mother.'

The flat was at the end of an unsignposted rabbit-warren of corridors and landings. The lift stopped at alternate floors, and a single staircase served three different buildings. Just like the place Natasha lived in, muttered Katya balefully. But the flat itself was distinctly gemütlich. At some point in my career, they had taught me to assess things like furniture and decorations and I took in the sitting room at a glance. Solid, Western-made furniture, and a large amount of serious electronics. Ludmilla was a lady with access. Beyond that, her taste ran to fringed lampshades, hanging plants and frilly cushions. Ludmilla herself was an energetic-looking woman of about fifty, in a T-shirt and flowered skirt. Heinz introduced us as Dieter and Magda. 'Stoltenberg,' she said briskly, holding out her hand. She reminded me of a teacher I once had. The room she was renting opened off the sitting room. She showed us in and started explaining about cupboards and light switches, but then the phone rang and she went to answer it. Heinz had elbowed aside some cushions and settled himself on the couch with a beer. I shut the door and sized up the room. Wardrobe and bed in the same expensive light oak as the sitting room. Fitted carpet, brand new wallpaper, more frilly lampshades and another television set.

'This isn't like Moscow at all,' said Katya, testing the mattress.

'It's not like East Germany either. Far too well furnished.'

'You think she's a Party member?'

'She's more than that. Ordinary Party members don't have access to all this stuff.'

'What is she then? A Party official? Or . . . Stasi, do you think she might be Stasi?'

'Whatever she is, she's far too well connected. Look at those books over there.'

Katya followed my gaze. 'Russian books?' Her voice rose incredulously.

'Don't take your coat off,' I said, 'it's dangerous here. We're going to have to leave.'

We waited in the bedroom until Heinz had gone. He took his time drinking his beer, but at last the murmur of voices from the outer room fell silent, and we heard the slam of the door. After another five minutes, we got up to leave. If Ludmilla asked, we would say we were going to dinner.

But when we opened the door leading to the outer room, Ludmilla was waiting for us. She had stationed herself in an armchair facing the bedroom door. On guard, one might almost have thought, were it not for her relaxed pose and friendly smile. On the table in front of her stood a bowl of cherries and a plate of dry biscuits.

'Sit down,' she said. 'You have time for a chat, don't you? I'm all alone since my husband died, and I enjoy having people to talk to.'

'Thank you. We'd be glad to.' I sat on the couch, motioning to Katya to take the second armchair, and unzipped my anorak.

'Help yourselves to cherries. I picked them this afternoon. I have a piece of garden, just two tram stops away from here. It's very convenient. That phone call just now,' she went on, with no change in inflection, 'was from an old contact of mine, from before the Change. He said he saw you getting into Heinz' car. Apparently the KGB are looking for you.'

This time I felt no twinge of fear, merely a kind of resigned lassitude. The Beretta came smoothly out of the anorak pocket and into my hand. In all my years of service, I had never used a gun, but I felt as if I had been doing this all my life. 'Don't move, Frau Stoltenberg. Magda, see if you can find something to tie her hands. And a gag of some kind.'

Katya looked at me, at the gun, at Ludmilla, and stood up uncertainly.

'Put that away, young man,' said Ludmilla. 'And you, sit down. You're in no danger. I told my friend that Heinz dropped you at the bus station.'

'Do you expect me to believe you? Magda, the gag!'

Ludmilla tucked her feet up on the chair, and leant forward to take a cherry. 'Heinz's hobby is doing up old cars and re-selling them. He has one he just finished yesterday. He's willing to sell it to you. He's gone to get it now.'

Silence. We all looked at each other. I was completely baffled.

'Your friend told you . . . who we are?'

'He told me who wants you. He didn't tell me why.'

'And you're prepared to help us get away?'

'Yes.'

'Why?'

She looked me in the eye. 'Last November, the Russians betrayed us. They stood by and did nothing while that fool Krenz opened the Wall. They could have put a stop to it while there was still time. Like they did in Prague in '68. But they didn't. They didn't raise a finger to help us.'

She had pulled her knees up under her chin and her eyes were fixed on me in a dark intense stare. I relaxed my grip on the gun. She was right: we were in no immediate danger. I had encountered this attitude once or twice before, working with the Stasi people. It wasn't the careerists who felt this way, it was the believers. The ones for whom East Germany had been a way of life. The ones who could neither forget nor forgive.

'And now, *Comrade* Gorbachev is selling us out to the West. We're going to be colonized by West German capitalism and taken over by NATO. Thanks to the Russians, we're losing our country, our ideals and our past. I don't know who you are, young man, and why they want you, but I'm going to have no part in helping them get hold of you.'

Heinz returned with the news that the police were out in force in the town, especially in the vicinity of the bus and train stations.

'That means there'll be road blocks on the way out of Weimar,' I said.

'No problem,' said Heinz, 'I'll show you a back way out of town. But it might be better to wait till it gets dark. Why don't you make us all something to eat, Mutti, and then I'll take them out through number 19 around half-past nine?'

Ludmilla hummed and hawed a bit at this – taking private vengeance on the Russians was one thing, harbouring two wanted persons in her flat was another – but finally gave in and went off to the kitchen. Katya followed, leaving me to negotiate car prices with Heinz. After some haggling for appearances' sake, I took out my cheque book and wrote him a cheque on my West German bank account, in the name of Dieter Fischer, for operational purposes only. It was lucky Heinz was young enough to be dazzled by a real West German cheque. I didn't have anything like enough cash on me to pay for a car. I doubted there were enough funds in the account to cover the cheque, and I doubted it would be honoured even if there were. Heinz was hopelessly naive, but I wasn't going to tell him so. Maybe I would send him a real cheque if I ever got the chance.

Dinner consisted of sausages and boiled potatoes.

'I told Frau Stoltenberg that she must let us pay for the meal,' said Katya, 'and for the room too of course.'

'Of course,' I said, getting out my wallet.

'Thank you,' said Ludmilla, accepting a sum which was probably double the usual cost of the room. 'It's hard for people like me on a pension to afford the prices of all the new things in the shops, you know.'

'On a pension?' I said, startled. Surely she was too young to be retired. But she preened like a peacock and told me complacently that she was sixty years old and had retired from her job in local government that spring. I took a closer look and deduced that the hair colour came out of a bottle, the same as Katya. When she was younger, she must have been a beauty, and from the way she behaved, she was used to being the centre of attention. So I ventured a question about her unusual first name, and she needed no further prompting to tell me all about her family. Like me, she was of mixed parentage. In her case, a Russian mother and German father. She had been born in Leningrad, but the family moved back to Germany in the 1930's. Most of her mother's family had died during the Siege of Leningrad, but she still had a nephew in Moscow and had made several visits to the USSR.

'Last summer, I spent two months in Moscow,' she went on. 'On the Arbat, I saw people singing satirical songs and drawing caricatures of Brezhnev. In the press, you could read authors who hadn't been published in decades. It was clear to me that glasnost and perestroika were really working. I got back here in August. People were pouring across the Hungarian frontier into Austria by the thousand. At a meeting I went to, the Party secretary stood up and said, "We don't understand what Gorbachev is trying to achieve with his perestroika. We don't need any of that here. Our reforms have been carried out already." I realized then that there was going to be an explosion of some kind. But they were so blind they couldn't see it coming. Gorbachev told them himself when he came here last October. "Wer zu spät kommt, den straft das Leben. Life punishes those who come too late." That's what he said to Honecker. He saw it coming, but they didn't. If they'd taken action, it wouldn't have been too late, even then. They could have averted the worst. The Wall might still be in place. We might still have a country of our own.'

'You don't think the two Germanies should be reunified?'

'The two Germanies are not going to be reunified. What's going to happen is completely different. Your country is going to take over our country.' She stopped for a moment and peered at me, opened her mouth to speak, and then shut it again. I guessed what she was thinking. Heinz might believe I was a West German, but his mother knew better, even though she had decided not to voice her suspicions. 'You Westerners are going to come in here and tell us how to do things. You're so convinced of your own superiority, you can't admit that there might have been some good things here too. It's not reunification, it's annexation. You're making us give up everything. First, you take away our money. The next to go will be our Constitution. Can you imagine what it feels like when they tell you that everything you believed in, everything you've been fighting for for the past forty years is worthless? I was thirty-eight when they put the Wall up. I thought it was the right thing to do. I believed in it, I thought it was the only way we could build socialism. And now they've pulled it down again, I'm sixty years old, and the best years of my life have gone. For what, I ask myself. For what?'

Heinz said irritably, 'Oh come on, Mutti, you know

perfectly well that the communists ruined this country. They destroyed everything.'

Ludmilla gave him a look that was half weariness and half exasperation, and said to us, 'My son is an ecologist, you know.'

'Really?' said Katya, 'that's wonderful,' and Heinz needed no further encouragement to tell us all about it. He had been involved in semi-clandestine environmental activities since he was at school, and was now an enthusiastic member of the new, legal, East German Green party. As we trudged through our sausages and potatoes, he deluged us with statistics. In Leipzig, the air was so bad there should be a smog alert every day. Bitterfeld was the dirtiest place in Europe. In Erfurt, the human lifespan was demonstrably shorter than normal. Parts of East Germany were unfit for human habitation.

'Is it as bad as that?' said Katya. 'I had no idea.'

'The factories spill out their wastes anywhere. Into the water, into the air. The air here is five times more polluted than in West Germany. The only forests still intact are those where the leadership used to go shooting. Honecker and the other communist leaders used to take bottled water with them when visiting parts of the country where they alone knew the water was unfit to drink. At least two-thirds of the rivers and lakes are polluted.'

To judge by the expression on Ludmilla's face, exasperation was winning out over weariness. It occurred to me that she might be capable of changing her mind and calling her friend as soon as we were out of the door. In any case, Heinz' earnestness was beginning to get on my nerves.

'What you have to remember,' I said, 'is that this country had no heavy industry after the war. Everything was in West Germany, in the Ruhr and the Rhineland.'

'Exactly,' said Ludmilla, picking up her cue. 'We had to build it all from scratch. We were the ones who fought off the Fascists, but the West Germans took everything, and we were left with nothing at all.'

'It's understandable that people should have cut corners,' I said. 'Especially then, forty years ago.'

'Germany was in a bad way after the war,' said Ludmilla. 'That's what you young people don't realize. Everything was in ruins. We had no housing, no water, no electricity, no jobs.'

Katya was staring at me as if I was bewitched. I said, 'That's why these tower blocks were built. They may not be beautiful, but at least they're functional. It was the only way to rehouse huge numbers of people with the least possible delay.'

'At least people had a roof over their heads and didn't have to sleep under a bridge or in a doorway like in the West,' said Ludmilla.

Katya rolled her eyes and looked down at her plate. Heinz got up and put the bowl of cherries on the table.

'Don't talk nonsense, Mutti. You know perfectly well these flats weren't built till the Seventies. If they're shoddy and ugly, it's not because of the war and the Fascists, it's because everything in this country was built that way. What we need to do is raze it all, get rid of it, and start afresh. They used the Fascists as an alibi for forty years, but there are no Fascists any more. They all died years ago. It's time to stop fighting the war and join the twentieth century.'

When it got dark, we said goodbye to Ludmilla, who was relieved to see the back of us, even though the conversation had turned out better than she expected. Heinz took us down the maze of passages and out of the building by a back way. Parked across the road was a beat-up Trabant.

'Is this our getaway car?' said Katya disbelievingly.

'What do you expect?' I said, smiling at Heinz. 'A Porsche like in the James Bond movies?'

'But we're never going to get to—'

'Magda!' I said, and she broke off just in time.

'A car like this is better, because it's less noticeable,' said Heinz soothingly. 'It doesn't go very fast, but you don't get away from this kind of people by going fast.'

He took Katya's arm and steered her gallantly into the passenger seat, leaving me to get in the back. The engine started on the third attempt. We drove cautiously out of Weimar on back roads and country lanes.

'You know, Magda, not everyone here thinks like my mother,' said Heinz, apparently feeling obliged to apologize for Ludmilla's Weltanschauung. 'People of her generation have known nothing else: it's natural that they should cling to the past. They can't see that reunification is the only hope for us. We should be thankful that the West is prepared to move in and take things over. They ruined us, the communists. They poisoned our countryside, they poisoned our minds.'

I braced myself for another onslaught of statistics.

'You mean through propaganda?' said Katya.

'No, worse than that. I mean through informing. Making us spy on each other. They turned us all into collaborators of the police state. They dragged us all down to their level. And now that they've gone, we have to deal with what they left behind.' He paused to negotiate a bad bend. 'Two weeks ago, I learned that my best friend has been informing on me for years.'

'Oh God,' said Katya. 'That must be terrible.'

'He was assigned by the Stasi to report on our environmentalist group. He and I joined the group at the same time; we've known each other since we were boys. When I found out, I didn't sleep all night.'

'It must be like having the ground dragged from under your feet.'

'Exactly, Magda, that's exactly how it was.'

'What did you do?'

'We tried to talk to him about it, we tried to get him to confess what he had done, we told him we wanted to understand why he had done it. But it didn't work. He wouldn't talk, he volunteered nothing we didn't already know about, he went on lying. He told us he had been working for the Stasi since 1987, but we knew he started when he was still at school. He wouldn't admit it. He doesn't want to recognise that he was guilty. We would have forgiven him, you know. His family doesn't have much money, he needed to study at university, we can imagine what it might have been like. But he doesn't want our forgiveness, he doesn't want to repent. What can you do with people like that? There are thousands like him. No one wants to acknowledge their guilt, no one wants to admit that what they did was wrong. This country is rotten to the core. We have to cleanse ourselves, sweep everything away, and make a new start.'

Where I came from, repentance used to take place in public. It was part of the old Russian Orthodox tradition. Ivan the Terrible confessed his sins to his people in Red Square. Raskolnikov, in *Crime and Punishment*, confessed his crime in the Haymarket in St. Petersburg. Of course, that was a long time ago. In our century, things had changed. The only people to make public confessions were those whose acts of repentance had been written in the basement of the Lubyanka. The others went on believing right to the end. Neither Lenin nor Stalin saw repentance as a useful exercise, and neither did any of their successors.

Here in East Germany, they weren't Orthodox, but Protestant, and I didn't know if repentance was supposed to take place in public or in private. I was inclined to think it wouldn't take place at all. The German Democratic Republic had set itself up as a custodian of socialist values, the "better" German state, occupying the moral high ground over the Nazi-ridden, capitalist, materialist-minded West. After the Wall was opened, a number of prominent intellectuals had even appealed to the people to reject the 'dirty' materialistic values of the West and hold fast to the 'humanist' moral values of the GDR, somehow managing to ignore the question of how a state that had discredited reputations, destroyed relationships, undermined confidence, sown distrust and betrayed its people could lay claim to any moral virtue whatsoever.

Self-deception was of course a common phenomenon in all the communist states of Eastern Europe. How could it be otherwise? We had all colluded with the regime. We were all guilty. Not so much because we had failed to stand up and denounce the crimes being committed – that took the kind of courage that few people possessed. What we were guilty of was the low-level but essential complicity without which the State could not have functioned. We had denounced people we knew to be innocent, agreed with positions we knew to be unfounded, obeyed orders we knew to be wrong, violated our own moral standards over and over again. The State had made sure that our mouths and our hands were as dirty as its own. I could forgive the East German intellectuals anything they had done while the regime was in place, all their mediocre compromises and sordid little surrenders. We were all guilty of that. What I could not forgive was their wilful blindness once the Wall came down, and their refusal to admit that their utopian socialist state had made a mockery of its own dusty forty-year-old ideals.

The advantage of their position was that, since they had no sense of wrong, nothing could be required of them in the way of repentance. They were the eternal victims: first of the Stalinists, and then of the West. I wasn't sure how things stood for the rest of us. Should you have to repent of things you were forced to do? The whole point of a police state was that it was impossible to decline an invitation to inform on your neighbour, or denounce your colleague. You did what they told you to do. You had no choice. You just went ahead and did it. Even though you knew it was wrong, you did it anyway. But where did that leave you once the force had gone? Was coercion enough to exonerate you? Where did that leave the guards in the Gulag, the soldiers at the Berlin Wall, the KGB officers who realized they had made a bad career choice?

I honestly didn't know.

Heinz pulled in by a bus stop at the side of the road a few minutes later, and I took over the wheel. If we went straight on for another mile, he explained, we would find ourselves on the Autobahn. West was Eisenach, east was Dresden, north was Leipzig. He didn't ask which way we were going. As for him, he would take the bus back into Weimar. He shook hands with Katya and wished her a schöne Reise, and nodded more coolly to me. A few minutes later, we were on the Autobahn, heading for Dresden. There were no signs of police activity. They must have been concentrating all their efforts on Weimar. The Trabant chugged valiantly along in the nearside lane.

'How far do you think we're going to get in this?' said Katya after a few miles. Her voice was studiedly neutral.

'With luck it'll hold out till Czechoslovakia.'

She looked at me sharply. 'Is that where we're going?'

'That's the nearest frontier. I want to get out of Germany as fast as possible.'

'Wouldn't it be better to go back to the West?'

'We won't be safe in the West. Remember the Berlin plates we saw this morning? The whole of Germany is mined. We'll be better off in Czechoslovakia.'

'I see.'

'Besides, I have a friend in Prague who might help.'

Another look. 'Then you don't want to go to Moscow any more?'

I took her hand. 'It's too far, Katyusha. We'll never make it.'

For a moment she was silent. The end of the journey was suddenly in sight. 'When will we get to Prague?'

'Some time tomorrow. We're going to leave the Autobahn in a few miles and cut across country into the mountains. I don't want to risk the main road from Dresden to Prague.'

'Oh God,' she said abruptly, 'I'm so tired. I'll be so glad when this is over.'

I didn't answer. I didn't feel too good myself. Ludmilla's sausages were settling like little balls of lead in my stomach. I rubbed my side, trying to get rid of the ache that had appeared.

'What did you want to talk to me about this morning, Axel? You said you had something to tell me.'

I kept my eyes on the road and tried to organize the words

in my mind. Katya, I've been lying to you. Nothing is the way you think it is. I lied to you in Moscow, I lied to you in London, I'm lying to you now. But I was too scared. My courage failed me. I couldn't face her accusations, even less her pain. So I took the coward's way out. I told her that I didn't remember. I said it couldn't have been important. She didn't answer. We drove on in silence. The light drizzle that had begun to fall as we left Weimar grew heavier as we drove east. By the time we left the motorway and struck off towards the mountains, it was raining in earnest.

Five

Katharine

That night, we slept in the Trabant. It was past midnight by the time we reached the Czech border, and pouring with rain. The frontier was closed for the night. We might have risked staying at a hotel out here in the mountains, but they were all closed too. Axel found a track leading off the road and drove the car out of sight. He took the front seat and I took the back. Despite the physical discomfort, which increased as the night wore on, I was glad that things had turned out like this. Tonight I didn't want to sleep in Axel's arms. I didn't want him to make love to me. Tonight I needed my body and mind to myself. I needed Lebensraum and Denkraum. Room to live and room to think.

For it was becoming increasingly clear that Axel was not what he claimed to be. Each time he had used his gun to influence the course of events, I had been too bemused to wonder what it meant, but this evening I had been in fuller command of my faculties. An information officer who spent his time in an office in Hamburg, handing out brochures on cotton production to journalists and schoolgirls, was unlikely to have the skills to grapple with would-be assassins, evade pursuing cars, and threaten old ladies. Why did Axel refuse to talk about the past ten years? Why was he lying about Stephen? How had he paid Heinz for the car? I lay stiff and cramped on the narrow seat, with the rain dripping down outside, and tried to make sense of it all.

Towards dawn, the rain eased, and we drove up to the town on the border. Oberwiesenthal, the road signs informed us, was a spa and a ski resort. Square grey fraternal housing overlooked the ski runs. Axel said the East German ski team came here to train. We overtook an antiquated steam train puffing doggedly along the valley and drove into town to find a café. Breakfast was a dismal meal: we barely spoke. Axel was in his frontier-crossing mood: tense and withdrawn. He rubbed his chest once or twice abstractedly. But as we got back into the car to drive the few kilometres to the border, he put his arms round me and kissed me.

'I love you.'

I didn't answer. We drove out of the square towards the frontier. We were to leave the Trabant at the border, walk into Czechoslovakia, and take a series of buses to Prague. The road ran round the edge of the town and climbed into the mountains. Axel's knuckles showed white where he was gripping the steering wheel. On the German side of the frontier were a restaurant and a snack bar. Axel ran the car into the parking lot next to the restaurant. He turned off the engine and put the keys in the glove compartment.

'This is where we start walking. If they ask, we're off for a day's hiking in Czechoslovakia.'

We got out of the car. Axel grabbed hold of my hand and held it fast. With our anoraks and backpacks we made fairly convincing Wänderer. If we were German, no one would look at us twice. The trouble was that we had British passports, and they would have seen us drive up in the Trabi.

Clearly, we hadn't come all the way from London in that. I wondered why Axel hadn't left it out of sight of the frontier post. The sky was heavy with cloud, and a mean drizzle was falling. There were one or two cars waiting to cross, but no other pedestrians.

'Have you got the passports?' I said.

'Yes,' said Axel.

He reached into his anorak, produced two passports, and handed them to the guard. The guard was young, with blond hair and red cheeks, and bore a vague resemblance to the last passport official we had encountered, at Dover, a week earlier. He flipped through the passports and handed them back. We walked a few yards to where the Czech guard was standing in his green shirt and trousers. The examination was equally bored and perfunctory. The passports did not belong to Stephen and me. They were not the colour of British passports, they were a much lighter shade of blue. I wondered what they had in them to calm everyone's suspicions so effectively. Axel put an arm round my shoulders and led me into Czechoslovakia.

We walked down the hill towards the village on the Czech side of the frontier. Neither of us spoke. It was still early, and there were few people about. I had a vague impression of shops and restaurants, and then we were through the village and out the other side. I walked carefully: I was treading on perilous ground. Under the tarmac surface of the road were swamps and marshes, rocks and craters and holes. Axel guided me off the road on to a track that plunged downwards into the woods. There was no one in sight.

'Could I possibly see those passports?' I said, in my politest Petrov voice.

He passed them over.

They were East German passports. Deutsche Demokratische Republik, said the words embossed on the cover. They were made out in the names of Magda and Dieter Fischer. Magda had been born in Rostock in May 1956, and Dieter in Berlin in November 1954. The photos were authentic, and so were the birthdates.

'You can't enter Czechoslovakia on a British passport without a visa,' said Axel apologetically.

'So you brought these along too. Where did you get them from?' Axel didn't answer, so I supplied the response myself. 'You had them with you the whole time. When you came knocking on my door in London, you already had these passports in your pocket.'

I stopped. That didn't work. Something was wrong. I turned over a page of Dieter Fischer's passport and Jessica's photo looked up at me. No, it was all right, she was there too. Helga Fischer, born in Berlin in October 1980. He had known everything: he had thought of everything. It seemed pointless to continue, but Axel was waiting to hear how much I had figured out.

'You had this trip planned right from the start. You knew I was going to France last Friday night. You knew Stephen was away. You knew Jessica existed. You tricked me into driving you across Europe. You knew from the beginning we were going to Prague, not Moscow—'

Axel grabbed hold of me, pulled me off the track into the trees, and held me tight. Not like a lover, like a jailer. Above the beating of his heart, I heard the sound of someone coming down the mountain, at least two people, walking with a fast, purposeful tread. His arms were like iron bands around me, and my head was wedged firmly against his chest. Maybe he had driven across Europe with abused and unsuspecting females before, and knew that by this stage of the operation they were capable of throwing themselves on the mercy of any stray passers-by: Vopos, Grepos, Stasi, KGB – whoever showed up. Over his shoulder I caught a glimpse of two men in the green uniform of the border guards heading down the hill at a brisk pace.

We didn't move for several minutes after they had gone. Axel's grip didn't slacken. I remember wondering confusedly why he was still pretending to hide. Surely he knew that when I saw those passports I would realize that all the sightings of the KGB, from Petrov to Ludmilla, had been set up as part of a carefully conceived plan to convince me of the danger we were in and the need to keep moving. But why? Where were we going? What did he want from me?

Finally he let me go. 'It should be safe to move now. Unless the army's set up an ambush, we should get down to Jáchymov with no trouble. It's only a few kilometres.'

'Leave it out, Axel,' I said irritably. 'For God's sake stop play-acting.'

He looked distinctly nonplussed. I remember wondering if he had natural acting ability, or if that was something the KGB trained you in too. Like firearms and disguises.

'Play-acting?'

'First the KGB, then the Stasi, now the Czech Army. Bogeymen for all occasions. Could we just stick to reality, please, from now on?'

'Reality,' said Axel. It sounded like a word he had learned in a foreign language, which he wasn't quite sure how to pronounce. He took my hand and led me back on to the track. 'So, Katya, let me explain.'

Reality. As I should have guessed, a relative concept. In

Axel's world, reality was contingent on who you were trying to manipulate, and how soon they found you out. On the day he walked back into my life, I had been well and truly manipulated. Nothing that had happened in London was real. When Axel arrived on my doorstep, it was not by chance, and he had not walked all night to get there. Nor would he have bothered to come, if he hadn't already known that I was leaving for France, and that Stephen was out of the way. Find a credulous female, and play on her sensibility. Bring in a friend to play the part of a KGB officer, enlist a few others to sit in cars and look alert for a few hours. By the end of the day Axel was on his way across the Channel, with the first stage of his journey successfully completed.

'What about the man you killed in Normandy? Was that more stage effects? To panic me into driving you a bit further?'

Axel looked pained. 'I didn't kill him.'

'Or was the corpse faked too? Was he dead, or just unconscious? You'd know I wouldn't go near the body.'

'He was unconscious. He banged his head rather badly, I think. He was just beginning to come round when we got to Verneuil.'

'Verneuil! You took him to Verneuil? But the lake—'

'Katya, he wasn't dead! In any case, I couldn't possibly have put him in the lake. Soviet dental work is very distinctive. They'd have identified him in no time at all. I left him at the station. In plenty of time for the six o'clock train to Paris.'

'I'm surprised you didn't finish him off as soon as my back was turned.'

'For God's sake, Katya, I'm not a contract killer!'

'Do I have your word for that, Axel?'

We walked without speaking for several minutes. The sodden woods dripped quietly around us.

'Tell me exactly what happened,' I said, and Axel, after a moment's thought, obliged.

'We'll go right back to the beginning,' he announced, with the air of one conferring favours. The beginning, it seemed, was about a month earlier, when he had been sent to London to talk to Stephen.

'Sent by whom?' I said.

'The KGB,' said Axel, and explained smoothly that since he had known Stephen in Moscow, it was felt that he would be the best person for the task.

I kept my calm. I had already guessed that Axel and Stephen had seen each other recently. I remained as impassive as I could and asked what the KGB wanted with Stephen.

'They wanted me to persuade him to moderate his extremely anti-Soviet coverage of events in Lithuania.'

'Good grief.' I was momentarily distracted. 'What did you say to persuade him?'

Axel smiled faintly. 'Well, nothing at all, obviously. They don't always realize that what they want might not be feasible. I told him what they were asking, he told me they could go to hell, I reported back that he had declined to cooperate. It might have stopped there, but a week later he published a rather scathing piece about Soviet policy in the national republics. That annoyed them, they decided he had to be taught a lesson, and that was why they sent me back last Friday.'

'Knowing that Stephen was away?'

'Yes.'

'Why? Did they want to intimidate me?'

'No. They wanted to make it look as though you were

having an affair with me. They knew you were going to France, and they wanted it to look as though you were smuggling me off to your country house when your husband was out of the way.'

My mouth fell open.

'Once in Morigny, I was supposed to plant bugs to record our conversations, make sure the neighbours saw me, get you into bed, of course, take some photos . . .'

I was unable to speak.

'Of course I didn't do any of that,' said Axel delicately, 'because I had other things in mind.'

'Of course. You wanted me to drive you to Prague. But then the KGB found out you'd left for your country weekend with a number of confidential documents and came chasing after you.'

'Yes. When I heard someone was looking for La Morosière, I considered leaving at once, but I had no means of transport. It was plain that you weren't going to cooperate. I could have stolen the Volvo, but I didn't think I'd get very far. So I decided to wait up that night and see what happened. I was pretty sure they'd try something during the night. And of course they did, and— Well, you know the rest.'

'Except that the corpse wasn't dead.'

'At first I thought he was. It gave me quite a shock.'

'When did you realize he wasn't?'

'When I was examining him. I finally found a pulse.'

'But, Axel, when you told me he was dead— You were so convincing. I never doubted you for a moment.' I cast my mind back to the darkened living room, the body crumpled on the floor, and Axel holding on to me for dear life. 'You were afraid, then, I know you were.'

He was silent for a moment. Finally he said, 'Yes, I was.

But for other reasons. I was scared because they'd found out I'd been double-crossing them, and because Pavel had just tried to kill me. I was scared because I knew they'd stop at nothing to get the papers back, and I still had to get all the way to Prague.'

'Pavel?' My voice rose. 'You mean you knew his name?'

'His workname,' corrected Axel. 'Yes, I'd met him before. He was supposed to show up at La Morosière later in the week, to provide back-up if needed.'

I quickened my pace, forcing Axel to do the same. *Go, go, go, said the bird.* Grit your teeth, close your mind, keep moving. 'Was he really trying to kill you?'

'Yes.'

'Why didn't you kill him, then, when you had the chance?'

'And upset them even more?'

'Do you really have these documents? The ones that Stephen wrote about?'

'Of course I do,' said Axel irritably. 'You've seen the envelopes – you gave me them yourself. Why else do you think they've been chasing us all the way across Germany?'

'One envelope had passports in it. What was in the others?'

He barely paused. He must have known I would take no excuses this time. 'A secret order from Kryuchkov, the head of the KGB, stating that, whatever happens, the Party must continue to lead Soviet society.'

'Yes?'

'A memo to the Politburo from the Central Committee recommending that Party assets should be transformed into hard cash to prevent them from falling into other hands.'

'Go on.'

'Copies of bank transfers showing that large sums of money have been sent from East Germany to Moscow during the last six months, and that even larger sums have been sent from Moscow to banks in West Germany and Switzerland.'

'What else?'

'A memo to the Politburo from the Soviet State Bank proposing that an offshore company should be set up in Jersey to handle Party funds, and that five hundred tonnes of gold should be sent abroad.'

'My God.' My knees suddenly felt weak. 'So they really were chasing us.'

'Of course they were.' He seemed offended that I should put his word in doubt. How could he have faked the pursuit in the Mercedes? he demanded querulously. By then I was pretty sure he could fake anything he chose, but I remembered his shaking hands on the way to the frontier, and grudgingly conceded that the chase might have been in earnest. We went on walking down the hill and I thought it through, the whole journey, from Alsace to here. I could believe that the car bomb was not part of his plan, given the way he had snapped my head off when we heard the news. And he definitely hadn't been expecting the terrorist warning on the radio. I remembered looking up and seeing his chalk white face in the gloomy interior of that little East German grocery store. Nervousness can be feigned, and so can fear. It's harder to make the blood move around in the body at will.

I concluded that he was probably telling me the truth. Or at least an expurgated version of it.

The main street of Jáchymov was long and wide. The houses had red roofs and peeling yellow paint, and a lot of broken windows. The glass industry found it more profitable to make Bohemian crystal for tourists than window panes for home-owners. Axel steered me expertly through town to the bus stop. It transpired that he had been here before, on holiday with his ex-wife, the red-haired Marxist-Leninist. The bus was crowded. We had to stand up all the way and it was impossible to talk. The journey took three-quarters of an hour. After a while the hills flattened out and the narrow mountain road widened into dual carriageway. The villages where the bus stopped were shabby but less dreary than those we had seen in East Germany. There were more cafés, more shops, more people on the streets.

The bus took us to a spa town called Karlovy Vary. Under its German name of Karlsbad, it had been frequented by Goethe, Schiller, and Karl Marx. Even Lenin's grandfather had been there. Lenin is always with us, said Axel, trying to lighten the mood. I caught a brief glimpse of well-tended lawns, elegant colonnades and gracious nineteenth-century buildings, before we crossed the river and chugged up the hill to the bus station.

The next bus to Prague left in an hour's time. We went to the hotel by the station to wait. It was less gracious on this side of town, but the restaurant was clean and welcoming, with red walls and white tablecloths. I selected a table with a view over rusty wire and railway tracks, while Axel went to the phone box on the other side of the road to call his friend Viktor in Prague.

He was gone for less than five minutes. I looked at him in mild surprise. 'That was fast. What did Viktor say?'

'We haven't talked yet. I have to call back in fifteen minutes.' A languid waiter materialized beside us and Axel ordered two beers.

'What happens when we get to Prague?'

He gave me a sudden charming smile. 'I don't know exactly. I'm supposed to meet someone there.'

I smiled back. 'Well, Axel, while we're waiting, I believe we still have a few loose ends to clear up.'

'Katya, please. Don't talk to me like that. Don't be so hostile.'

'Am I being hostile? Oh, I'm sorry.'

The waiter ambled over with our beer.

Axel sighed. 'What do you want to know?'

'Let me make sure I've got it straight so far. The KGB sends you to see Stephen. He refuses to cooperate. They decide to set me up instead. You play along, but in reality you have other plans. They want some compromising photographs, you want me to drive you to Prague. And then an unexpected problem crops up. They find out you stole these papers, and Pavel comes to get them back. There's a fight, he winds up unconscious. You tell me he's dead, to convince me to leave and take you with me.'

'Ye-es,' said Axel, not altogether convinced by this schematic version of reality.

'Just out of curiosity, what would you have done if Pavel hadn't appeared?'

'I don't know,' said Axel, pulling out his charming smile again. 'Frankly, I was in a bit of a quandary. Originally I thought Stephen would arrive in a day or two, and I could just give him the papers and leave. But then I found out he was going to be gone much longer. I couldn't hang around and wait. It was clear I would have get myself to Prague to see this other person. But first I had to work out how to get there.'

'So a fake corpse, in fact, was exactly what you needed?'

'You could put it like that, I suppose.'

We drank our beer.

'How did the KGB find out you'd got the documents? Do we assume they read the Sunday papers?' Axel nodded. 'So it was you who gave Stephen his information?'

'Of course. When they sent me to London, it was a golden opportunity. I already had some of the material in my possession, and I'd been wondering what to do with it. It was much too risky to contact the German press. The leak would have been traced straight back to me. So I told Stephen about it.'

'Then you lied to me the other day?'

'I'm afraid so.'

'The German journalist – that wasn't true either?'

'No.'

That left the question of how he had got hold of his material in the first place. I was about to ask how a mere consular official came to be in possession of all these Central Committee documents and secret memos, but he looked at his watch and said he had to continue the contact procedure. The contact procedure? I pulled aside the heavy net curtain shrouding the window and watched him dial. When was he going to admit that Viktor was not just a helpful friend but a fellow officer? When was he going to admit that they both worked for the KGB? By the look of it, the phone was picked up on the first ring. Axel spoke briefly into the receiver and hung up. He was grinning with relief as he came back across the road to the restaurant.

'I just spoke to Viktor. He'll call me back from a safe phone in twenty minutes. Where were we?'

'These photos you were supposed to take. What were they going to use them for?'

'Blackmail. Either Stephen would do what he was told and

write about the need to stop the Soviet Union collapsing, or else they'd show the photos to his editors.'

'But even if I had been having an affair with you, what would that prove? Stephen doesn't know any secrets, or if he does, he prints them.'

'Don't be naive, Katya. He'd have been thoroughly discredited. How objective is a Western journalist whose wife has been having a long-running affair with a Soviet official?'

'Long-running? Hardly.'

'Remember what I told you about disinformation the other day. The art of the plausible. They can prove we knew each other in Moscow. They can make it look as though the affair has been going on ever since.'

'Axel, we haven't been physically in the same city for ten years!'

Axel sighed and looked round the room. It was half-empty. The other clients were Czechs, sitting decorously in their chairs and exchanging the occasional low-voiced comment. No one was indulging in what could be termed a conversation. Walls had until recently had ears. Finding neither emergency exits nor other forms of inspiration, he announced reluctantly that, actually, there might have been a period of two or three years, or maybe not quite as much as that, when, in fact, he might have been in Bonn, at probably much the same time as Stephen and I.

I put my glass down. 'You were in B-Bonn? While we were there? And you knew I was there? But you n-never . . . you never . . . oh my God, Axel, do you know what you're saying?'

'There was no way I could get in contact with you.'

'But how could you be in the same town and not—'

'It was impossible.'

'Axel, I didn't know if you were still alive. You'd disappeared off the face of the earth. That first year in Bonn, I was . . . It was one of the worst . . . And you didn't even call! For three years, you didn't call!'

'It was impossible,' he repeated stubbornly. 'In any case, I was married.'

Anger helped me to get a grip on myself. 'Married? Oh, then that's quite understandable. I'd like another beer, please.'

We sat in silence till the beer arrived. I thought about Bonn. I thought about how different my life could have been. And then it occurred to me that if the KGB could fake evidence to prove that Axel and I had been lovers in Bonn, it would be even easier for them to prove we had been lovers in Moscow. The beer came but I didn't pick it up because my hands were shaking too badly.

'Did you take ph-photos of me in Moscow, Axel?'

'Of course not!' He avoided my eyes.

I kept my hands tightly clenched under the table. 'But?'

'Everyone who works for a foreigner is in contact with the KGB. I was supposed to report on you and Stephen. You knew that.'

'So you told them you were having an affair with me?' My voice was rising. One or two of the well-behaved Czechs turned their heads in our direction.

'I had to,' said Axel. 'It was the only way. You wanted me, I wanted you, sooner or later something was going to happen. If I hadn't told them, they'd have found out anyway, and we'd both have been in trouble.'

'Oh my G-God. What did you say?'

He kept his eyes on the tablecloth. 'I told them about a month after you arrived that I thought it would be possible to get an affair going with you. They liked the idea.'

The atmosphere in the restaurant was getting stuffier and more oppressive by the minute. An elderly couple got up and left: a group of three young men arrived. A cold sweat broke out on my forehead. I was alone in a foreign country with no money, no papers and not one word of Czech, my only companion a man who was moving further away from me with every word he said. Axel drank his beer and looked nonchalantly around him. I didn't speak. I waited till he had finished drinking his beer, and the comings and goings in the restaurant had ceased, and I had his full attention.

Then I said, looking him full in the face, 'Why don't you tell me the truth, Axel? Admit it. The affair was their idea in the first place, wasn't it?'

We were unable to find seats together in the bus to Prague. I made sure of that. Axel sat in the front of the bus, next to a Czech lady in an old-fashioned floral skirt, and I sat in the back, beside a young American tourist with cut-off jeans and a serious backpack. From time to time, Axel turned round and gave me an anxious look: I avoided his eyes. My neighbour tried to talk to me in English: I pretended not to understand. If you didn't talk to people, they couldn't lie to you. That was easy. The hard part was to stop lying to yourself.

Three weeks after Stephen and I arrived in Moscow, I had left the apartment building with Axel to visit some Soviet administrative office. It was raining quite hard. The guards at the gate, who were busy giving a visiting Russian a hard time about his papers, refused to let us pass. We waited in front of the barrier for two or three minutes, getting wetter and wetter. Suddenly Axel snapped something at one of the guards. The effect was instantaneous. Without consulting his colleague, the man sprang to attention, saluted, and opened the barrier. He didn't bother to check our papers. I turned to Axel with a question on my lips, he smiled at me, made some comment about Russian weather, and took my arm to guide me across the road. I did not pursue the matter. I wiped it out of my mind, just as I erased my doubts about microphones in the walls three months later. Of course Axel wasn't worried about the bugs. He had obtained prior permission to fuck the correspondent's wife in her own bed: what was there to worry about?

Looking back on my behaviour of the past few days, I could see how thoroughly I had been abused, and how eagerly I had helped to pull the wool over my own eyes. Axel knew who he was dealing with. Not until he was safely in France had I begun to ask questions, and not very probing ones at that. I had spent the past three days busily suppressing evidence that all was not as it seemed. What on earth had possessed me to leave La Morosière and drive Axel to Germany? Why had I abandoned Jessica in Munich? I remembered the wondering look in Gudrun's eyes, and shuddered. How was I going to face her when I went back to Munich? How was I going to look Stephen in the eye again? I had been putty in Axel's hands. He had done exactly as he wanted with me, just as he had in Moscow.

The drizzle that had been falling on and off all day intensified, and the bus driver switched on the windscreen wipers. After a while, I began to cry too, for the sun that had gone, and the games that had turned sour, and the stupid, naive, selfish woman that I had been.

It was early evening when we got to Prague. For a moment, I forgot about Axel and looked curiously out of the window. The working day was over, the rain had stopped, and people were emerging into the tenuous evening sunlight. The castle loomed in the pale blue air over the Vltava river. The streets were full, there were flowers and people and smiles and laughter. The rooftops gleamed damply in the sun, the birds swooped low over the water. The city was in full bloom. The drab, grey years were behind it. The East was coming in from the cold.

The bus drew into the terminal, the passengers collected themselves and their packages together and clambered on to the pavement. I was the last one off. Axel was waiting for me: I looked down at him resignedly from the steps of the bus. All I wanted to do was crawl into a corner and never see him again. He took my arm and led me into the terminal building. Producing a handkerchief that I recognized as Stephen's, he began to wipe the traces of tears off my face. I wanted to tell him to leave me alone, but it was too much of an effort to open my mouth. I stood there passively and let him do what he wanted. The crowds swirled round us, buying carrots and turnips, sweets and soft drinks, blurrily-printed magazines and Dick Francis novels in Czech. Axel stood back and inspected me.

'You look terrible, but I suppose it doesn't matter till we get to the safe house.'

The words jerked me out of my trance. 'Until we get where?'

'To the apartment Viktor's arranged for us to use tonight.'

'A *KGB* safe house?'

'Keep your voice down, Katya.'

'Is that what it is?'

'Of course it is. I told you before we got on the bus. Just for one night.'

'There is no way,' I said clearly, 'that I am going to sleep in a KGB safe house tonight or any other night.'

Axel glared at me. 'Then where are you going to sleep? Under a bridge? They don't appreciate that kind of thing here. This isn't the West.'

'They have hotels, don't they?'

'Yes, and they're all fully booked. You can't get a hotel in Prague unless you reserve three months in advance.'

'I don't care. I'm not sleeping in a KGB safe house.'

'Don't be unreasonable, Katya. There's nowhere else to sleep.'

'I don't care.'

'Fine,' said Axel. 'In that case, you can do what you bloody well want.'

He turned on his heel and marched off. I watched him make his way through the maze of kiosks. There was a taxi stand a few yards away, with two or three taxis waiting. Axel went to the head of the line and got in. The taxi drew away. He didn't look back.

Six

Axel

Two streets away from the bus station, I told the driver to go back.

I left the taxi waiting by the kerb and went to look for her. She was walking aimlessly across the forecourt. She caught sight of me and stopped dead. For an instant her whole face glowed with relief and joy, and then her features tightened into a mask of apprehension. That was when I realized that what had happened in the witch's hut had nothing to do with fairy tales. Nor even make-believe. Europe was changing, the ice was melting, people could decide for themselves what they were going to be. The time for make-believe was past. Nothing could stop me telling Katya all about myself. My real self, my real family. My sister's profession, my father's rank in the army. My non-existent brother in Kaliningrad.

I walked up to her and stopped a foot away. We looked at each other.

'Come with me. I can't leave you.' I held out my hand.

She didn't take it. 'Where are you going?'

'Wherever you want.'

'Do you mean that?'

'Yes.'

She allowed herself to be led towards the taxi. We got in. The driver jerked his head back inquiringly.

'Where to?' I asked her. 'Which bridge do you want to sleep under?'

'Would you really sleep under a bridge?'

'If that's what you want.'

'We won't have to do that. Is it safe to use the British passports here?'

I grimaced. That wasn't something I was anxious to do. The risk was minimal, since the remnants of the Czech security services were not in close contact with either the Stasi or the KGB these days, but it was a risk nonetheless. But if I had to take risks to persuade Katya to stay with me, then I would take them. Life punishes those who come too late. 'We can if you want to,' I said.

'What's the best hotel in Prague?'

'The Intercontinental, I should think.'

'Does it have a fax?'

'Probably. Why?'

The ghost of a smile flickered across her face. 'Cover, Mr. Maletius. Stephen would never stay in a hotel that didn't have a fax machine.'

We were supposed to be meeting Viktor at eight in a beer garden called U Fleku, but it was nearly half past by the time we arrived. Negotiations with the hotel had taken up a lot of time, but they had finally agreed to place one of the rooms that top-flight hotels keep free for unexpected VIPs at the disposal of Mr. Stephen Maletius, the correspondent of a prominent British newspaper.

'What did I tell you?' said Katya, as we waited for the lift. 'Stephen does this all the time.'

The room they had given us was a lot more luxurious than the safe flat would have been. If we craned our necks, we had a view of the river. We explored the bathroom and bounced on the mattress with the glee of children who had bamboozled the grown-ups. Her hostility towards me had, for the time being, evaporated. We were both mildly euphoric after our brush with separation. When I held out my arms, she came straight into them.

Before we went out, she insisted on making some phone calls: one to Gudrun in Munich, to say she would be back in a day or two, and one to the newspaper in London, to find out where Stephen was. The paper, it transpired, had no idea of Stephen's whereabouts. The article on Party funds had been published in error, as I had guessed, and Stephen was furious because it would compromise his source. To prevent further leaks, he had refused to leave a contact address. All they knew was that he had a meeting in Central Europe in the next few days. Katya hung up shaking with rage. He was the bloody limit, she'd never heard a word about this meeting, it would be Christmas by the time he got to La Morosière. Jessica was right, you couldn't count on him for anything.

Viktor was waiting in a corner of the beer garden, sitting alone at one end of a long table. The courtyard was dim and shadowy, overhung by chestnut trees. The place was packed. Mostly tourists, by the look of it, and mostly German. A good place for a meeting.

I had known Viktor for years. We were the same age, and we had met at the KGB training school at Yurlovo. He had been my room-mate in the little grey room where I had lain awake thinking about Katya. I trusted him. Not just because of our friendship – in the KGB it was unwise to place too much reliance on personal ties – but because he thought like

I did about the Party and the future of our country. He looked curiously at Katya, and I made perfunctory introductions in German. He had guessed ten years ago that there was a woman at the root of my insomnia, but we were forbidden to discuss our private lives, and he had no idea who she was.

The French people sitting at the table moved up to make room for us. I sat next to Viktor, and Katya sat opposite us. A stout waiter brought us large glasses of dark brown beer and plates of stew. Both tasted better than they looked.

'Why haven't you been to the safe house?' said Viktor.

'She refused to go. We found a hotel instead.'

Viktor looked at me and then at Katya. He was thinner than when I had last seen him. Here in the beer garden, under the chestnut trees, with his blond beard and ascetic smile, and his dark roll-necked sweater, he could have been mistaken for one of the monks who had long ago brewed beer in Central Europe. I could guess what he was thinking, but he made no comment.

'I checked the signals room before I left the Residency. There was nothing on you. Either they lost your trace, or they don't think you came this way. But there's a message from Chayka. He's been held up. He can't be in Prague before Monday.'

'Damn! That means I have to hang around here for another three days.'

The exclamation caught Katya's attention and she looked up. I smiled at her, but she didn't smile back.

Viktor didn't smile either. He stared intently into his beer for a moment or two, and then looked straight at me. 'Chayka is a journalist, isn't he? I thought so. Listen, Axel, why are you giving this material to the Western press?'

'Who else am I going to give it to?'

'To our own Soviet press, of course! You forget how far we've come in the past few years. We can handle this kind of material ourselves now.'

I ate a couple of mouthfuls of stew. 'Viktor, do you know exactly what I have with me?'

'I can guess.'

'No Soviet journal would touch it.'

'That's what I thought you'd say. So I brought this to show you.'

He took a folded newspaper from inside his jacket. I could see that it was in Russian. Before unfolding it, I looked carefully around. Katya was concentrating on her stew. A party of young Germans was giving their all to some Bavarian drinking song just behind us, and the French people were busy relating their experiences with illicit money-changers. No one was paying attention to Viktor and me.

KGB BREAKS THE SILENCE, said the headline. '*General Oleg Kalugin reveals the role of the State Security Committee in political decision-making.*' There was a photo of a man in a tweed jacket with his mouth set in a determined line. The paper was *Moscow News*, a former propaganda sheet which had built up a reputation for unbiased reporting and serious investigative journalism. These were still such rare commodities in Moscow that people queued up for their copy on publication day. I turned, as instructed, to page four. Another photo, another headline, a brief biography, and an interview. I read it through quickly. The KGB, said the General, was still a state within a state. After five years of perestroika, it was still untouchable. Its internal security service was still several times larger than any comparable service in the West. It still infiltrated workplaces and churches, political groups and workers' movements.

Its power was still immense, and it had no intention of relinquishing it.

Obviously, I had heard of Kalugin. He was a former head of the Foreign Counter-Intelligence Service, who had made general at the age of forty. At forty-five, he had been demoted and posted to Leningrad, and at fifty-five, he had been forcibly retired. A year or so earlier, he had written a letter to Gorbachev outlining his proposals for reform of the KGB. His suggestions had been a little too revolutionary for the Party reformers. He wanted to abolish the KGB's links with the Party, liquidate the political police, and reduce KGB personnel by at least fifty percent.

I looked up from the newspaper. Kalugin's information was not exactly new, but in the mouth of a KGB general it was frankly astounding. Viktor was watching me with an I-told-you-so smile.

'I've never seen anything like this before.'

'He's paved the way. All you have to do is follow suit.'

'Why does a KGB general give an interview like this?'

'Disillusionment with the socialist dream. The same as you and me, Axel. I met him once, you know, about four years ago. When I was in Paris, I had to take part in an operation involving a dissident from Leningrad. They sent me to Leningrad to be briefed. Kalugin wasn't responsible for the operation, but I met him while I was there. He struck me as disenchanted even then.'

'Hardly surprising. It must be quite a shock to find yourself in Leningrad after twenty-five years with Foreign Intelligence.'

There was a long silence. The French people were chattering ecstatically about the Velvet Revolution. One of them produced a badge with a capital 'I' and a big red heart and the name 'Vaclav Havel'. Katya watched us dourly for a minute and then looked away again.

'Forget your British journalist, Axel. Go back to the Union and talk to *Moscow News*.'

'How can I? You forget they're looking for me.'

'Not in Moscow.' He gave me a sardonic grin. 'They won't expect you to go there. It's the safest place in Europe.'

'I don't know, Viktor. I'll have to think about it.'

'I've been thinking about it for years.'

I looked at him. 'What?'

'This or something like it. You and I have a lot on our conscience, Axel. We've done things we should not have done. Maybe it wasn't our choice, but we did them anyway.' He stared unseeingly across the courtyard. 'For our own sake, for the sake of the people we harmed, we need to admit this. At least to ourselves.'

'What happened to your dissident?'

Viktor grimaced. 'What do you think? Since then, I— What I did was wrong. If I had a chance to make amends—'

He broke off. We were both silent. It was stuffy in the courtyard and I was finding it increasingly difficult to breathe. I had confronted the fact that the KGB was guilty of criminal acts a long time ago, but I had never brought myself to consider my own role in those acts. Viktor had put into words the ideas that had been lurking on the edges of my consciousness for months. I had done terrible things to Katya, and to Stephen too. And they weren't the only ones. There was the SDP official in Bonn, the woman in Munich whose husband worked for Franz-Josef Strauss—

'Fly out tomorrow,' said Viktor. 'Don't wait for Chayka. There's a military plane leaving for Moscow at 0500. If you want I can get you on it.'

He paused, waiting for an answer. I couldn't speak. The ghosts were strangling me. I ran a hand over my forehead to wipe away the sweat.

Viktor misinterpreted my silence. 'If you don't want to take the risk, give the papers to me. I'll go to Moscow and give them to *Moscow News*.'

I looked over at Katya. Our eyes met. 'No,' I said, 'I'll do it. I'll go to Moscow.'

'In any case, you can't stay here till Monday. They'll catch up with you for sure.' I was still looking at Katya. He followed my gaze. 'I can't do anything about her, though.'

'I know. I'll leave her here.'

'Once it's all out in the open, you'll need to watch your back. The best protection is publicity. Make sure you stay in the public eye. Give interviews. Go on television.'

'Television?' When I decided to steal the papers, I had planned to hand over the documents and melt discreetly back into the shadows. Now it looked as though I was going to find myself in the full glare of the spotlights. 'Viktor, I need to warn my father before I do this.'

'How will he react?'

'I think he'll approve.'

'Is he in Moscow? I'll let him know you're coming.'

The French people were putting away their badges and guidebooks and getting ready to leave. Viktor got to his feet and prepared to follow.

'I'll pick you up at four on the far side of the Cechuv Most. That's the bridge by the Intercontinental. Cross it, and you'll see a flight of steps going up to the Letenské gardens. Wait for me there. Dark-blue Peugeot, Belgian plates.'

Katya was watching us curiously. How much Russian did she remember? Had she understood the conversation?

Viktor kissed her hand and told her in German it had been a pleasure meeting her. She managed a smile. The French people began pushing their way across the courtyard, Viktor drifted unobtrusively in their wake, and Katya reverted to her grim expression. I wondered what she was thinking. Even if she hadn't understood the words, the meeting must have destroyed any remaining illusions she might have had about my career as an information officer. At some point, I was going to have to explain that I worked for the KGB and had always done so. Even before they assigned me to Stephen. The truth was, I didn't want to. I knew the reaction those three letters provoked in the West, and I wasn't sure Katya was capable of making the distinction between an officer of the First Chief Directorate and the thugs who had guarded the gates of her Moscow apartment building.

We looked at each other in silence. Two elderly German couples came up and asked if the rest of the table was free.

'Yes,' I said, 'we're just going.'

When you've been operating under cover nearly all your life, joining the KGB is the logical thing to do. I was eight when I discovered I had things to hide. 'Nazi, fascist, SS.' The Great Patriotic War had been over for almost two decades, but the scars had not yet healed. 'You're a German,' they hissed in the school playground, 'you've got a German name.' By a stroke of good fortune, my father was transferred to an army base at the other end of the Kaliningrad administrative region a few months after my identity was revealed. 'You don't belong here, you're our enemy.' While my mother oversaw the packing and moving of our household goods, I withdrew behind the dustbins at the far end of the courtyard and worked on what I later learned was called a legend. Everything was ready for the first day at my new school. Axel was a Lithuanian name, I told my new classmates, a Baltic version of Alexei. You can call me Alyosha, if you want. Why do I have a Lithuanian name? Because my mother's Lithuanian, that's why. My father's Russian though. He's a general, and he's in charge of all the military bases in Kaliningrad oblast.

Nobody swallowed the second part of this, but that didn't matter. It was a red herring designed to distract attention from the rest, and it worked perfectly. My classmates would have found out the deception soon enough if they had ever come home with me, for we all spoke German at home, my father included. But I never invited anyone home, and I never accepted invitations to their houses. After the age of eight, I had no close friends, and I confided in no one.

The KGB approached me in my last year at the Moscow Philological Faculty. The recruiting officer explained that they were interested in me because I could pass for a native German. He made it clear that I could expect to spend most of my career abroad. That was fine with me. I had no desire to spend my life as half a Russian in Russia. In any case, I believed in socialism. I was proud to be singled out by the KGB, I was intrigued by the opportunity to discover the internal workings of the system, and I believed it was my duty to do everything in my power to make it function better.

Stephen Maletius was assigned by his paper to Moscow when I was halfway through my training. My instruction was interrupted: my background was too good to pass up. I was transferred temporarily to the Second Chief Directorate, and entrusted with the task of compromising Stephen. I was at an age when it is easy to tell oneself that individual destinies count for nothing in the fight for a greater cause, and I did not examine the moral aspect of what I was expected to do. But then I fell in love with Stephen's wife, and was forced to confront the fact that my own individual destiny counted for nothing either. I was a Soviet citizen, Katya was not, and we had no future together. Theoretically, I knew it was no hardship to make sacrifices for the sake of something I believed in. But it was so hard to give up Katya that I found myself wondering whether I really believed in the Party after all. Lying awake in the little grey room at the Institute, with Viktor sleeping peacefully in the next bed, I found myself beginning to question the values I had grown up with. Was it right that the State should be able to determine the fate of each individual citizen? Shouldn't everyone have the freedom to choose what they wanted and decide their own course in life? I didn't want to break with the Party. I was used to them, I had known them all my life, I didn't want to have to do without them. But because of Katya, in the end I had no choice.

Outside the beer garden, the streets were narrow and silent, stalked by the shadows of Middle-European angst. We walked slowly towards the river. We didn't touch and we didn't speak. Katya was deep in thought, and I had no desire to talk. The conversation with Viktor had shaken me. It was cooler out here than in the courtyard, but I was sweating again, and the pain was back in my chest.

We crossed the river on the Charles Bridge. After the empty streets of the Old Town, the bridge was noisy and cheerful, with guitar-strumming youths and long-haired girls and backpackers from a dozen Western countries. Water colours of the city were laid out on the pavement alongside badges with skulls and crossbones commemorating the death of communism. The tanks had been withdrawn; the fear had gone. What came next, no one knew. Heinz had seemed to think it was possible to wipe it all out, all the false, destructive years of communism, and start again with a clean slate, as if nothing had happened. But I doubted he was right. They had done their work too well, those hard-eyed re-makers of mankind, and what they had done could not be undone. The young men who had died resisting the tanks could not be brought back to life. The lies that had been told could not be un-told. There was no way to efface past suffering, no way to wipe out accumulated resentment, no way to make reparation. The only thing we could do was make sure it didn't happen again.

Katya walked silently by my side, ignoring musicians and vendors alike. I wondered what she was thinking. I wondered if I had already lost her. We left the bridge, and the city sank back into shadows. As we began the long walk up to the Castle, I told her I was leaving for Moscow in a few hours' time. She took it more calmly than I had expected.

'Will you be all right?' I asked anxiously.

She gave me her best Petrov smile. 'Of course I will.'

'What will you do?'

She seemed mildly bewildered by the question. 'Drive to Munich. Collect Jessica. Go back to Normandy. Wait for Stephen to come.'

'Stephen?'

'Well, yes, of course. He can't stay in Central Europe forever.'

'You said you were ready to divorce him.'

She didn't answer. A wave of rage and jealousy swept through me. Before I knew what I was doing, I had slapped her hard across the face. She took a step back. We stared at each other in amazement.

'Listen, Katya. Listen to me. I'm going back to Moscow tomorrow. If I could, I'd take you with me, but that's impossible. Viktor wouldn't agree, and in any case you have to get back to Jessica. But after that I'm going to come back and get you. As soon as I can.'

Her voice was almost inaudible. 'Why? Because they want you to?'

'Because I want to. Do you remember the day we saw each other for the first time?'

She looked away.

'Do you really think the KGB had anything to do with that?'

She was silent. Our footsteps echoed hollowly in the empty street.

'How can I believe you, Axel?' she said at last. 'You've lied to me about everything else. How can you expect me to believe you when you say you love me?'

'I don't understand. Surely you must know I'm not lying to you? These past two days—' She shook her head. My patience snapped. 'You don't want to believe me, do you? It's safer not to. You want to go back to Stephen and your safe little existence – what was the phrase you used? Emotional hibernation? You want to go back to all that again.'

She stopped walking and turned to face me. I had got through to her at last. The words came pouring out: I doubted she even knew what she was saying.

'No, I don't. That's the last thing I want. I want you, Axel. I love you, I'll never love anyone as much as you, I would even be willing to move to Moscow for you, and live there with Jessica, the three of us, but there's no point in doing it, because we'll never be happy together. There's no future for us. There's one vital ingredient missing from our relationship. Trust. Because of what you are and who you work for. The way you came into my life: you were KGB put there to entrap me. All right, so later, it turned into something else, but the fact remains that you started off making love to me under false pretences. We're never going to be able to get away from that. I'm never going to know where your loyalties lie. With them, or with me.'

She turned away and leant wearily on the wall. There were fruit trees growing on the hill below the Strahov monastery, where the land sloped gently down to the river. Faintly in the distance came the sound of voices and laughter from the bridge, but up here in the shadow of the Castle, the houses were shuttered and the streets were deserted. I looked at Katya: she was crying. I looked at the apples gleaming in the moonlight and remembered the story of Tsarevich Ivan and the Firebird that I had told our child a few nights earlier. It was no use: I was going to have to tell her the truth.

'Katya. Do you remember me talking about the journey Stephen and I made to Koenigsberg?'

She stared at me blankly. Koenigsberg was the last thing on her mind.

'That trip was organized by the KGB. That was the reason they assigned me to Stephen. My mission was to entrap Stephen. It was nothing to do with you.'

'Entrap Stephen?'

'We didn't just visit Stephen's old family home, we paid a visit to his aunt and uncle too.'

'What aunt and uncle?'

'His father's sister Sophie and her husband.'

'Stephen has an aunt in Koenigsberg?'

'As soon as we got back to Moscow, I was ordered to disappear from Stephen's life. The day after that, someone paid a visit to your husband and told him that unless he cooperated, his aunt and uncle would be sent to the camps.'

'You m-mean Stephen's been spying for the KGB all these years?' She put a hand on the wall to steady herself.

'Spying? Of course not. Writing for them. Planting information the party wished to leak. Disseminating opinions they wished to make known. Doing what he could to improve our public image. Stephen never attacked the Soviet Union over Afghanistan. That was the main reason they recruited him when they did. There was such an outcry over the invasion in the West that they needed as much positive coverage as they could get.'

'But this morning you t-told me that the KGB wanted him to moderate his coverage of Lithuania.'

'Don't you read what your husband writes, Katya? For years, Stephen was a model of restraint when he wrote about the Soviet Union. Never a word out of place. But lately, he's been making up for lost time. The uncle died two years ago, and his aunt died earlier this year. He has no other relatives in Koenigsberg.'

'He never told me he had an uncle and aunt in Koenigsberg.'

'He never told you he went there.'

She put up a hand and touched her cheek. A red mark was beginning to show. 'Axel, is this true what you're saying? It's not some tale you've cooked up to trick me into leaving Stephen?'

'No,' I said as forcefully as I could. 'It isn't.'

'Because there's one thing you're forgetting. There aren't any Germans left in Koenigsberg. They were all deported in 1947.'

'Sophie married a Pole. He had a Polish name – Kuczinski or something – and he was actually born in Poland. Because of that, they slipped through the net. A few people did, you know.'

'All right, tell me about them. Who were they? What did they do?'

'They were farmers. They worked on a collective farm.'

'Come off it, Axel! Stephen's father was a doctor. His grandfather too. Don't tell me Sophie made a career as a kolkhoznik.'

'She had no other choice after 1945.'

'Oh. Yes. I see. Well, go on then.'

'They lived about fifty kilometers from the town of Kaliningrad in a place called Zelednogradsk. On the coast. I got hold of a car, and we drove out there. They were old, in their seventies. They had retired from the kolkhoz a few years earlier. The place where they lived was terrible. There were four houses standing side by side. Three of them had been bombed out since the war, and they lived in the fourth. They were miles from anywhere. The house needed repairs, they had hardly any furniture, they said they didn't have enough to eat. I asked them why they didn't grow vegetables in the garden behind the house. They said there was nowhere to buy seeds. They were stupefied by the sight of Stephen. It took them a good ten minutes to understand who he was. The old lady hadn't seen her brother for nearly forty years, and she thought he was dead. It was a shock to learn that he was alive and living in England, and that this was his son. It was hard for her to take in. And then she realized that Stephen was English, he was a foreigner, he had no right to be in Kaliningrad, and here he was in the middle of her living room. She got very frightened, they both did.

She kept telling him he had to leave. Stephen was put out by that. It wasn't what he had expected.'

'How did he know where to find her if she wasn't in touch with his father?'

'He asked if I could find out whether she was still in Kaliningrad. We had the address already. I just passed it on.'

She had been standing slumped against the wall. With an effort, she pushed herself upright, and began to walk towards the Castle. I fell into step beside her. The old houses slept crookedly in the chill summer night. Our footsteps echoed on the cobbled street.

'Were you really born in Kaliningrad?'

'Yes. That's why they assigned me to Stephen. They knew his family came from Kaliningrad, they assumed he would attempt to go there. My job was to plant the idea in his head if it hadn't already occurred to him, and make things easier if he'd thought of it already.'

We reached the square in front of the Castle. The cathedral spires gleamed in the floodlights and the soldiers in their blue uniforms stood stiffly on either side of the gate. There was no one about. The ghosts of the socialist utopia had slipped peacefully away, and the Castle drowsed in its thousand-year silence.

'Did Stephen do anything to help them? His aunt and uncle, I mean.'

'I don't know,' I said. Privately, I doubted it. Knowing Stephen, he probably figured he was helping them enough by keeping them out of the camps. On the way back to Kaliningrad, his only comment had been, 'To think they had the chance to get out in '47, and they didn't take it.'

'I wish I'd known,' said Katya, half to herself. 'I could have sent them some seeds.'

'I sent them some.'

'*You* did?'

'When we got back to Moscow. I went out and bought all the seeds I could find, and sent them to the old people. I don't know if they ever planted them.'

'Why did you do that?'

'Why do you think?'

'I'm sorry.'

'Because the KGB wanted me to?'

'I'm sorry, Axel. I shouldn't have said that.'

I was beginning to feel slightly desperate. In six hours I would be on the plane to Moscow and nothing I said seemed to be making any impact on her.

'Do you believe what I've just told you about Stephen?' I asked, and to my relief she nodded immediately.

'Yes. I've always known he's kept part of himself shut off from me. But I didn't realize—' She stopped.

'I wasn't trying to turn you against him.'

'He told me they were all dead. I remember now. He said his grandfather was killed on the Russian front, and the rest of the family died in the bombing.'

'They didn't put me there to have an affair with you. It was him they were interested in.'

We started down the steps by the Castle wall. Virginia creeper trailed down the walls and gleamed against the old stones in the lamplight. I pulled her into a patch of shadow and kissed her. When we had finished, we were both slightly breathless.

Katya said, 'I understand now why he published that piece last Sunday.'

'What do you mean? They said it was a mistake.'

'Stephen's capable of making it look like one. To cover himself, with them and with you. He's done this kind of thing before, you know.'

I thought back to my meeting with Stephen. It had been cool, but businesslike. 'I'm sure Stephen would like nothing better than to denounce me to the KGB, but he was very interested in what I had to offer. I don't think he did it on purpose.'

'I do. I've never met anyone like Stephen for harbouring grudges. You got him involved with the KGB. He would never have forgiven you for that. When you walked back into his life ten years later, he must have thought the chance was too good to miss.'

'I don't believe it. Journalists protect their sources. Especially when there's more information to come.'

It took her a moment or two to respond, and when she did, her tone was markedly cooler. 'So there is. I'd forgotten about that.'

'Stephen wanted documentary evidence. He said he couldn't publish anything that hadn't been substantiated.'

'Right,' said Katya. 'Documentary evidence. Orders from Kryuchkov, memos to the Politburo, bank transfer forms. When were you intending to give him that, Axel?'

I looked at her dumbly. I couldn't speak.

'Stephen has a meeting in Central Europe, and you have a meeting in Prague. What a coincidence.'

We went on staring at each other. After a minute, I couldn't stand it any longer. I closed my eyes. It was all the confirmation she needed.

'You've come here to meet Stephen! My God, I don't believe it! You've driven all the way across Europe, and you've brought me with you! What kind of deal are you planning? Stephen gets the papers and you get me? Or is it the other way round?'

'No, Katya, no, I didn't mean it to happen this way.'

She hugged both arms round her body, shielding herself, as if she were cold or in pain. 'How could you do this to me, Axel?'

'I didn't mean to bring you here.'

'Then for God's sake what did you mean?'

'I admit I started out using you, but along the way, everything changed. I didn't want to let you go. I wanted to keep you with me.'

'How can I believe you, Axel? How can I believe anything you say to me?'

She flung away from me up the steps to the square. I would have followed her, but she stopped at the top and leant against the railing. I waited. After several minutes, she turned round and walked slowly back towards me. She stopped two or three steps away.

'Is Stephen in Prague now?'

'No, he's been held up. He can't get here till Monday.'

Her face relaxed slightly. 'Are you meeting him in Moscow?'

'No, I won't see him at all. I've decided to give the information to *Moscow News*.'

'Then you really are going to Moscow? Oh God, I can't take any more of this.' She passed a hand over her eyes. 'Which way is the hotel? I need to go back there. I need to sleep.'

Without waiting for an answer, she set off down the steps. I followed. We walked down to the bottom in silence, and trudged through nondescript buildings towards the river. It was a long way. Occasional cars went past, but there was no one in the street.

When we got to the bridge that would take us across the river and back to the hotel, our steps slowed. We stopped walking. On the other side of that bridge lay the irreparable. We stood at the entrance to the bridge and looked each other up and down.

In the end, she said wearily, 'What do you want from me, Axel?'

'Everything,' I said.

'Then you have to tell me— If you want everything, you have to tell me everything. What you've done, where you've been. You have to be honest with me. You have to trust me. I need to know it all. Otherwise, I can't—I have to know who you are.'

I was unable to speak. The pain in my side was back, worse than ever.

'Will you do that?'

'You know who I am already, Katya. You know me better than anyone.'

She gave me a twisted little smile. 'When did you join the KGB?'

I didn't answer.

'What have you been doing for the past ten years?'

'Katya, I'll tell you everything when all this is over. I promise.'

'When will that be?'

'It's hard to say. When I get to Moscow, I don't know what will happen.'

'So I could be waiting for some time?'

'Right now, it's true, I have nothing to offer you. But it won't be like this forever. I have the right to German citizenship. When this is over, we can settle in Germany. You can leave Stephen and come with Jessica and we can bring her up as our child.'

Her eyes filled with tears, but she didn't hesitate. 'I won't do that, Axel.'

'But you just said you would! You said you'd move to Moscow.'

'No, I didn't. You weren't listening. I said I wouldn't. And the reason is that I don't know who you are, and I'm never going to know.'

There were hardly any street lamps. It was too dark for me to see her face. Her voice was very soft.

'You told me the other day that you wanted Russia to make a new start, but if all Russia has is people like you, it's never going to happen. Can't you see that with all your secrets you're still clinging to the old ways, still helping to keep the old system going? You need to open the cupboard and let out the skeletons, explain what you've done, admit your mistakes, maybe even say you're sorry for screwing up people's lives – but you aren't capable of it. You're too used to hiding things, denying them, pretending they don't exist. It's second nature to you, it's the only way you can function. You don't want to tell me about yourself, you don't want to tell me about your work. If you won't tell me now, you'll never tell me. You aren't going to change. You were like that already when I first knew you. I'm sorry, but that's not what I want. I've been through all that with Stephen. I've lived with Stephen for eleven years, and what I know about him after all that time is the tip of the iceberg. Next time, I want the other nine-tenths too.'

Seven

Katharine

When I awoke the next morning, he had gone, leaving nothing but a wet towel on the bathroom floor and a note on the bedside table.

Katya,
I started off lying to you, but everything I told you last night was the truth. Try to believe me. And remember what I said: I'll be back to get you. That's the truest thing of all. After today, I don't know what's going to become of me: but one thing I'm sure of, I'll be back. And this time, it won't take ten years. I love you, Axel.

I read it through, crumpled it up and threw it on the floor. All right, Axel, you love me. I'm not arguing with that. Whatever role the KGB had played in our affair – inventor, authorizor, facilitator – I was willing to concede that in the end events spun out of their control. I believed the way he looked when he came back to find me in the bus station yesterday. I believed the way he made love to me last night, grinding himself into me as if he wanted to leave permanent traces of his passage, doing his best to leave the imprint of his body on mine. I went into the bathroom and scrutinized myself in the mirror. Bites and bruises on my neck and arms, soreness between my legs. Axel, his mark. Last night I had welcomed the pain, provoked it even. It had seemed the logical expression of the conflict in my mind. Now I was less sure. I wanted to leave him behind, here in Prague. I didn't want any reminders to take with me.

In the past week, Axel had turned my world on its head. He had shown me that my life was not what I thought it had been – not now, not in Moscow, and not at any point in the intervening years. Everything was altered, betrayed, destroyed. The ground had shifted under my feet, and I was looking at the world with new eyes. And the worst of it was that my vision was still faulty. Axel had lied to me in Moscow, he had lied again in London, and he had deceived me most of the way across Europe. It was impossible to say where the lies stopped and the truth began, or if there was a dividing line at all. Last night, perhaps, he had been telling me the truth, but what I had heard was only part of it. There were things he was simply unable to tell me. The habits of a lifetime were too strong. The words would not come.

The trouble was, love wasn't enough. I wanted more than that.

I rented a car and drove back to Munich. On my way out of Prague, I suddenly remembered that this was the city where Rainer Maria Rilke had grown up. He had spent the first twenty years of his life here, written his first poems, taken his first steps in literary circles. His family house was still standing. I knew I ought go and look at it, but I had no desire to do so. Rilke belonged to my real life, to London and Stephen and Jessica and the house with the Laura Ashley chintz in the sitting room and the high hedges round the back garden. Once I got back there, I would be able to think about him, but out here in the middle of Europe, in the place where he was born, with Axel's note in my pocket and Axel's words in my mind, it was impossible. Navigating through dreary high-rise suburbs in search of the motorway to Plzen, I recalled that Rilke had characterized Prague as 'enigma and disorder'. Based on the twelve hours I had spent there, it struck me as a pretty fair description.

I got to Munich shortly after midday. At the border, my passport attracted no attention. Either the KGB had failed to track us this far south, or they weren't interested in me now that my passenger had flown. I drove up to Elisabethplatz on back roads to avoid the traffic, and drummed my fingers impatiently on the steering wheel at red lights. I had no time to waste. I was going to pick up Jessica and leave at once for La Morosière. I needed to get back to my house and my garden and the world I was used to. I wanted to cycle round the country lanes, and sit in the garden, and wait for Stephen to return. I wanted to act as if Axel had never been there.

A male voice answered the buzzer at the Heislers' flat.

'Hello, Volker, it's Katharine.'

He pressed the button to open the door without answering. I took the lift to the fifth floor and crossed the landing. The door was standing ajar. I pushed it open and stopped dead.

Stephen was standing in the hall waiting for me.

He was leaning against a chest-of-drawers with his arms folded. In his eyes were neither hostility, nor affection, nor even curiosity. He looked me over imperturbably, taking in the short brown hair, the red-rimmed eyes, and whatever other traces the journey across Europe had left on me.

'All alone, Katie?'

'What are you doing here?'

'I flew to Frankfurt—'

'Frankfurt? I thought you had a meeting in Central Europe.'

'Is that what the paper told you?' A slight smile flitted across his face, but the amusement was for himself alone. 'No. I decided against it. I called Volker from the airport, and he told me Jessica was here. I thought it might be as well if I came to collect her.'

'Where is Jessica? And everyone else for that matter?'

'Volker's at the *Süddeutsche*. Gudrun took the children to the zoo. All the children.' Including the one you abandoned here, he added, though he didn't say it aloud.

I looked at him more closely. It was odd, although Axel had reminded me of Stephen, Stephen didn't make me think of Axel. Not at all. My husband looked tight and contained. Not anguished, not even annoyed. Whatever feelings had been aroused by my trip with Axel rated fairly low on the Richter scale.

'So you flew to Frankfurt and you called Volker,' I said. 'What a fortunate coincidence.'

Stephen wasn't going to answer that. 'Where's Axel?' he demanded.

'He's not here.'

'Are you going to see him again?'

'No. Stephen, I want to explain what happened—'

'There's no need. Shall we go in here?' He stood aside to let me pass. We sat on opposite sides of the sitting-room and watched each other. 'Gudrun told me where you'd gone. And why. I must say, it hadn't occurred to me that you'd been pining for him all these years.'

Pining? The word sounded limp and Victorian. I was about to protest when the implications of what he was saying sank in.

'You m-mean, you knew? About Moscow?'

'Of course I knew,' said Stephen. 'The way you two behaved, one would have had to be blind not to know.'

'You n-never said anything.'

'No.'

'Why not?'

'Because it was a blessing in disguise,' said Stephen in the same patient parental tone. 'It was clear that you weren't going to be able to cope with Moscow if you didn't have something like that going on.'

'If you'd paid me more attention I wouldn't have needed him.'

'Katie, I was there to do a job, for God's sake, not to hold my wife's hand. We're not going to go through all this again, are we?'

'It was you who brought it up.'

'In the circumstances, it's rather difficult not to bring it up. It's not the sort of thing one can keep quiet about.'

'Why not? There are plenty of things you do keep quiet about.'

'I fail to see—'

'Axel told me about your trip to Koenigsberg.'

Stephen went rigid. The colour drained from his face. I watched him, spider to fly, just as he had watched me a few minutes earlier. If I'm a whore, my darling, then you're a traitor to your country, and that's not much better, is it?

'What did he tell you?'

'He said you went in through Lithuania, looked for your father's old house, and went out to the country to visit your aunt. And that the KGB forced you into an . . . arrangement with them when you got back.'

The silence was broken by the sound of a key in the lock, followed by a couple of crashes and the clatter of high-pitched voices. 'It's my turn.' 'No it's not, you had it last.' 'I did not.' 'Yes you did, after supper last night.'

'Nobody gets it until after lunch.' Gudrun's voice.

They rolled as far as the sitting room, saw us sitting there, and piled up in the doorway.

Jessica disentangled herself and hurled herself across the room. 'Mummy! Mummy, you're back! What have you done to your hair? Did you have lots of adventures? Where's Axel?'

'Back in Moscow,' I said, and immediately wondered if it was a wise thing to say in Stephen's hearing. I had no means of knowing who had tipped him off about Jessica's whereabouts, and why.

'He didn't come back with you?' There was no mistaking the disappointment in her tone.

'No, Jess, he told you he wasn't coming back.'

'I know, but I just thought . . .'

I looked instinctively at Stephen over the top of her head. His face was impassive.

Eight

Axel

When I left Prague, she was asleep, looking so wan and exhausted that I didn't have the heart to wake her to say goodbye. I stood looking down at her for a long while. Then I pulled the blanket up over her shoulders and kissed her cheek. She didn't stir. The morning was cold and black, and the image of her pale, tear-stained face stayed with me all the way out to the airport and into the plane. From now on, it was all I had left.

The plane took off, the blackness waned. The dawn came up, grey and grubby, over the lands that had once belonged to our fraternal allies. The only other passenger was an army major travelling on official business. We did not exchange names. Somewhere between Wroclaw and Warsaw, a desultory conversation began, and we talked idly about Lithuania, the Party Congress, and German reunification. Neither of us ventured a personal opinion. I was back in my own universe, speaking what the East Germans called Sklavensprache. Slave speech. The code words and the veiled allusions came naturally off my tongue. It was the language I had spoken all my adult life. No wonder I didn't know how to talk to Katya. I felt in the pocket of my anorak, and touched the locks of hair lying next to the manila envelopes she had given me in London.

When the pilot announced we were crossing into Soviet air space, the conversation tailed off. We stared silently down at our homeland. We were approaching the seat of Bolshevik power, the heart of old Russia. Lenin had moved his capital here from St. Petersburg soon after the Revolution. A man like him would have seen at once the advantages of a city turned in upon itself, surrounded by fortified monasteries, hidden from the gaze of the outside world. I had seen Eisenstein's film *Ivan The Terrible* when I was still quite young, and in my mind Moscow was irremediably marked by poison and plots and shadows. I remembered terrifying councils in smoky churches, where priests crept in silken procession, deep-eyed icons brooded, murders were decided, and destinies sealed. Ivan had created the oprichnina to destroy his enemies. Four centuries later, Lenin had founded the Cheka for much the same reasons. The cabin seemed suddenly airless, and I swallowed painfully.

The plane landed at a military airfield outside Moscow. It was mid-morning local time. The sky was a limpid blue with thin strands of cloud, and the birches at the end of the runway swayed in the wind. The major had an official car waiting, so I requested a lift into town. It was plain that he didn't like it. I had caught one or two sidelong glances in the plane, and guessed he was more scared of me than me of him. It was understandable. I had been taken to the plane by a known KGB operative. The travel pass I carried bore no name. I wore clothes that had clearly been designed for an undercover mission. When I asked him to drop me on Gorky Street, he seemed relieved that I had no more compromising destination in mind.

In the car, we sat well apart and looked out of our respective windows. It was two and a half years since I had been to Moscow, but the traffic on the way into town was just as I remembered. Belching brown lorries and sludge-coloured cars: Volgas and Zhigulis bucketing along with smashed radiators and dented sides. It was a world away from the purring Mercedes and cheerful little Volkswagens of West Germany. We might have won the war, as the generals attending the Party Congress were fond of pointing out, but it sometimes seemed that we had won precious little else. I kept an eye on the rear-view mirror, but could see no signs of pursuit.

After a while, the first apartment blocks of the Moscow suburbs hove into sight: square, grey and unadorned, and soon after that the crowds began. Not the purposeful flood of shoppers and office-workers who strode possessively through the streets of London or Hamburg, but a lumbering army of uprooted peasants, trudging towards the city in search of subsistence or permits or an audience with the tsar. I remembered how Katya used to complain about their zombie-like gait and unfocused faces ten years ago. I paid no attention to them back then, I was used to them, but looking at them now, I could see what she meant. Moscow was grey. The people were drab, the buildings were discoloured. The air was heavy with despondency.

The major dropped me on the corner of Pushkin Square. For the next half-hour, I walked down Gorky Street towards the centre of town, moving slowly, stopping every now and then to pretend to study something, crossing the road, turning into side streets, tying my shoelaces, watching the faces, watching the body language, alert for anything out of the ordinary. The crowds shoved past me, clutching their shopping bags. The air smelt of low-grade petrol and cheap scent. There were typists in high heels, babushki in raincoats, veterans in medals. The older people were grim with sacrifice and lost hope. The young people were on the lookout for something better: Levi jeans, Western rock music, new slick television programmes like *Vzglyad* and *Fifth Wheel*, Estée Lauder, Coca Cola and the Marlboro Man. As far as I could tell, no one was following me. To be absolutely sure, I would have had to take more precautions, but I didn't think it was necessary. There was no reason for anyone to assume I was back in the USSR.

I crossed Manezh Square, skirted the dark red bulk of the History Museum, and entered Red Square. My father was waiting for me by the Lenin Mausoleum.

When I was young, my father and I had had our differences, but these days we saw mostly eye to eye. We had taken separate routes to the same place. The turning point for both of us was the war in Afghanistan. No military man, my father asserted, would have given the order to invade. The Party's decision showed a lack of responsibility unworthy of the leaders of a great nation. They were sacrificing young men, men the age of his son, on the altar of ideology. For that he could not forgive them. Like everyone else, he had overlooked or rationalized unwelcome evidence against the Party for years, but the war forced him to recognize once and for all that there was a difference between the way things were, and the way the Party said they were. Losing the Party was harder for him than for me. I asked him once how he had made the break with a way of life he had known since he was a child. He said that it was better to abandon something which had been proved wrong by history than to carry it to the end in his soul.

Viktor had called from Prague and told him to expect me. He had put on weight since I last saw him, and the pouches under his eyes were darker than I remembered. These days, he was involved with Shchit, or Shield, a group of reform-minded army officers. We began to walk towards St. Basil's, melting into the crowd of shoppers, sightseers and tourists. Beside us rose the vast archaic walls of the Kremlin. My father was in full military uniform and I was wearing my East German anorak. No one gave us a second glance: if anything, they averted their eyes. Here, in the very heart of Soviet power, we were invisible. We paced slowly over the cobbles towards Saint Basil's Cathedral and I told my father why I had come to Moscow.

He grew progressively more alarmed. 'You're proposing to give these papers to the press?'

'I have to. It's the only thing to do.'

'It won't stop the Party.'

'At least people will know what they're doing.'

'You think they don't know already?'

'Knowing something, or suspecting it, isn't the same as hearing the accusation made out loud, with evidence to back it up.'

A black Zil limousine shot out of the Kremlin through the Spassky Gate and cut sharply across the square towards the Central Committee building a few streets away. The tourists scattered respectfully. My father eyed it with misgiving.

'Don't take on the Party, Axel. It's too much for you, it's too much for anyone.'

I didn't know what to say. I hadn't expected him to react like this, and his opposition disturbed me. But whether he supported me or not, I couldn't go back now. I pointed out that nothing had happened to Kalugin.

'No, but I've heard they're sticking close. Surveillance in the metro, threatening phone calls. And what he said isn't as damaging as what you're proposing to say.'

'Ten years ago, he would have had to defect. And so would I.'

'What?' He looked at me, startled.

'It was the only way to survive, if you didn't want to collapse at your desk. There's a very high rate of heart attacks in the First Chief Directorate.'

My father was silent.

'But now things are different. We don't have to withdraw, we can fight openly. We can go to the press and say, "Look, this is what they're doing, I believe it's wrong, and I want to speak out against it".'

'It's suicide, Axel!'

'Is it? Is it so different from what you're doing for Shchit?'

He glared at me. 'You know it all, don't you? No one could ever teach you anything, even when you were a child. You were always so sure you were right.'

'Yes,' I said. 'You always used to say I was so sharp that one day I would cut myself. Well, now I have.'

I touched the hair in my pocket. He sensed my distress.

'What do you mean?'

'I'll tell you some other time.'

He put a hand briefly on my shoulder. 'You'd better come out to the dacha with me tonight. Your mother will want to see you.'

'All right.'

We were a few steps away from the Spassky Gate. Beyond lay the Kremlin.

'Come on,' said my father, producing an official pass, 'let's go in. I want you to breathe the air in here. I want you to feel what it's like.'

The air of the Kremlin is like nowhere else in Russia. Here, where the Soviet palace of congresses stands beside the terrible candlelit cathedrals, the Bolshevik rulers trace their lineage back to the blood-hungry sixteenth-century tsars, and Stalin, the Father of the Peoples, meets Eisenstein's Ivan. If the Bolsheviks had stayed in the cool baroque palaces on the banks of the Neva, Russia might have resisted the ferocious dream of the communist utopia. Under those rational Baltic skies, sanity would have intruded sooner. It would never have come to this.

The guards inspected the pass and waved us through. A few men in dark suits hung round conferring in front of the Supreme Soviet. My father and I walked towards Cathedral Square, and he began to tell me about a visit from my sister and her family the previous week. I tried to listen, but it was hard to concentrate. The ghost of Ivan strode beside me through the courtyards. I could hear the swish of his robes, I could taste his fear in my own mouth. All his life he was surrounded by enemies. Boyars and pretenders inside the frontiers, Poles and Tatars outside. And the solution reached in those fearful whispered conferences was always the same. Extermination. Always. I could smell the incense swirling around me. It was getting hard to breathe, and I felt the inevitable stab of pain in my chest.

'Do you feel it, Axel? Do you understand what I mean?'

'Yes.' I knew exactly what he meant. It was he who had introduced me to Eisenstein.

'Nothing's changed. Nothing's ever going to change.'

'I know.'

'Good.' He took out a handkerchief and mopped his forehead. 'Let's go this way. I have to get back to the Ministry.'

We headed for the Borovitsky Gate, and he went on talking about Irina's visit. They had all come up from Leningrad for a few days, not just her and the boys, but Ruslan, her husband, too. The weather had been fine, and they had all gone out to the dacha. Misha and Sasha had climbed trees and gone swimming. My parents didn't see as much of their grandsons as they would like, and they had been delighted to have them for a whole week.

'Pity you couldn't have been here too. I don't know when was the last time we had the whole family together.'

'Yes,' I said mechanically, 'it's a pity.' A week ago, I had been in France, in the garden at La Morosière, playing cards.

'The boys asked when you were coming to see them. They still remember the time you took them camping in the woods. What would it be, two years ago? Three? Such a pity you never had children of your own.'

Maybe it was tiredness, maybe it was loneliness, maybe it was confusion. Maybe it was the incense. Maybe it was the satisfaction of being able to put an end to a long-standing reproach.

'But I do have children, Papa,' I said.

Nine

Katharine

Munich glittered in the afternoon sun. After the greyness of the East, it felt odd to be back in a country where people dressed to be looked at, and shop windows dressed to be bought. We walked slowly in the direction of the Englischer Garten. Gudrun had sent us out to talk, while she gave the children lunch. So far, Stephen hadn't said a word. There was a small hard lump of fear in the pit of my stomach.

'Tell me about Koenigsberg,' I said, when I couldn't bear the silence any longer.

'What do you want to know?'

'I don't know. Just what it was like. Was it what you expected? Were you disappointed—'

'Of course I was disappointed!' said Stephen. 'You should see what they've done to the place.'

'The Russians?'

'Yes, and the British too. The British bombed it, and then the Russians besieged it. There wasn't much left after that. Nearly two-thirds of the city had been destroyed by the time the Germans surrendered in April '45. The population was decimated. Most of those who hadn't been killed during the fighting died in the early days of the Russian occupation.

Less than a quarter of the civilian population survived to be deported by Stalin.'

'You mean the Russians killed them?'

'No, they died from neglect. Starvation. Epidemics. A lot of people were living in camps, since their houses had been destroyed, and the conditions were appalling. They were buried in mass graves carved out of the earth with excavators. There isn't a single memorial to the German dead in the entire city. They even razed the German graveyards. But everywhere you look, you see memorials to Soviet soldiers, terrible ugly things, old torpedo boats and aeroplanes, rusting away on top of huge blocks of concrete. There was one right across the road from where my father's house used to be.'

'You didn't find the house?'

'No. It was in a district that had suffered a lot of bomb damage. Almost all the buildings were new. They'd built a sports field where the house used to be.'

'So the lilac tree had gone.'

'You remember that? Yes, it had gone, but there was an oak tree which was several hundred years old in the garden. That was still there. Not the same tree, that must have been destroyed. Or else they chopped it down for firewood after the war. But there was a young oak tree, about the right age. I'd like to think it grew from the same roots.'

'Then there was still something left.'

'Not much, but better than nothing. My grandfather had always wanted to cut down the oak. He was convinced it was taking nourishment away from his flowers. So he finally got his wish, but not quite in the way he expected. Of course, there aren't any flowers any more.'

It was getting harder and harder to hide my amazement. I had long ago decided that Stephen was incapable of emotional involvement, but here it was at last. A ten-year-old excursion into the traces of a much older past. It had been there all these years, and I had never guessed.

'Where else did you go?' I asked.

'We drove out to Cranz. That's where my aunt and uncle lived.'

'Cranz? That's not the name Axel mentioned.'

'Of course not. They changed its name, just like everything else. "The history of Kaliningrad begins in the year 1945." That's what they used to teach the Russian kids in school. Koenigsberg was German for seven hundred years, but for the past forty-five years, they've been trying to erase all traces of Germany. All the old German buildings in the city centre were levelled by bombs, and they've put up those faceless Russian apartment blocks instead.'

We reached the entrance to the park and turned north, towards the lake. Stephen went on describing the indignities inflicted on the city of his ancestors. The stock exchange turned into a Seaman's Palace of Culture. An entertainment park built on the site of the oldest graveyard in the city. A statue of Mother Russia with the inscription 'Come here to me, you children of Russia, this is your home'.

'What about Jacob?' I asked. 'The Rector of the University? Did you find any trace of him?'

'I wasn't really looking. After three centuries, I doubt there's anything to find.'

'I thought he had a famous collection of books.'

'Not any more. The University library was pillaged after the war and the books ended up all over Russia and Lithuania. When they put their minds to something, the Communists are thorough. There's nothing left of the past any more. It's gone forever.'

'Why didn't you write a piece about it?' I said unthinkingly. 'For the Review section.'

'You're forgetting I wasn't supposed to be there. If it hadn't been for your friend Axel . . . He did tell you he was the KGB officer sent to entrap me, I suppose?'

'Yes.'

'He was clever, I'll say that for him. He did good work those six months he was with us. By the time he'd finished, he'd screwed both the husband and the wife.'

I flinched: he must have sensed it: but he didn't look at me.

'The story on the Party funds wasn't a mistake, was it?' I said. 'You published it on purpose.'

For the first time that day, Stephen smiled. The pure, self-satisfied smile of the cat who got the cream. 'Of course I did. I wasn't going to miss a chance like that. Did he tell you he was my case officer for three years while we were in Bonn?'

I stared at him. Axel had been Stephen's case officer? In Bonn? For three years? Seeing Stephen, but never me? 'Yes,' I said coolly. 'Yes, he did.' The trees were swaying slightly in the bright afternoon air. How much more was there that I still didn't know?

Stephen smiled again. 'What remarkable honesty,' he said. 'And what about you? What did you confess? Come on, don't look at me like that! I'm not the only one who's been hiding secrets for ten years, am I?'

We were treading on the grass now and our feet made no sound. We walked past a group of picnickers, laughing raucously amid a stack of empty beer bottles. Their laughter sounded as if it was travelling a long way to reach my ears, echoing amid empty spaces, reflecting off dark stars. A few yards farther on a woman was lying on her back, her face turned towards the sun and a book with the Harlequin logo spine up on the grass beside her. *It would be nice if Axel was my Daddy. Can one have two fathers ever?*

'I didn't have to tell him,' I said. 'He guessed.'

I smiled involuntarily and Stephen saw it.

'Does she know?'

'No.'

We came in sight of the Seehaus. We were both hot and the tables were spread out invitingly at the edge of the lake. Even Stephen, who was never thirsty and rarely drank alcohol, seemed tempted by the sight.

'Let's go and get a drink,' he said.

We sat at a table with steins of beer in front of us and avoided each other's eyes.

'I didn't realize you knew about her,' I said at last.

'There's a lot you didn't realize, Katie.'

'The way you've always behaved towards her, it's not as if— Why have you never said anything?'

'Because I look on Jessica entirely as my child. Biologically speaking, Axel may have fathered her, but I have been responsible for bringing her up and forming her character. Background can eradicate heredity, any intelligent person can see that.'

'You've never given any sign that you knew. How could you—?'

'That's not quite true. You must have noticed how I reacted when I learned you were pregnant. If you didn't have your head in the clouds all the time, it might have dawned on you then that I knew about your affair with Axel.'

I stared at him. Of course, he was right. The evidence had

been there all along, had I but a mind to see it. A memory flashed unbidden into my mind: Axel and I standing in each other's arms in a corner of our sitting room in Moscow, Stephen opening the door, but not entering the room, pausing to say something to the maid over his shoulder, Axel and I, out of his line of vision, seeing him reflected in the big mirror over the mantelpiece, moving apart before he came into the room . . .

And Stephen had seen us too, reflected in the same mirror.

Human kind cannot bear very much reality.

'How long have you known about Jessica?'

'Since the moment you told me you were pregnant.'

'You can't have! We slept together about a week after Axel and I—'

'Katie, I really don't care to hear about that.'

'And another thing. You can stop calling me Katie. I'm not a child, Stephen. My name is Katharine.'

'That's not what he calls you.'

'No it's not. But if *you* want me to answer, you can call me Katharine. Tell me how you knew about Jessica, please.'

'Well, you see, my dear *Katharine*, there's something you don't know about me. I caught mumps when I was nineteen. There were complications.' He paused, waiting for the kill. 'I'm sterile, Katharine. I can't have children.'

He raised his beer to his lips and watched me stare at him. I could feel myself going white, then red, then white again. 'You n-never told me that. Why didn't you tell me that before we were married?'

'I'm afraid I took it for granted that you weren't interested in having children.'

'My God, Stephen, that's an awful lot to take for granted.'

'Not really, given the kind of person you were. I must say I was surprised you coped so well with Jessica.'

'What about your father? He never said a word. When I got pregnant, he must have—'

'He didn't know about the mumps. I was away at Cambridge when it happened. No one knows – apart from the doctor who treated me.'

I got up then and walked away and left him sitting there. He made no attempt to detain me. I walked on through the park, choosing paths at random, paying no attention to where I was going. What kind of man could hide illness from his parents and sterility from his wife? What kind of man could stoically accept infidelity and illegitimacy, and conduct a clandestine relationship with the KGB without ever arousing the slightest suspicion in the person closest to him? With Axel in the past few days, I had inhabited a world where nothing was what it seemed, where the dead came back to life, identities changed, motives were camouflaged, destinations masked. What I had seen had given me no desire to penetrate further, yet now I was discovering that I had been living in a world like that all my adult life. Axel had betrayed Stephen, abandoned me, twisted our lives beyond recall. Stephen had done all of that and worse. Both of them had lied to me and used me, but, of the two, it was Stephen's betrayal that disgusted me more.

I turned in the direction that would take me back to Gudrun's house. The sickness and repulsion were dying down, and I felt better able to control myself. I was going to do what I had originally planned: collect Jessica and drive back to Normandy. On the way, I would tell her that Stephen and I were going to be divorced.

Ten

Axel

In his excitement over his unexpected new granddaughter, my father forgot all about getting back to the Ministry. We left the Kremlin and wandered towards Arbat Square, while I did my best to answer his questions. Why had I never told him, how had I found out about her, where did she live, what was she like? What about her mother? he added, as an afterthought, but I shook my head, and he didn't pursue it.

'Just think, a little girl at last,' he said, grinning happily to himself. 'Wait till I tell your mother. She'll be so pleased. You don't have a photograph, do you?'

I looked around, but no one was paying any attention to us, so I pulled out the East German passport and showed him Jessica's photo.

'Beautiful,' he said, 'such beautiful red hair. Nine years old, you said? Think of it: Misha is ten and Sasha is eight. They would all get on so well together.'

'Yes, I suppose they would.'

'Does she speak Russian?'

'Only English and German.'

'That doesn't matter. She'll pick it up very fast. They learn fast at that age. She can come here and—'

'Papa, I don't know if—'

'No. Of course not. Of course she can't. What was I thinking?'

We started down the Arbat, one of the few remaining streets of old Moscow. It was lined with big old houses built after the fire of 1812. Their facades were painted pistachio and primrose and duck-egg blue, and ornamented with gables, pediments and columns. During my years away from Moscow, they had turned it into a pedestrian precinct. My father was sunk in thought. I gazed idly around me, and then began to look more closely. The sun had come out and the street was crowded. There were jugglers and pavement artists, bookstores and cafés. Vague young men in sweaters declaiming mildly seditious poetry about commissars and glasnost. Sharp young men in jeans selling matrioshki of the Soviet leaders. Tourists in Reeboks hesitating over Yeltsin and Brezhnev, doing deals with cigarettes, sliding dollars into rolled-up newspapers. The touts took everything, with no more than an occasional glance over their shoulders. I couldn't believe what I was seeing. My father was wrong. Moscow was changing. We passed a jazz band playing Moscow Nights and an artist bent over a caricature of Gorbachev. I could see why Ludmilla had been impressed. The ice was melting, the sap was rising. The city was awakening from its seventy-year sleep. We wandered on past the coloured facades. It took me several minutes to grasp what else was different. It wasn't just the life and the colour and the movement. It wasn't just the feeling of spring. There was something new in the atmosphere, something which should have hit me right away, because of course it was that which made everything else possible.

The fear had gone.

I stopped dead in the middle of the street, next to a young man with an array of hollow wooden dolls laid out on a convenient window sill. Next to a self-important Gorbachev, with a red ribbon saying 'President USSR', were a smaller, sneering Brezhnev, a smug Khrushchev, an enigmatic Stalin, and a Lenin too small to distinguish any expression at all. The vendor smiled at me invitingly, and gestured towards his wares. He didn't care who I was: KGB, Party, tourist – it was all the same to him.

Leaving my father staring after me, I stumbled into a side street and sat down on a low wall. I had to get away from the matrioshka-seller: I couldn't look him in the face. My heart was beating too fast, the pain in my chest was back, and I was gasping for breath. During the whole of my career I had managed to convince myself that I, an officer of the First Chief Directorate, had nothing in common with the people in the domestic service of the KGB who were responsible for intercepting mail, tapping phones, searching apartments, following, watching, guarding, threatening, maintaining whole populations in a state of fear. But that was purely wishful thinking. I had been fooling myself. I was paid by the same organization, I identified myself with the same initials. I could be transferred from foreign service to domestic duty at any time. I was one of the people who had made Moscow grey and lifeless. I had helped to take away the expressions on the white peasant faces, and sent them plodding hopelessly through their drab, leaden world.

'Axel, are you all right?' My father was leaning over me anxiously.

I managed to smile at him. 'Don't worry. I'll be fine in a minute.'

'You're as white as a sheet. Should I try to find a doctor?'

'No, it'll pass. I've had pains like this for months.'

'But what is it? Shouldn't you—'

'I saw a doctor in Hamburg. There's nothing physically wrong with me.'

He stood beside me and waited. The pain grew less acute, and my heartbeat seemed to be slowing. An elderly man with thinning hair and a shopping bag asked if everything was all right. My father reassured him. A child came up beside him and stared at us. The man took her hand and they moved away. I thought about the families who had been separated by the Wall, the handkerchiefs fluttering across no man's land, the unmarked crosses behind the Reichstag. I looked at my father with his rows of medals and the granddaughter he might never see. I thought about all the lives that had been destroyed by that ruthless, seventy-year-old fairy tale.

'Papa,' I said, 'I can't just throw those papers in the garbage.'

What I did was terrible. I twisted people's lives, I ruined their careers. I used them, manipulated them. I did a lot of harm, a lot of damage.

Moscow News: *What kind of acts are you referring to?*

I used people for political ends in a way which damaged their personal lives. I cannot give you details which might serve to identify the people I am referring to. They have suffered enough. There is no excuse for what I did: I do not intend to try and exonerate myself.

Moscow News: *But you were an officer of the KGB, and you were bound to obey orders.*

Yes, that is true, but I should not have committed these acts, even though I was ordered to do so. It was wrong. I wish it were possible to go back and act differently.

***Moscow News**: For most of your career, you were working abroad, serving your country –*

I wasn't serving my country, I was wasting my country's resources! For most of the past ten years, I've been fighting an enemy that never existed, and helping to undermine a government that hasn't had hostile intentions towards us for several decades.

***Moscow News**: Still, you have less on your conscience than certain of your colleagues, those responsible for domestic repression.*

Although I was never personally responsible for repression, harassment or illegal imprisonment, what I did helped to perpetuate the system which did all these things, and therefore I have a certain responsibility for that too.

***Moscow News**: Would life be better in the Soviet Union if the KGB had been less active against foreign governments?*

Of course it would. The KGB employs some of the most brilliant men in Russia. It skims the cream of Soviet resources. If people like that were allowed to work in other fields, our country could lead the world, instead of using subversion and deception and intimidation to pretend that we lead it. If all the money spent on following foreign spies or entrapping foreign politicians had been used to develop the economy, our country wouldn't be on the verge of bankruptcy today. Our people wouldn't have to put up with bad food, shoddy consumer goods, and primitive medical care.

***Moscow News**: Is this why you have decided to speak out publicly?*

That's one reason. The other reason is that I do not believe we can build a better society if we do not admit what we have done. If we are to choose the right path, we have to understand our mistakes. For years, I deceived myself into thinking that what I did was justified, that it constituted acceptable and normal behaviour, and that I was obliged to carry out orders which I knew, in my heart and conscience, were wrong. I hope some day that I may be reconciled with those I harmed. I hope they can find it in themselves to forgive me.

Epilogue

Katharine

November 1990

Wer jetzt kein Haus hat, baut sich keines mehr.
Wer jetzt allein ist, wird es lange bleiben . . .
Rainer Maria Rilke
Herbsttag

On the first day of November, at the end of the afternoon, I left the house and walked towards the lake. It was about half-past four. The sun had shone for most of the day, but the brightness was dying now, and the shadows were crawling through the woods and across the lane. The book was going well. With no one to distract me, no shirts to iron and no homework to supervise, I was working longer hours and concentrating better than I had ever done before. The draft was already half complete. By spring, the biography would be finished.

I crossed the lane and turned on to the track through the woods. When I had walked down here with Axel the previous summer, the forest had been green and lush. Now the leaves were darker and sparser, and they crackled underfoot. I had told Marcel, my neighbours, and the people in the village that I was staying here on my own to work on a book. If they suspected that there was more to it than this, they gave no sign. They were used to eccentric Englishwomen in Morigny and, as far as it went, the story was true. The computer sat on the big oak table in the living room, surrounded by papers and reference books. To all intents and purposes, I was leading a peaceful, industrious and creative life.

My journey to Koenigsberg had ended where it began. Jessica and I got back to La Morosière a week after we had left. It was still only the middle of July. I felt as though we had been gone a lifetime. Marcel asked if we had enjoyed our week at the sea, and we said we had. Didn't get much of a tan, he observed, looking us over. It's because we have red hair, Jessica informed him. Redheads don't tan, you know. Where's your father then, he said, and she explained that Daddy had to work and might not be coming this summer.

Jessica had taken the news that I was leaving Stephen with an equanimity that kept me lying awake, shivering with guilt, for weeks. *Nobody suffers in our house.* That was what I had told Axel, but I had been a long way from the truth. We had all suffered. I didn't dare to ask Jessica how long she had been waiting for us to separate: I suspected it had been for always. I had told her that for the time being we would live at La Morosière, and she seemed to find this acceptable. For the next few weeks, life went on as it usually did. She spent a lot of time at the farm, I read my books on Rilke. We went for bicycle rides. If the weather was bad, we played cards. At the beginning of August, Stephen called and asked me what my plans were. I said I didn't know.

Although I had spent a certain amount of time contemplating the mess I had made of my life, I had reached no conclusions on what to do next. For ten years, my existence had revolved around two men: the husband I didn't love and the lover I couldn't forget. All I knew was that I had no desire to spend the next ten with either of them. Why don't you send her back to London? said Stephen casually. She can stay on at her old school till you finish your book and get yourself sorted out. He had hired a housekeeper, he explained, who had agreed to look after Jessica when he was away. I was speechless. Think about it, Katharine, he said. After a couple of days, I called back and accepted. I had not expected such generosity from Stephen, but when I tried to thank him, he cut me off, and said he would come and pick her up at the end of the month.

'Guilt,' said my sister, who had come to stay for a few days. 'After the way he treated you all these years, it's the least he can do.'

We were sitting in the garden under the parasol with the remains of dessert, and a bottle of cider the farmer had given me. The weather was as hot as it had been in July, but the garden was not so green. There were yellow patches on the lawn, and the trees were changing colour.

'Are you going to marry Axel now?' inquired Jessica.

It was the first time Axel's name had been mentioned since we left Munich. 'No,' I said.

'You can tell me, you know,' she assured me in her most worldly tones. 'My friend Gillian's mother got married again. I won't be shocked.'

'Axel's in Moscow. He won't be coming back.'

'Would you like him to come back?' she demanded.

I looked at her and felt like bursting into tears. What else did she know? How much else had she seen? What else was she keeping wisely to herself? 'I don't know, Jess,' I said. 'I think maybe we're better off on our own. Just you and me.'

'But we're not going to be just you and me,' she pointed out. 'I'm going to be in London with Daddy, and you're going to be here on your own. You're going to need someone to keep you company.'

'I'll have the kitten,' I said feebly. The farmer's cat had just had kittens, and I had been inveigled into adopting one.

'My God, Mummy, you are so stupid sometimes,' said Jessica, and went off to ride her bike.

'Tell me about your new husband,' said Juliet, who had been listening with interest. 'This can't be the Axel you knew in Moscow, surely?'

The day after that, we went to Chartres. Juliet had never seen the cathedral, and Jessica seized eagerly on the prospect of a day out. She had confided to her aunt that she was relieved to be going back to school in London. She had been worried that the children at the village school would laugh at her French. I did not enjoy Chartres much: I was too busy brooding about my inability to provide my daughter with emotional stability and appropriate schooling. In any case, there were too many tourists. When we had finished in the cathedral, we walked down to the station to buy the English papers. It was the newsstand where I had bought Stephen's paper on our previous visit, and when Jessica said suddenly, 'Look, Mummy, there's Axel,' I spun round, half expecting to see him in the flesh. Instead, I found myself staring at a photograph. It was a week-old French-language edition of *Moscow News*, and Axel's photo was on the front page under a banner headline that said, 'KGB OFFICER REPENTS'.

'That's Axel?' said Juliet. 'Good grief.'

'What does repent mean?' said Jessica.

'I'd never have recognized him,' said Juliet.

'Are we going to buy the newspaper?' said Jessica.

'And repenting too,' said Juliet. 'Maybe you should marry him after all.'

'Can I have the picture?' said Jessica.

'Let's go and sit in the café over there,' I said. 'The one we went to before. You can both have an ice cream while I read the article.'

The interview sent shockwaves through the Moscow political establishment. It was picked up by the Western and Soviet press, and a number of follow-up interviews were published. Axel became a minor celebrity. Foreign journalists in Moscow sought him out, newspapers dispatched special correspondents to interview him. The spectacle of a KGB officer apologizing to his victims overshadowed even the documents he had carried across Europe. Here and there, the theme of repentance was taken up by other prominent citizens. An academic expressed regret for his own failure to speak out during the Brezhnev years. A prominent reformer deplored the lack of remorse shown by those who had repressed human-rights activists.

Juliet went back to London, urging me to let her know the minute I heard from Axel. Jessica and I made several trips to Chartres to buy more copies of *Moscow News*, plus whatever English papers we could find. Gradually we fell into a routine: newsstand, ice cream, cathedral, and a walk in the forest on the way home. Jessica got addicted to stained-glass windows, and I developed a passion for blueberry sorbet.

Not everything we learned was to our advantage. One evening, at Marcel's house, I caught a glimpse of Axel on the television news, looking pale and tense and speaking near-perfect French. I had already discovered that he had spent two years in Munich, and that his father was an Army general who worked for the Defence Ministry. By now I was getting inured to Axel's revelations. It wasn't too much of a surprise to learn that a lot of the Party bank transactions had been routed through Hamburg, and that Axel had handled a good many of them himself. What had not occurred to me was that he might have had a hand in preparing post-reunification Germany. In a second interview, published two weeks after the first, he explained that he had been responsible for interviewing ex-Stasi officers being considered for re-hiring by the KGB, and briefing them on their future activities.

'You really do pick the most frightful men,' said Juliet admiringly on the phone. 'First Stephen, now him.'

'I agree that Stephen was a mistake.'

My sister sighed noisily. 'I really do not understand you.'

'He's confessed, hasn't he? He's said he regrets what he did. What more do you want?'

'So you've forgiven him?'

'He was talking to me in that interview. He was saying the things he couldn't say to my face.'

'Have you heard from him yet?'

'No, but I don't expect to. Not for another few weeks. He'll wait till the fuss has died down.'

At the end of August, Stephen came over to take Jessica back to London. School would be starting the following week. He brought me my clothes, my reference books, and a computer that he said he didn't need any more. More guilt, Juliet would have said, or perhaps it was simply relief. He had bought a new car, another Volvo. Surprisingly little was said about the fate of the other one. He stayed at La Morosière for three days, sleeping in the spare room Axel had used two months earlier. Relations between us were less strained than they had been for years. There were no rows and no recriminations. He did not broach the possibility of my returning to London. I think he was as thankful as I was that our marriage was over.

When he and Jessica had gone, I got down to work in earnest. The kittens moved in, not one but two, and I was glad to have them for company. One was black and one was grey, and in deference to Rilke, I christened them Rainer and Maria. The days were growing shorter, and we had a week of rain. I got in a load of firewood, and unpacked the sweaters Stephen had brought me. For the time being, I was all right. I had the book to finish, and it kept me occupied. I thought rarely of Axel, though he was constantly in my mind. I had his note, and that was all the reassurance I needed. When he could, he would come. Until then, I would wait.

September slid by unnoticed. The rain stopped and we were treated to a glorious Indian summer. I went for long walks and picked mushrooms and blackberries. I stopped going to Chartres. Instead I listened to the radio. Gorbachev and Kohl had reached an agreement in July, and Germany was preparing for reunification. The four World War Two allies signed a treaty formally relinquishing their rights over German territory. East Germany left the Warsaw Pact. Reunification was set for October 3. In contrast to this orderly progression, the news from Moscow was a mixture of the ominous and the bizarre. All kinds of wild rumours were flying around. The murder of a reform-minded Orthodox priest was said to prove that the KGB was cracking down on reform. Some odd military manoeuvres, passed off by the army as potato picking, were deemed to be evidence of a forthcoming coup. It was too byzantine for me, but Juliet took it seriously. The hard-liners, she informed me, had begun to take control. An anonymous KGB officer, writing in *Pravda*, accused Axel of betraying his fellow officers and violating the sacred trust of the Party. One week after the piece appeared, Axel was fired from the KGB, deprived of his pension rights and stripped of his awards. Juliet said it was only to be expected. They had done the same thing to Kalugin.

'If he has any sense,' she went on, 'he'll have kept something back to use as a negotiating counter. He'll try and do some kind of deal with them.'

I knew that already. As far as I could tell, he had kept back the memo from Kryuchkov and the information about the offshore company in Jersey. Of course he would do a deal with them. Juliet was worried that I still hadn't heard from him, but I was as confident as ever. The negotiations would take time, I told myself. It wasn't the kind of thing you could sort out in a couple of hours. The sun shone from a cloudless blue sky, Marcel and his wife were coming to dinner, and I had enough blackberries for a blackberry and apple pie.

The November day sank quietly into the dusk. I reached the edge of the lake and stood gazing out over the vast expanse of water. A wind got up and ruffled the surface into little waves. The reeds cracked and the trees sighed and I turned my collar up around my neck. The summer had gone, and the autumn would soon be over too. '*Who has no house now will not build him one. Who is alone now will be long alone.*' The lines I had been reading earlier in the day came into my mind, and I shivered involuntarily. Today was All Saints' Day: the Day of the Dead. I realized it must be Jessica's half-term. I wondered what she was doing, who was looking after her, whether Stephen had taken her away somewhere. Neither of them had mentioned the subject last time we had talked on the phone. If I had thought of it earlier, she could have come here.

Last year, we had all stayed at La Morosière for a week in late October. We had roasted chestnuts and swept up the leaves in the garden and played Monopoly. Stephen, who normally hated any kind of game, had got quite involved when it became clear that he had a good chance of buying both of us out, and we stayed up playing till one o'clock in the morning, much to Jessica's delight. Jessica . . . I became aware that there were tears on my cheek. The idea of spending the winter here on my own filled me with dread. If Axel didn't come back, I was going to have to find an alternative plan for the future.

It had dawned on me only the week before that I might not see Axel again. Writing a cheque in the supermarket one day, I had suddenly realized it was nearly the end of October. Over three months, and I still had no news of him. I didn't sleep that night. Part of the time I spent pacing round the silent house, occasionally falling over one or other of the kittens. The night was made for hunting: they skittered around me and attacked my ankles. I began to think seriously about what could have happened to him. If he were in custody in Moscow, I would have read about it in the press. The KGB would have made sure of that. It would have served as a warning. The same if he had been in a car crash, or some other kind of 'accident'. I had to face it: Axel was free and alive and had made no attempt to contact me. Had he changed his mind? Did he think I didn't want him? I had heard nothing from him since that July night in Prague when I had told him we had no future together, and I had no means of contacting him to tell him I had changed my mind. *I'll be back*. The note by now was torn and crumpled, barely legible from all those nights I had sat huddled in my dressing gown reading it. Why did you write those words, Axel, if you didn't mean them?

Or was there something else going on, something too far below the surface for me to grasp? Since Germany had reunified, it seemed that every day there was some new revelation of treachery and manipulation. A list of East German deputies who had worked for the Stasi was read out to a closed session of the Volkskammer, and fifty-six names were cited. The East German official charged with dismantling the Stasi turned out to be Stasi himself. A high-ranking official in West German intelligence confessed to being a double agent in the pay of the Stasi. As Axel had said, the whole of Germany was mined. There were subterranean channels and treacherous currents that could drag you under. The West German official turned himself in after being asked to transfer his services to the KGB. Everything was linked: there were invisible threads holding vast obscure networks in an inextricable knot. Once they had you, they never let go. *I'll be back*. Will you, Axel? Will they really let you go? They have you for life, just like all the others. Fate gives no third chances, far less the KGB.

The temperature was dropping by the minute and the wind was getting stronger. Away in the distance, the sound of a car broke the early evening hush. I turned away from the lake and began to plod wearily home. However much I longed to see Jessica, I couldn't leave here. Not yet. I had to finish the book first. In the spring, I would sell La Morosière, go back to London, buy a small flat, and find a job to support Jessica and myself. What else could I do?

Twelve years ago, I had married Stephen to avoid having to cope with the real world. But reality catches up with you in the end. Lawyers, judges, estate agents, employers. And at the end of it all, a cramped flat and a boring office. With my qualifications, I would be lucky to get a job filing invoices.

The noise of the car was growing louder. It must have turned off the main road into the lane. On that quiet road, a passing car was the event of the day, and I waited to see it go past the end of the track. But the engine slowed and then stopped. I realized that it must have taken the turn-off to La Morosière. Someone to visit me? Perhaps Marcel. He dropped in from time to time, though usually not this late in the day.

I quickened my pace, crossed the lane, and reached the access road in time to see the car drive into the courtyard in front of the house. Not Marcel: he usually parked on the road. In any case, it wasn't Marcel's car. It was a dark blue Renault, with Paris plates.

Someone closed the gates behind it. I stopped short as I recognized Jessica. She didn't see me standing there in the dim light. I tried to call out, but no sound came. They must have flown to Paris and rented a car. I walked slowly towards the gate. My chest felt tight: I was torn between exhilaration and fear. Stephen didn't believe in surprising people: there had to be some ulterior motive to the visit. I stood at the gate and watched. Jessica was running towards the house, yelling at the top of her lungs. 'Mummy, Mummy, we've come to get you!' The light spilled out into the darkening garden as she opened the door and disappeared into the house. A cry of thrilled surprise rang out, and I guessed she had found the kittens.

The driver of the car was in less of a hurry. He got out and stretched, reaching skywards, taking his time. I would have recognized him anywhere: his legs, the shape of his back, the dark-blond hair that he pushed back off his forehead. My apprehension dissolved. *I'll be back*. My Teutonic knight on his noble dark-blue steed. He had kept his promise after all. I lifted the latch of the gate. He heard the click, turned round and saw me, cried my name and began to run towards me.

I opened the gate and went into the garden.

Author's note

The lines from 'Burnt Norton' by T.S. Eliot are taken from *Four Quartets*, *Collected Poems 1909–1962*, published by Faber and Faber Ltd and reproduced here by their kind permission.

For their help with various aspects of this book, I would like to thank Laure Mandeville and Charles Lambroschini of *Le Figaro*, Barbara Momenteau, Valentina Berthélémy, and Dr. Jean Kemeny. I am grateful to Eckart Gusovius for giving me access to his private archives on Koenigsberg. My thanks to everyone who was kind enough to take the time to read and comment on the manuscript, in particular Ellen Hampton, Natalie Leroy, and Christopher Macann for substantive help at different stages of the revision process.

The Research Reports of Radio Free Europe/Radio Liberty are an unequalled source of information on Soviet politics. Also useful were:

Handbuch der Historischen Stätten: Ost- und WestPreussen, Dr. Erich Weise, Alfred Kröner Verlag, Stuttgart, 1966

KGB Today, John Barron, The Reader's Digest Association, Inc., 1983

Berlin, Coming In From The Cold, Ken Smith, Hamish Hamilton Ltd., London, 1990
The Saddled Cow, Anne McElvoy, Faber and Faber Ltd., London, 1992
The First Directorate, Oleg Kalugin, St. Martin's Press, New York, 1994
The Haunted Land, Tina Rosenbaum, Vintage, London, 1995
Memoirs of a Spymaster, Markus Wolf, Pimlico, London, 1997.

A brief glossary of Soviet and East German political terminology

Stasi: East German security police (contraction of Ministerium für Staatssicherheit, the Ministry for State Security)

inoffizielle Mitarbeiter: Informers working for the Stasi (literally "unofficial collaborators")

Grepo: Grenzpolizei, East German border guards

Vopo: Volkspolizei, East German police force

Red Army Faction: Rote Armee Fraktion, also known as the Baader-Meinhof Gang. West German left-wing radical group responsible for terrorist actions including bomb attacks, bank robberies and kidnappings, most of which took place in the 1970's.

Shchit: A union of Soviet reformist military officers, founded in 1990 (literally 'Shield')

First Chief Directorate: The section of the KGB responsible for operations abroad.